Dark Intent

By Brian Reeve

 New Generation **Publishing**

Chapter 1

Durban, Republic of South Africa

After evading Jan Krige and the three men, members of the group of no name, James Steiner reversed his car out of the *donga* and headed for Durban, reaching the city four hours later. He went to his flat near the centre and put a call through to Peter Smith, a high-ranking operative in the Directorate: Special Operations, the Scorpions. He got through to David Johnson, Smith's assistant, and after introducing himself was told Smith was out of the city for two days. It meant waiting before he could tell Smith a copy of the file, desperately wanted by the group of no name, had been sent to him by Krige's lawyer, David Staples. He left a message for Smith to ring him when he got back; it was urgent. Johnson knew Steiner had been on the Andrew Cartwright case.

Steiner had a shower, changed clothes and left the flat to get in some food. He had just entered an arcade when he saw a South African girl, Sophie Carswell, leave a shop. He remembered her well. He had met her a year ago in Johannesburg and more recently had come across her in London when he was on his way to Japan, the place he regarded as his spiritual home. She was bitter when they parted in London. He had taken sexual advantage of her in her flat, an act he regretted afterwards.

Steiner didn't know if she would still be angry with him when she saw him but decided to greet her. He increased his pace and when he was close said: 'I didn't think I would see you again.'

She turned quickly and he was surprised when she smiled and seemed pleased to see him. 'How are you? This is a long way from London and Japan.'

Before she could say any more he said: 'I regret the way I behaved and I hope you are not still angry with me.'

3

'That is forgotten,' she said. 'Would you like some coffee?'

'I would love some. There's a place over here.'

They got a table and ordered. For a while they talked and then she said: 'You told me you were going to Japan. When I told my boyfriend Paul Adams what you had done to me he was incensed and from a friend of yours in London found out where you had gone. Paul did not find you and returned to London. He said you were known in South Africa and had returned there.' She pushed him to see if there was something she hadn't heard about. 'Is that all? Clearly it was not much of an adventure for either of you.'

'I will tell you what I know,' said Steiner. 'Adams got a friend to try and kill me. I evaded him and then two *ninja* were sent after me. I was a step ahead and they lost me. That is when I came back here.'

For a while she was quiet. She knew Steiner had killed Adams' friend and the *ninja*. 'Paul and I parted soon afterwards and I came out here,' she said. 'I'm staying with close family friends near the University of KwaZulu-Natal on the Berea and teaching dance classes until I decide on my future.'

'Let's have a drink sometime,' said Steiner.

'That will be great,' she said.

They exchanged phone numbers and left the bar.

Chapter 2

Durban, Republic of South Africa

Two days later Peter Smith arrived back in Durban. He had been working on a case in the provincial area of KwaZulu-Natal, previously Natal before apartheid was abolished in 1994 and the ANC party became the elected government.

After entering his office he phoned Steiner at his flat to find out what was happening in the Cartwright affair. It was his priority and they arranged to meet at the flat in five minutes.

When the two met Smith went straight to it. 'The stage is yours,' he said. 'Tell me where you are in this affair.'

Steiner began. 'You told me before I went that you believed these men were after something of great importance, the evidence you have been after for years. The something is a file.' Steiner was mildly amused to see no response from Smith. 'The file was stolen on the night Cartwright was killed. That was when I phoned you, but I knew nothing about the file except that the safe in Cartwright's room was open. It appears the file was compiled by the group of no name, or the group, and contains the names and details of the leading white players who were in government, security, the police, the military and business during the apartheid period. In addition the file makes reference to vital information that if revealed would provide the evidence to convict the men and women named. Needless to say all those in the file refused to attend the TRC hearings.' Steiner poured water into two glasses and gave one to Smith.

'Three men from Pretoria went to Durban and this group orchestrated the operation with information they had acquired. The leader of the three was Jan Krige, a tobacco farmer who owns a spread outside White River near the Kruger Reserve. These three had a boss in Pretoria who set the thing up. His name was Johan Muller. Of these four only Krige is still alive.' Steiner drank some water.

'I won't ask how they were killed,' said Smith. 'I assume they had nothing to offer.'

'No, they didn't,' said Steiner. 'But Krige did. The names of the three dead men were given to me by John Bryant, your informer in the group. I am afraid he is also dead. He knew too much.'

Smith blanched. 'I hope there are some people left in Pretoria.'

'Krige's name was given to me by Muller before his end,' said Steiner. 'At last I had found the leader. I went to Krige's farm. One of the men who went to Durban and was still alive had gone to kill Krige. He hated him. He shot Krige, who appeared after he got there. The man, Johannes Koch, was busy trying to rape Krige's wife Kirsty when he was rudely disturbed. At that point I arrived and managed to save Krige.' Steiner drank more water and went on. 'At last I got the full picture. Krige told me they had broken into Cartwright's house to get the file. Krige found it in a safe. It appears the other two had already gone, if they were ever there. After Krige had left I arrived and found Cartwright dead, which I told you over the phone at the time. I can only believe Krige killed him but he did not admit it and there is no evidence.' Steiner got up and went to the glass doors. 'The final turn in all this is that Krige went back to Pretoria alone and the next morning contacted his lawyer. He gave him the original of the file and instructed him to send a copy to you in the DSO and the press. By now it would have been in the newspapers if they had received anything. You haven't got a copy either and that is important.'

Chapter 3

Durban, Republic of South Africa

A day before Smith arrived back in Durban from KwaZulu-Natal, a man in the DSO, John Kallis, was going through Smith's mail and noticed a large package. It had been sent by courier and marked Urgent, Addressee only. Smith's secretary would have signed for it and placed it on his desk for his attention.

Kallis, tall and well built, looked at the package and decided to open it. He and a few others had the authority when Smith was away. He closed the door and with a paper knife cut into the package. He extracted a file with State Security 1960 to Present, File A written on the cover and a letter attached to it by a paper clip. The letter had no name or address and simply said the file was the missing file wanted by the group of no name and sent to a Durban lawyer, Andrew Cartwright. Clearly the file had been removed by someone in the group before being sent to Cartwright. He was interested and flicked back the cover to the introduction.

Kallis had read a page when a colleague entered the office. He saw the black file in Kallis' hands and said: 'That looks interesting. Is it a good read?'

Kallis shut the file and said: 'Yes, I will have to contact Smith. It might brighten his day.' His colleague picked up a newspaper on the desk and left.

Kallis put the file back into the package, opened the door to see if anyone was about and walked from the office. He held the package under his jacket and left the building.

When Kallis got to his flat he sat down and started to read the file. He read part of it and then skimmed the remainder. He took a pen and paper and wrote a short

7

letter. He destroyed the package's envelope and after placing his letter, the covering letter and the file in a white jiffy bag called for a courier from a company he used frequently. Ten minutes later the package was collected and he sank into a chair, pleased with himself. The package was addressed to Johan Teichmann, a leading member in the group of no name.

Chapter 4

Pretoria, Republic of South Africa

The package sent by Kallis reached the group in Pretoria later that day and was sent to Teichmann. When he opened it and saw the file he could not believe their good fortune in getting it back. He read Kallis' letter and the letter that accompanied the file, and then contacted the man who led the team responsible for compiling it.

The man Teichmann summoned to his office was pleased when he saw the front cover of the file. He took it from Teichmann but after inspecting it showed disappointment.

Teichmann saw the look on the man's face and knew something was wrong. 'What is it?' he said, knowing the answer before it came.

'This file is a copy of the original and the person who made it did not try to pretend otherwise,' said the man. 'In the group, the original will have a small Oriental seal heavily stamped on the inside of the back cover under the synthetic backing. You have to peel away part of the backing to find it. The seal is virtually undetectable unless you know exactly what to look for and where it is located. It is a near certainty that the file is the original if the seal is there. Only five men, and now you, are aware of what I have just revealed to you. You have always worked on copies, and will continue to do so, but the system I have just described was created and applied to the original in case it fell into the wrong hands, which it did, and a copy, was made by the person who stole it.

'The way to use this system is first to see if the seal is where it should be. Final and absolute confirmation that the file is an original is to get an independent expert who

9

specializes in assessing the authenticity of produced works to conduct a scientific examination.'

'Thank you for enlightening me,' said Teichmann, dropping his body into a leather seat. Two questions came to mind. Where was the original file and who took it from Cartwright's house? He knew Jan Krige had killed Cartwright and he believed Krige had not retrieved the file. That meant there was a man working alone, a man who had killed Muller, the two others and the DSO plant Bryant. Bryant's death indicated that the man was not working for the Scorpions. If he was working for another organization, who were they?

Chapter 5

Durban, Republic of South Africa

When he got to his office after seeing Steiner, Smith went through his mail without interest. That he had not received a copy of the file promised by Krige angered him and he knew he had to find out what was going on. He believed Krige had told Steiner the truth when he said he had given the file to his lawyer and a copy was to be sent to him in the DSO. Krige would have been stupid to lie because others would have been sent to get him.

After dwelling on the matter a little longer Smith shut his door and picked up the phone. He had Krige's number from Steiner and soon after dialling a man lifted the receiver.

'Krige. Who do you want?'

'I'd like to have a word with you,' said Smith. 'My name is Peter Smith. I work for the Directorate: Special Operations and I believe you met one of my operatives, James Steiner, a couple of days ago. He went to your farm to speak to you and the reason for his visit was to find out what happened recently in Durban and your involvement.' Smith went to the window and looked out over the old part of the city, a part he loved. He continued. 'I know the essential details of what went on. These go up to when you gave Steiner your word that your lawyer would send a copy of the file to me in the DSO. You can easily guess the file to which I refer is the one you took from Cartwright's safe, the file the group of no name sent you to retrieve and which I want. Something has gone wrong. I have not received the copy. If your lawyer did send it, it has been intercepted.'

'My lawyer assured me it had been sent by courier two days ago. I trust him implicitly but I will ask him again.'

'Thank you,' said Smith, rather liking Krige. 'If nothing happens I will phone you again. In the meantime I want your lawyer's name and contact details. When you speak to him you can tell him I phoned.'

'These are the details you want,' said Krige. He read them out and Smith terminated the call.

Smith did not think he would get much out of the lawyer, David Staples. If a copy of the file had been sent by courier it would have reached his office. That meant someone in the DSO had taken it.

Smith appreciated that Staples would never have parted with the original and that meant he had it. He knew a copy was interesting, but the original was everything as far as evidence was concerned. It was quite literally the cream.

A couple of hours later Smith phoned Staples. After telling Staples what the call was about, Smith said: 'Did you make any copies of the original other than the copy you sent to the DSO?'

'No,' said Staples, lying. 'That was the only one. In this business the fewer the number of copies you make of anything the better and it's advisable to know each recipient in person. The DSO is a special case and a copy was sent only to you.'

Smith coughed and said: 'It is apparent you didn't send copies to the press. You told Krige you would.'

'I decided to send a copy only to you,' said Staples. 'You're the major player in this game.'

'Where is the original?' said Smith.

'Krige and I agreed, out of a sense of responsibility, to send a copy of the file to the Scorpions,' said Staples, 'not the original in case it went astray. The original came into Krige's hands by chance and is in a safe place. Our intention was to keep the original secure until the copy had been examined and then if required send it to the appropriate authorities. I am not releasing the original now under these circumstances.'

12

'I would like another copy of the file in case we can't find the first,' said Smith, guessing the reply before it came.

'I emphasize that to prevent further replication of the original and avoid the danger of another copy disappearing, the copy I sent to you has to be found.'

Smith knew there was no way of getting another copy. And, the chances of getting the original, which is what he really wanted, were not good.

After lunch Smith phoned Steiner and they arranged to meet at Steiner's flat. The flat was sparsely furnished with a hint of Japanese styling. When they were seated, Smith said: 'I don't like Staples. He is very confident and I don't know when he is telling the truth or lying. I am sure you know most of what I heard. He did say the original is in a secure place and will be released when the copy sent to us is found and examined. I couldn't believe what I was hearing when he said Krige had come across the file by chance. He seems ignorant of the fact that Krige admits taking the file from Cartwright's safe to satisfy his masters in the group. That meant killing Cartwright, if the lawyer got in the way. Even though Krige would not admit it in front of his wife, he definitely killed Cartwright but that is not my problem now. I simply want to nail the person who took the file off my desk; and, I want the original.'

Chapter 6

Near the Kruger Reserve, Republic of South Africa

A day after Smith spoke to David Staples, Krige received a telephone call on his farm. The man introduced himself as Johan Teichmann and said he was one of the leaders in the group.

Teichmann did not waste time on pleasantries. 'I would like to meet you. I have something to say. It is between you and me and I suggest White River.'

Krige was quiet for moment and then reluctantly agreed. He was curious. 'I can meet you tomorrow,' he said. 'There is a large café in the centre of town. I will get a table opposite the door. I'll wear a navy blue blazer.'

'I'll recognize you anyway,' said Teichmann. 'I've seen photographs of you.'

Krige terminated the call.

The next morning Krige met Teichmann in the town café. No one else was there.

After ordering coffee, Teichmann went to the reason for the meeting. 'I know you, Richter and Koch went to Durban to retrieve the file from Andrew Cartwright. Cartwright was killed, by you I believe. Richter and Koch had refused to accompany you to Cartwright's. They lost their nerve and decided to return to Pretoria without you. That was bad behaviour and I have heard they hated the sight of you.'

'I told them to wait for me and that I wanted to do the job alone. We agreed they would wait for me where the main road out of Durban begins. When I got there they had gone. In many ways that was great. We despised one another. It was down to class and they had none.'

Teichmann grinned, his mouth a rictus. He said: 'I have been led to believe you did not get the file from

Cartwright. Perhaps you killed him before he could tell you where it was kept. After hearing the facts I conclude that either the file is still concealed in the house or someone else came along after you had left and found it. If there was someone else, we have absolutely no knowledge of his name or identity. My feeling is that there definitely was an outsider who got the file and who has since systematically killed the people involved in the operation. Muller, Richter, Koch and Bryant were, I believe, all killed by this man and we in the group are certain he was the stranger seen on your farm and wounded by one of my predecessor's men. Unfortunately, the wound did not stop him from escaping. You are the only one who survived his rampant taste for killing and I don't know why he spared you, except that you were of his breed and he liked you.' Teichmann swallowed a large mouthful of coffee and then said: 'The reason we believe it was the outsider who took the original file is that a copy was sent to the group a day ago. This means the stranger has the original.'

Krige realized the group were playing in the dark and merely skimming the surface. They would know as much as he knew if they had more information, which they weren't going to get. Crucially, he had not told the group that Steiner had asked him for the file when he was in his lounge on the farm. The fact Steiner did ask for the file meant he knew he had retrieved it from the safe. Steiner also knew he had not killed Cartwright and he accused him of doing the killing. He did not deny the accusation and confirmed his guilt.

Teichmann waited a short while after making his statement about the file being sent to the group and then changed the subject. 'You are probably aware that it is group policy to hunt down the men who committed heinous crimes during the apartheid period against whites. It is well known these men escaped prosecution and conviction and now have positions of power in government, the security services and business. They run the country which belonged to us.' Teichmann looked straight at Krige. 'You might have heard of the black file, entitled State Security 1960 to Present, File B. It was developed through years of research and development and, like the white file, State Security 1960 to Present, File A, contains details of blacks who are guilty of major crimes against humanity. This file is a mirror image of the stolen white file in terms of structure, except that the white file was prepared to protect white leaders. Conversely, the black file was created to convict blacks who brutally and violently opposed the state. The file has four men in the top ten who are amongst the most reviled men ever to draw breath. One of the men is a self-proclaimed Zulu warlord, Moses Shozi. How he got the name Moses I will never know. The other three were in exile and returned to South Africa a few years after apartheid was abolished. They are Xhosa guerrillas and amongst the most despised of men; details of their activities makes you puke. All four men are in KwaZulu-Natal. The Zulu lives there permanently and is a member of the National Council of Provinces. The Xhosas are apparently just passing through, most likely on their way to greatness, but they spend most of the time in KwaZulu-Natal.'

Teichmann breathed deeply. He was in his late sixties, tall and overweight. Krige sat quietly, at first wandering what all this had to do with him and then slowly realizing Teichmann wanted him to do something for the group that involved the blacks.

Teichmann went on. 'These men are pure killers and they deserve to be eliminated. If the government can't do it then others have to. After the excellent work you did in Durban the group wants you to take on the job of getting rid of these four. For support you would be accompanied by a man we trust. He is highly capable and well endowed both mentally and physically. In other words he is no slouch and will back you all the way unlike Richter and Koch. His name is John Dalton.'

Krige was cold when he said: 'The group gave me their word I would not be asked to do any of their dirty work again. And now you're breaking it.'

'You have the ability,' said Teichmann, confident that with persistence he would get Krige to comply. 'There are few like you and a selection process takes time. We don't want anyone else. After the demise of the blacks there will be extensive press coverage and black and white will rejoice and wish the state had done its job. The world has no place for them and they are the same as the brutal dictators controlling African states and other countries.'

'Why don't you let the law play its part and arrest these men?' said Krige. 'It would leave the group out of a nasty business and allow them to run a viable political party.'

'We do not believe the evidence that would convict them is easily found, if it can be found at all,' said Teichmann. 'After years of analysis and research the group has the evidence in detail and it is this stuff that is referred to in the black file. Excerpts from this file will be released when these men die and put the government and investigative agencies to shame. All confidence in them will be lost and, in their humiliation, will realize they have to get their act together. People will be made painfully aware the deeds perpetrated by these men are rife and this country could easily lapse into civil war.'

One side of Krige could see why the group had created the two files in such detail and wanted revenge against blacks who had taken their country from them. The other side was that the Truth and Reconciliation Commission had, under Archbishop Desmond Tutu, done the best it could, including convicting and prosecuting hard criminals who had applied for amnesty but were refused. It was time for the country to move on, even if the criminals from the past, blacks and whites, still remained free. But, all this did not help him and his fear was that he would be asked again, as Teichmann had just done. He said: 'I still can't understand why you ask me when you must have other

17

men. And, what assurance do I have that I will not be asked again?'

'Leadership in the group has changed,' said Teichmann patiently. 'The men you knew are either dead, like Muller, or have been sidelined, like Gerrit Viljoen. They would not have asked you again. But, in answer to the first, I repeat that you have exceptional operational qualities and the innate ability of a leader. I am not surprised that as an ex-major in the now defunct Johannesburg murder and robbery squad you have acquired such attributes.' Teichmann scratched his cheek. 'In answer to the second I cannot control some of the men in the group, men at my level, and if you refuse they will not forget and will come after you. I cannot offer a guarantee they will not approach you again, but I would do everything I could to deter them.'

'Why are you a member of the group?' asked Krige.

'I believe that most of the top men are very intelligent and capable, and share a strong interest in the welfare of the Afrikaner people. There are those I disagree with and asking you to do this work again goes against me. But, cooperation is often necessary to make organizations effective.'

'At my expense,' said Krige, without humour. He thought about what Teichmann had said and realized he had no choice. It was as before when he had been asked to get Cartwright. 'I need Dalton's contact details, particularly his telephone numbers. From you I want details of the men, their habits, what they have committed in the past, photographs, their backgrounds, a pattern of their movements past and present. I want precise details of where they live, who they see if anyone, their contacts and their daily routine. Throw in anything else you can think of which might assist us. I want all this information to be sent to me by courier. That shouldn't take more than two days. As soon as I get it I will contact Dalton and get ready to move. We will use his car and it must have Natal plates. I

18

will drive for part of the way and give him the time to read the stuff you send me. I also want Dalton to bring along a rifle, a Winchester chambered for a 7mm Remington magnum cartridge. He will need a handgun and I want a Beretta 93R 9mmx19 Luger/Parabellum pistol. The three guns must be silenced. I want no more contact from you. When the job is done, I will contact you by telephone.'

'I will do what you ask,' said Teichmann. 'The information you want will be sent to you in two days. Be careful in how you deal with these men. They are some of the most dangerous men ever to walk on South African soil and they are natural killers.' Teichmann got up and with a brief smile left the café. Krige stayed for a few minutes more and then left.

Chapter 7

Krige's farm

Two days after meeting Teichmann, Krige was on the verandah with his wife Kirsty when a van drove up to the house. It was an express courier service and Krige waited calmly for the driver to take a slim, A4 envelope from the van and approach him. He wanted identification and when he had gone, Kirsty looked curiously at the envelope.

'What's that?' she asked. 'You seem to have been expecting something.'

'It's just some routine reports from the Farmers' Cooperative,' said Krige.

'I've never seen you get them before,' she said, unconvinced. 'Open the envelope and let me see what they are up to now. I'm interested. Why do they use a courier?'

'It's usually pretty boring stuff,' said Krige, wishing she had not been there. 'I'll show you later.'

Kirsty suspected the delivery had nothing to do with the Cooperative but decided to wait and see if her husband kept his word.

Krige was keen to read the papers sent to him by Teichmann and make a start on the job. It was early in the morning the next day, just after sunrise, and he extracted the contents from the envelope. They comprised a number of pages neatly structured to form a composite document and he began reading it on the verandah. He had nearly got through what he thought was a very comprehensive piece of work, when Kirsty appeared. It was forty-five minutes before she usually got up.

She stood in the doorway and said: 'What are you reading? Is it that the stuff you received yesterday? You said you would show it to me.' She walked closer.

Krige stopped reading, ordered the papers and folded them over. He knew he again had to lie and hope she believed him. 'The papers are not from the Cooperative,' he said. 'They cover the details of a business deal I might get involved with. I have to go to Pretoria for a few days to see these people. When I get back I'll let you know what it is all about. We could be onto something good.'

She looked at him in disbelief. 'Why can't you tell me before you go? And, when are you going?'

'Probably tomorrow,' he said. 'I want to go and get back here as soon as I can.'

'I hope you are telling me the truth this time and not going on another operation for the group.' She couldn't help being suspicious. 'You lied to me then and I don't want your lies now. Those men are evil and I don't want you near them.'

'I am certainly not involved with them,' he said, compounding the lies. 'Last time was something I got into, after they put pressure on me to retrieve the file that had been stolen from them and sent to a Durban lawyer. I got the file but the copy sent to the DSO by David Staples went astray and it is up to the DSO to find it. The DSO want him to make another copy but for security reasons he will not. One copy has already disappeared and he does not want copies flying about all over the place.'

'Someone killed Cartwright,' she said. 'I hope it wasn't you.'

'It wasn't me even though that was implied by James Steiner. He wasn't there and has no idea who shot Cartwright.' Krige refrained from saying Richter and Koch had not gone to the house on that fatal night. If she knew she would instantly conclude he had done the killing.

She mellowed a little and said: 'I am glad those thugs, Richter, Koch and Muller, got what they deserved. If the group were civilized men, with respect for the human race and did not behave like the old Nationalist Party that used to rule this country, I would not despise them so much.

They deserve death. She did not mention Steiner and that he had killed Richter and Koch; to her he was in a different class. She wished she could see him now.

'I have to trust you or our relationship is finished,' she said with finality. 'Go to Pretoria and sort out your business. I can run the farm for a few days. We have good men. You must phone me.'

'I will,' said Krige. 'I am beginning to think it will be a waste of time. I can't say it really interests me. Let's have breakfast. I want to go to town for essentials.'

Krige reached town at eight and parked his Land Rover near the public telephone box. He fished in his pocket and took out Dalton's number. He had Teichmann's papers with him when he dialled. In less than a minute a woman answered and he asked for Dalton. He soon heard Dalton's voice.

Krige introduced himself. 'I have received the information from Teichmann.'

Dalton listened quietly.

'You can read it in the car on the way,' said Krige. 'I will drive for the first part. We can meet here in the town cafe tomorrow morning at nine.'

'I'll be there,' said Dalton.

Krige cut the call and crossed the road to the general store. He had to return with something.

While Krige was in town, Kirsty noticed the envelope sent to her husband had gone. She let it pass and felt she had said what was on her mind. She knew she would not find out any more without a fight.

That evening Krige said he was leaving early the next morning. He looked at her on the sofa. 'I assure you there is nothing devious going on. The deal is simply something I want to look into. If we agree to it, I think it will benefit both of us.'

Chapter 8

North of Pretoria

The next morning Krige kissed his wife and left the farm. They said little to one another. She felt it had all been said. He loved her, but since the job in Durban, he sensed she had distanced herself from him. If she ever found out what he was going to do now, she would leave him.

In town, Krige parked his Land Rover in a quiet side road not far from the café. He walked to it and waited outside. After a while, a man arrived in a Ford and parked. Krige was the only young white around and the man approached him.

'Jan Krige?' he said and held out his hand. 'John Dalton.'

Krige nodded and led the way inside the cafe. He could not help being impressed by Dalton's excellent physical condition. Perhaps he was just the right man to have along.

They found seats in a corner and after ordering, Krige put the envelope he was holding on the table in front of them. 'You can look at some of this in here while we drink our coffee and then you can read the rest in the car when we get going.'

A pot of coffee came and they filled their cups. 'The first part of this covers the background of these four men,' said Krige. 'Read it and you will see why some members of the group hate them so much, particularly the older men who lived through the apartheid period and believe these men are as virulent now as they were then.'

Dalton slid the papers towards him and started on the first section. It read:

Three of the men are Xhosas with extensive guerrilla training. These men, Elijah Ngubane, the recognised leader, John Nofomela and Paul Ngwenya are three of the most dangerous and violent men ever to operate in South Africa. They first came to prominence six years before 1994 when apartheid ended and Mandela was released to form a majority government. But these men, like others, did not stop their murderous activities. They are around thirty-five years of age.

In the past fifteen years the three have appeared to reside permanently in South Africa. Before that they spent time training in Angola and Russia in constant preparation for all the raids and skirmishes they organized and executed in South Africa. Since their return they have left South Africa periodically but these were very short breaks. Their activities are essentially secret but they are not benign. They left the country a few weeks ago but soon entered again. It is highly likely they are here now, if the pattern of their movements is anything to go by. When they returned they were followed to a house in Malakazi township, KwaZulu-Natal. It is a place we know about and, judging by the amount of time they spend there, we are confident they are there now.

These men do not only hate whites; they also have an intense dislike for some blacks. They killed several blacks in high positions during apartheid and this has not stopped. They have pretended to be part of political organizations but have used party cover to conduct their evil work. The African National Congress or ANC in particular regarded them as their sons and it is believed still do. But you will never rid a political movement of its criminal element, men who use the cause as a catalyst to kill. Sometimes it is directed against their own people. A brief account of the way these men operate is exemplified by the following.

Years back a man named Thami Zulu, a nom de guerre for Muziwakhe Ngwenya, came to a bitter end at the hands of one or more killers. He was a celebrated member of the ANC, a gifted leader and tipped to replace Mandela. He died in strange circumstances, or rather he was murdered, but the killers got away with it. He was an intelligent, sensitive man and after being turned down for Witwatersrand University went through the University of Botswana and then on to Moscow for training in guerilla warfare. He wanted to stay away for longer but he was needed and he returned to the camps in southern Angola. Chris Hani, the murdered chief of staff, spotted him and made him regional commander of operations in KwaZulu-Natal. His predecessor, Nyanda, was assassinated by South African agents.

Thami Zulu wanted peace but in those days the whites were in no mood to listen. In 1988 nine ANC guerillas were massacred in separate ambushes as they entered the country from Swaziland. The killings had a paralyzing effect on the ANC leadership which was reduced to paranoia about informers in its ranks. The ANC security section, independent of the military and with draconian investigatory powers, recalled Thami Zulu to Lusaka. He was placed under house arrest and then formally detained.

Chris Hani and Joe Modise, commander of MK or Umkhonto we Sizwe, made furious demands in the National Executive to have access to him. They were refused. After seventeen months in detention, a large part in solitary, Thami Zulu was released. Five days later he was dead, at the age of thirty-five. That started bitter controversy in the ANC and a commission of inquiry was set up. The findings were never made public but it is generally believed there was no evidence that Thami Zulu was a South African agent, the reason for holding him. Cause of death was given as tuberculosis, which he had had for some time. The real cause was something else. The English newspaper, the Guardian, obtained a copy of an analysis made of Thami Zulu's blood and stomach after his death. Diazon, an organo-phosphorous pesticide, was detected in both specimens. The pesticide is a particularly toxic poison. Only three men were known to have seen Thami Zulu in the twenty-four hours before he died, Ngubane, Nofomela and Ngwenya. They served under him in Natal as part of the regional command structure. These three were the most wanton, ruthless killers ever to see service in the ANC military. Their absence was clearly noted when they refused to appear before the Truth and Reconciliation Commission set up after Mandela became president. This was allowed and many refused, particularly senior whites previously in national security and government and members of the predominantly black Inkatha Freedom Party. If Ngubane, Nofomela and Ngwenya had appeared they would never have got amnesty for political crimes and would probably have been arrested and prosecuted if the evidence was there. Now, because they refused to apply to the TRC for amnesty they are at large. These men are the three guerillas we want.

The fourth black is a Zulu gangster named Moses Shozi. He plays a prominent role in the Inkatha Freedom Party who want their own state as much as we do. They are natural enemies of the ANC who have been in power since Mandela's release. Shozi is guarded and extremely dangerous. He should be the first hit followed by the guerillas.

Shozi's a member of a gang called Amasignora. It is the Zulu equivalent of the Afrikaner Broederbond as it used to be known although the reason for its existence is less subtle, quite simply the murder of those who obstruct the political ambition of Inkatha. Their favourite target is the ANC and ultimately they're behind much of the head-on violence in the townships. Apparently some of our people would have been content if the activities of this gang remained at that but some of them were too clever. Before and after the ANC was unbanned it is no secret that there have been a number of attacks on white farmsteads. Invariably these were attributed to Umkhonto we Sizwe and Azapo, the Azanian Peoples Organization, but evidence shows this is not true. Inkatha were the villains in some of these attacks and quite cleverly stamped the

26

carnage as the work of their black enemies. As recently as four months ago, three families were killed on farms in northern KwaZulu-Natal. Years before they had moved down from where they farmed near the Zimbabwe border. One of the families was related to a senior member in the group and he never rested until he believed he knew who had done it. His findings pointed to Inkatha, specifically Shozi. That is one of the reasons why he is on the list.

Shozi lives in his own house in KwaZulu-Natal. He seldom leaves and then only for short periods when warring against those to whom he has taken a dislike. The three guerillas appear to spend most of their time in Malakazi township. The resting places of these four men should be ideal for your purposes and details are attached. Other information you will need are in other sections of this document.

'That is a comprehensive statement on these four blacks,' said Dalton. 'I'll read the rest in the car, where they are staying and their movements. Teichmann said you wanted to drive.'

'Yes,' said Krige. 'For part of the way you can concentrate on the document. First, I want to park further down the road or up a side road, somewhere less conspicuous. Wandering eyes soon take an interest in a vehicle that doesn't move for three days. Bring the Ford.'

Dalton followed in his car and when Krige parked in a side road he drew up behind. He opened his car boot and took out the 7mm Remington, in its scabbard, a Browning 9mm pistol and the Beretta 93R for Krige, both in holsters. The Beretta had the unique capability for a pistol in that it had a 20-round magazine and could fire, if necessary, three rounds in a single burst. It was the finest pistol Krige had used. There was a silencer for each gun.

The two men were soon on the main road that went through Pretoria and on to Pietermaritzburg 800 kilometres away. The turning to the heart of KwaZulu-Natal, home of the blacks, was in Pietermaritzburg.

'You will see in one of the sections the locations of the men,' said Krige. 'As far as their movements go it is a guess and we will have to find that out for ourselves. The group don't know the details and I can imagine their difficulty. Very briefly, Shozi's house is in the Edendale Valley, fifteen kilometers from Pietermaritzburg, five kilometers from Umbali township and four kilometers this side of Malakazi township. It is shown on the map. The area is very pretty, very quiet and the house, with quarters for the guards, is near the main road. It is the only road around. The Xhosas are staying in a room in Malakazi that belongs to the mayor of the township, a man named Dhlamini and is a few hundred metres from his house. I am confident both houses will be easy to find. If not we will have to call on the mayor.'

Krige paused then went on. 'As the document said we should go first for Shozi. Before then, I want to go and picture the layout of Malakazi. There is a footpath that goes along the side of the main road between Umbali and Malakazi and passes Shozi's house. The whole area is grass and woodland and I believe there are trees partly blocking the house from the path and the road.' Krige turned down the window. 'Amongst the trees there is a *kopje* and a trout stream that virtually follows the path. After Malakazi we will head for Shozi and take a vantage point in the *kopje*.'

'You have certainly prepared yourself,' said Dalton. 'I am impressed.'

'It is all in the document,' said Krige. 'There is quite a bit more. I have spent time reading it. Teichmann and his people did a good job. In a while we will stop for something to eat and buy some food and water for later. This could be a long job and we won't find a shop on every corner.'

Chapter 9

Berea, Durban

While he was involved with the Cartwright affair, Steiner had left a senior student to take the *karate* sessions. He did not know how he could help Smith any more and there would be little chance of getting the original file from Staples, unless the copy was found and the National Prosecuting Authority became involved. And, Smith had not asked him for any advice.

On a cool evening when he did not have a class he phoned Sophie Carswell.

She picked up the phone and was pleased to hear him. After a few words he said: 'Would you like to go to the beachfront for something to eat.'

'I would love to but I have been asked out by a guy at the dance school,' she said. 'I don't particularly like him but he was insistent and I said yes. He is a bit strange and before and after every class he parades himself in front of the wall mirror. I'll be back at around nine. Come up here for a drink.'

'You might be held up,' said Steiner. 'What about tomorrow night.'

'That's great,' she said. 'You can pick me up at eight.'

'That's fine,' said Steiner. 'I will see you then.'

After the call Steiner sat in the living room and thought about Sophie. She hadn't changed since he saw her before he went to Japan and he regarded her as one of the most attractive girls he had met. Her passion for life, the way she moved, only enhanced her good looks. He knew he could easily fall in love with her and in some ways that was something he feared. He was in part a loner and even though he knew his natural ability and determination had helped his development in life, it was the other that had put ice in his veins.

The following evening Steiner finished the class at seven-thirty. He went to his flat round the corner and after a shower drove up the Berea to where Sophie was staying. He rang the bell and she opened it. She wore a knee-length black dress and high heels, and her make-up was perfect. They greeted one another and she was about to lead him inside when someone came out of the shadows near the gate and walked up to the door.

Sophie was momentarily stunned and then said: 'John Kallis, what are doing here? James Steiner and I are going out for a drink.'

'I'll come with you,' said Kallis. He eyed Steiner. 'I hope you don't mind.'

'I do,' she said. 'You were not asked and I don't know what you are doing here, hanging about in the shadows. That's very strange behaviour.'

He laughed humourlessly. 'So this guy has got you all to himself.'

'Yes,' she said. 'That is the way I want it. Please go.'

He walked to within an arm's length of her. 'Just leave him and we will go alone.' He was starting to lose his cool and took hold of her arm. 'I'm getting impatient.'

'Leave her,' said Steiner. 'She's too good for you.'

Kallis let Sophie's arm go and stared at him. For a moment he was still, unsure. There was something strange about Steiner, something dangerous. He smiled at Sophie, turned and slowly walked towards the gate.

Steiner faced Sophie, who was amazed at the way he had dealt with Kallis.

'Let's go in.' he said. 'He won't come back.'

They went inside and locked the door. Sophie sat down in the nearest chair. Her mind went to what Steiner had told her about Japan and she wondered what he had done to the three men who came for him. When he had taken sexual advantage of her in London she had sensed his presence and feline strength and she felt it now.

Steiner stood near her. 'You will never rid the world of men who behave like that and enjoy it. The only chance you have of defending yourself is through the law or doing what you can to the best of your ability.'

She got up. 'After that I'm not in the mood to go out.' She walked over to him and held his hand. 'Let's have a drink here and call it a night. That creature has spoilt the evening.'

She led him into an adjacent room. There was a drinks cabinet against the wall. 'What would you like,' she said. 'Everything is here.'

He asked for a glass of water and she poured a Campari for herself. When they were seated on the sofa she asked: 'When were you last in Japan?'

'Just after I saw you in London,' he said.

'When you went for me?'

He was quiet and then said: 'Not the best thing I have done.'

'But you showed such passion,' she countered. 'I enjoyed it even though I was angry. You were so gentle. I heard you had left for Japan.'

'You were very attractive,' he said.

She smiled and stared at him. 'How would you like to take me to Japan? It's coming up for their autumn, apparently the most beautiful season in their year.'

'How do you know?'

'Paul Adams told me. That was before we broke up.'

'Why did you?' he said.

'We had nothing in common. All he was interested in was *aikido* and watching television. Essentially he was an empty shell. Not my type.'

'What is your type?' he said.

'I'll tell you one day,' she said, the hint of a smile caressing her lips. 'What about Japan? I would love a break from South Africa.'

31

'We will go,' he said. 'At the moment I don't know when. There is something I want to see concluded, even though I am not involved anymore.'

'That sounds very mysterious.'

He looked at her. 'We will go to Japan as long as you behave yourself,' he said cryptically and with a smile.

She was about to respond when he changed the subject. 'What will you say to John Kallis. People like that have to prove something and that is when they are dangerous.'

'I want nothing to do with him,' she said emphatically. 'He will get the message. He can be pleasant when he chooses but that is when he thinks he has a chance with me. He is very charming with women and very intelligent, though that did not show tonight. I must have been blind to go out with him, even if it was only now and again. I turned him down several times.'

'What does he do?' asked Steiner.

'Have you ever heard of the Directorate: Special Operations, the DSO?' she asked. 'They are known as the Scorpions and have a crime fighting capacity to investigate and prosecute national priority crime. I know his boss is a Peter Smith. He talks a lot about the DSO and is obviously drawn to his work'

They spoke for a while longer then he said: 'You need some sleep. I will phone you.'

She let him out through the front door and when she had closed it, said softly: 'Sleep well James Steiner. If you don't make a play for me, stay away. I'm falling in love with you.'

As Steiner drove home he thought about what Sophie had said concerning Kallis and the man's work with the DSO. It was incongruous that Kallis' boss was Peter Smith. He had had difficulty concealing his surprise when she told him. He thought about the file, the job Kallis might have and wondered if he got on well with Smith. He sensed by Kallis' accent that he was Afrikaans and he found that unusual. There weren't many Afrikaners in

Durban. He told himself to forget about the man. He wouldn't see him again.

Chapter 10

KwaZulu-Natal, Republic of South Africa

Moses Shozi held up his hand as he came to the crest of a hill, small in the vast theatre comprising the Edendale Valley. The land was KwaZulu-Natal, homeland of the Zulus.

'Which one?' he said, grinning.

Behind Shozi in the moonlight of the late evening were thirteen men, strong in stature and in their prime, their heads shaven and reflective like domes of polished wood. They were in single file, their bodies clad sparingly in shorts, loose-fitting shirts and heavy belts, their feet bare, impervious to the thorns and stones scattered among the grass. Firmly thrust into their belts, were wide-bladed *pangas*, half-axe, half-knife, the time-honoured implement for hacking through indigenous bush and cutting men to death.

'It's the third on the left.' Joseph Setlaba returned the grin. He liked it when his master was in a buoyant mood. 'They stay with their mother, Mrs Mkhize.'

Below them, several hundred metres distant and couched in one of the many shallow valleys lay half-a-dozen modern houses in a staggered row. Shozi glanced at the cans of paraffin carried by two of his men then urged the group on. The pounding feet crushed the long-stemmed grass as the men descended on the homes before them ignoring the silhouettes they etched against the top of the hill and confident of their authority behind the barrel-chested warrior they had elected to serve.

When they came to Mrs Mkhize's house Shozi drew his blade, adjusting the .38 Webley revolver poked into his belt. He cut into the door, exploding the lock and ripping into the jamb. Whining on rusting hinges the door surrendered and Shozi went through.

Seated on a sofa and cradling girl twins in her arms an obese woman cried out as Shozi appeared. She held the children tightly, the muscles of her arms hidden by the coating of fat that had accumulated from years of eating a high-starch diet of *mielie* porridge, sausage and bread.

Skirting his master Setlaba went to the room adjoining and peered inside, noting five untidy bedrolls, three near the window and partitioned from the others by a low sackcloth screen. There was no one there and he ambled back, shaking his head.

'Where are your sons?' said Shozi, hovering over her. She started weeping, the tears welling in her eyes and onto her cheeks.

'Please don't hurt them,' she begged. 'They are good boys.'

Shozi hit her on the face with sickening impact, a steel knuckle-duster, shaped into the horned head of a bull, biting into her, cutting a furrow from her cheek to her jaw, drawing a thin line of blood.

'Where are they,' he growled evenly. 'I'll not harm them but they must learn to be loyal to Inkatha.'

She sobbed quietly, her hand covering the wound, his words providing a measure of reassurance and reducing her fears. Deep within a voice warned that Shozi was a killer, one who operated with impunity, but she ignored it, choosing to believe her sons would be spared. 'They work in the city,' she said softly. 'Tonight they'll be late.' She drew the children closer. 'They're on the last bus.'

Shozi dug in a pocket for his watch. 'Thirty minutes,' he said, weighing up the information. He glared at her. 'Take your children and stay in the other room. We'll wait.'

She bowed, holding her hands together and to her face, as if in prayer to her chosen god. 'Please don't hurt them Mr Shozi,' she repeated pleadingly, bending lower. The girls cowered against their mother, terrified, but too young to understand.

Shozi hit her again, his fist brushing her hands away, feathers caught in a gale. She was thrown back on the sofa and he had drawn more blood, a seepage that spread like new red paint and ran down into her eye. But he was without remorse and gripped her arm, his fingers coils of wire, and jerked her bulk out of the seat, the children clinging desperately to her dress. She was spent, illiterate, unable to comprehend the hatred between men.

With a heave he shoved her towards the bedroom and she tripped, the children with her. Setlaba took over, pulling her onto her feet and pushing her through the doorway, cuffing the girls sharply on the ears as they huddled behind.

Shozi went to the front door. Outside on the sand his men stood obediently in a semi-circle waiting for his command. 'Hide them in the grass,' he directed as his lieutenant joined him. He examined the broken lock, casually peeling off flaking paint. 'By the time they see this it'll be over. We'll stay in here.'

Setlaba issued instructions to the men and they withdrew into the grass and clusters of bush. Satisfied, he returned inside, settling the door as firmly as he could against the frame.

Shozi nodded and went into the bedroom. Dabbing her bleeding face with a flannel, Mrs Mkhize stared up from one of the beds, the arms of the children around her waist, immersed like sticks in jelly. He locked the room and lowered himself onto a tomato box standing on its end. 'This night is ours,' he said. 'I've waited patiently for these two. For too long they have brazenly supported the men who now rule this land.'

When Moses Shozi rested his weight on the box in their mother's house, Thomas and Ephraim Mkhize caught the bus at the depot in the city. The journey home was nearly twelve kilometres, down the Edendale Road into KwaZulu and up the valley. In the old single-decker Leyland bus, labouring up every hill, the ride took a full twenty-five minutes to an unmarked stop on the dirt road a few minutes walk from the house.

After disembarking they moved well off the road, watching the bus depart and letting the cloud of dust settle. Thomas led and they went over the road and into the bush, hungry and tired after a day that began before dawn, hoping their mother had dried porridge and meat in the pot. For a while their path took them up through grass, waist high and subjugated in places by large rocks. Then it dipped and levelled out under low trees, the profuse interlinking foliage deflecting the light like an iron roof. In less than a minute they were nearly through, about to emerge and a few hundred metres from their house. Along the narrow track Thomas had remained ahead, the white splayed soles of his bare feet padding quietly in the sand. As he came into the open he stopped as if turned to stone.

'What's wrong?' asked Ephraim, startled by the abrupt halt.

Thomas did not answer, grabbing his brother instead and leading him to a crouch next to the trail.

'Someone's squatting in the bush in front of the house,' he said in an urgent whisper. 'I saw him.' He pointed to a spot below them. 'It's difficult to make him out but I saw him.'

Ephraim looked to where his brother was pointing. 'Who is it?' he asked, anxiety creeping into his voice.

'Inkatha's bullies are always sniffing around,' said Thomas angrily. 'Be patient. I'm sure he'll move again.'

They waited at the top of the slope, scarcely breathing. 'Perhaps I was mistaken,' said Thomas at last, beginning to feel annoyed with himself. 'I suppose it could've been an animal.'

As he spoke they saw a movement and someone behind a bush close to where he had pointed.

37

'There, I told you,' Thomas exclaimed, gaining some satisfaction that he was right. 'What do they want?' At that moment the door to their house opened and a bold figure, briefly outlined, walked onto the sand. He called into the dark and before him a group of men rose and came from the undergrowth. He directed them to him and they all went inside, closing the door.

At first the brothers were too numbed to speak. Then Thomas turned to Ephraim, afraid. 'Do you know that man?' he asked and without a reply said: 'It's Moses Shozi, our enemy.'

'They'll kill poor mama.' Ephraim cried quietly. 'What've we done to bring this man to our house?'

'Nothing,' said Thomas unrepentantly, trying to console his brother by placing his arm round him. 'Shozi's a murderer.' He poked his head up and studied the house, noting a thin line of light. 'The door's not shut,' he said, unable to see the shaved wood. 'Maybe they're preparing to leave.'

'They'll never give up,' said Ephraim, knowing how Shozi worked. 'If they leave they'll be back. We'll have to go into hiding.'

'We must see mama tonight,' said Thomas firmly. 'She may be hurt. Wait and see if they go.'

Chapter 11

Mrs Mkhize's house

Moses Shozi paced restlessly on the matting of the room, his hands held behind him, his countenance severe, that of a giant raptor. His men were seated on the floor in a ring round him, uncertain of his mood. It was ten-twenty and there was no sign of Mrs Mkhize's sons.

'Some of us should've waited on the road,' said Shozi, angry he had not thought of it before. 'They're not stupid. I think they saw you.'

The men were silent, not wanting to ignite the gangster's rage.

'I know how we can bring them in,' continued Shozi. He stopped near the door, rocking demonically on his large feet. 'Follow me. They're out there somewhere.'

Watching from their position on the hill Thomas and Ephraim shrank when after a few minutes Shozi reappeared in the yellow light, his men on his heels.

'They're leaving,' whispered Thomas, his hopes rising. 'When they've gone I'm going down.'

'I'm coming with you,' said Ephraim fiercely. 'If they've hurt mama I'll kill them.'

'There's nothing you can do,' interjected Thomas. 'The Zulu police are in their pockets, whatever evidence we manage to scrape together.'

They watched the men cross the sandy patch and begin their ascent of the hill. Within a short time the gang reached the top and went from sight, disappearing one by one.

'Give them more time until they get to the next valley,' said Thomas. The two stayed in the grass, eager to get to the house but wary in case Shozi decided to return. After a while Thomas went onto the track.

'Come on,' he said harshly. 'We must hurry to mama.'
They ran down the remainder of the path and accelerated
over the final stretch to the house.

'Wait,' cried Thomas, fearful again when he saw the
exposed white pine where the *panga* had cleaved. He
looked through a half-inch split that offered a partial view.
But his concern for their mother and sisters was too great
for him to deliberate any more and he went in.

Ephraim sprang past him and seeing the empty room
ran to the closed door, disengaging the bolt and going
through. His mother was still on the bedroll with the twins,
her lacerations drawing him inexorably to her. She rolled
her eyes and reached for him with a joyous cry.

'Ephraim, you are safe. Where's Thomas?'

They embraced, the twins snuggling and squealing
against his body. Then Thomas was next to them, throwing
his arms out like an octopus, encircling and holding the
family together. For minutes they smothered one another
with their love, sharing the pain.

'We must leave soon, mama,' said Thomas. 'He'll be
back. We have friends in Umbali.'

Mrs Mkhize rested her big head on Thomas. 'Oh my
sons, you'll be so tired when you get there. I must give
you what food I have.' She had wiped the blood from her
cheek and the cuts were clotted channels. Ephraim helped
her up and with Thomas holding the twins they made to
leave.

But like a bad dream Shozi appeared, his cracked lips
pasted to crowned teeth. 'I knew you were out there,' he
cried exultantly. 'How easy it was to bring you in.' He
moved over and Setlaba came in, two of the others next to
him. 'Take them,' said Shozi relaxing his arms in triumph.

Mrs Mkhize went to her knees, uttering a muted
scream. 'What do you want from us Mr Shozi?' she cried.
'We've nothing for you. Please leave us alone.'

Shozi ignored her, his attention only on her sons.

40

Thomas and Ephraim knew they were in trouble, that surrender was out of the question and as Setlaba came nearer they ran from their family, jumping over the bedrolls to the window. Ephraim reached it first and scooping up a blanket broke through the panes of glass and struts of wood. He started to climb onto the sill but one of the men was too quick and, grabbing his trousers below the groin, tore him from the window, throwing his skinny body effortlessly onto one of the beds. Giving up his bid to escape, Thomas hit the man on the neck, sending him spinning off like a toy top.

'You can't escape,' said Shozi, taking the gun from his belt. 'For this you'll die.' Setlaba closed in, slamming Thomas to the floor, the large muscles bunched and striated under his shirt. The other two men sprang onto the brothers taking them by the ankles and through the sitting room to the front of the house. In terror Ephraim and Thomas fought to stay indoors knowing that once outside they were doomed. But there were too many of them and they were helpless against the heavily built men.

They were dropped like sacks of grain onto the earth, discarded as carrion and the eight Zulus formed a circle around them. Inviting the men who carried the cans to do their work Shozi watched as they removed the caps and came up to the youths. When Thomas and Ephraim saw the half-gallon containers, cleaned of their labels and shining in the light, they screamed pitifully, their high-pitched cries slowly devolving to pathetic whimpering, the noise of the condemned.

Shozi was as if in a trance and started chanting, urging the bizarre show on, gyrating his body rhythmically in the dance of death. The others joined in, waving their *pangas* in the air, delighting in a ritual they had seen before. Swaying in concert, the men with the paraffin drenched their victims until their clothes were stained and the oily fluid clung like glue to their skin and short wire-brush hair. In a last flurry to save himself, invoking tenuous threads of strength, Thomas charged at the circle of men, his fuelled movements fanned by the deepest craving to survive.

As he neared the perimeter he lowered his head, an attacking goat, selecting a spot between two of the men, and charged. His move was unexpected and a metre from his goal he felt he could get through. But their reactions were as sharp as surgical steel and they converged, grunting excitedly, enjoying the exercise before the meal, the agony of the boys before them. As a coordinated unit they tripped him up, expertly taking him to the ground, his greasy face forced into the sand. With practiced ease they locked his arms behind him, causing him to cry heretically and threw him into the centre of the ring. Ephraim went to his brother's side and lovingly held his head above the dirt, no longer thinking about his own safety. His brother was going to die.

Bored by the foreplay, Shozi stopped his chanting and came into the circle. From point-blank range he fired his gun, the lead striking Thomas and Ephraim in their knees, breaking and splintering, turning the legs into useless sticks. They shuddered but could not cry any more, holding one another instead with brotherly love, resigned to the horrifying death that was to come, a dispensation from Satan himself.

Stuffing the Webley into his belt, Shozi looked at Setlaba. The tall lieutenant went to him, reaching into one of the pockets of his shorts for a box of matches. He lit two and flicked them in turn onto their victims' clothes, grinning savagely when he saw the flames leap, engulfing the youths all at once in the unbearable heat, scorching their young features in a crackling frenzy.

Shozi and his men did not stay to see the corpses reduced to charred remains and with the fire devouring its feast he led his band off, going to the grass and up the hill. Behind him was quiet, the neighbours, whatever they saw, not daring to resist and further incur his wrath.

Mrs Mkhize, the bedroom locked, knew when she heard the last screams of her sons that they were dying, the most recent act of murder by Shozi. She wept in gasps as if retching into a bucket, the misery and torment too much to bear.

Chapter 12

Moses Shozi's house

Moses Shozi lived nearly three kilometres from Mrs Mkhize's home on flat land in a double-storied house. It overlooked a running stream and *kopje* that in the rugged magnificence of its huge boulders, shear in places like an alpine face, was incongruous on the grassland. When he and his loyal file reached his stronghold, an hour after slaughtering Mrs Mkhize's sons, he went inside, telling Setlaba to dismiss the men and send them to their rooms, a white-washed abode across the yard from the house.

The house was worthy of no name, rectangular with a gabled roof of terracotta tiles. There were three bedrooms upstairs and a lounge and kitchen below. It was sparsely furnished but Shozi chose to have it that way, preferring to save the money he made from running *shebeens* and gambling dens in the townships.

After placing his *panga* and pistol on a chair the gangster went to the kitchen and took a bottle of beer from the fridge, popping the cap and injecting a copious quantity of the liquid down his throat. He seated himself at the table, placing the bottle on the synthetic surface.

Setlaba entered, thirstily contemplating the beer but waiting until his master gave him permission to take one.

'This evening we had a little fun,' said Shozi when Setlaba sat near him with a beer. 'Mrs Mkhize's sons deserved to die but weren't important. There are other men who are far more dangerous. In the coming years they'll be the new military commanders in this country.' He drained the bottle and got two more. 'These men belong to Umkhonto we Sizwe, the Spear of the Nation. They're Xhosas.'

'Who are they?' Setlaba watched the hatred simmer.

44

Shozi went on. 'For the last five years three of these men have been in self-imposed exile at a bush camp in Zambia. A year ago they refused to apply for political amnesty, which was permitted, because they feared prosecution for previous crimes running guerilla cells. They wouldn't have dared enter the country under the Nationalists but now with a new government they feel sure of themselves. A month ago they returned.'

Setlaba sat up, interested.

'Last week,' said the gangster, 'I was informed that these dogs are here under our nose, two valleys beyond Mrs Mkhize and four kilometres from here.'

Setlaba's handsome features lit up in expectation. 'They'll be more interesting than Mrs Mkhize's sons,' he said, traversing his tongue over frothed lips. 'When do we kill them?'

Shozi raised a finger in caution. 'This operation will take more preparation than tonight,' he said. 'These men are in the top league. They're like us. They fight like fanatics, like wild dogs, as if there is no tomorrow. And if they are cornered they go mad, like a buffalo with its belly full of shot.' He left the table and looked at Setlaba confidently. 'I already have a tail on these three bucks and it'll stay there until I know their movements. Then we'll execute them and burn their bodies for the rest of their breed to see.'

Chapter 13

Malakazi township

The three men whose deaths Shozi sought were together in a room in the township of Malakazi.

Also in the room, with his back to the door and dressed in an ill-fitting grey suit was the elderly mayor of the settlement, Joshua Dhlamini, a long-serving Zulu member of the ANC. A few minutes earlier he had carried the news of Moses Shozi's latest act of barbarism to the three men, news he had heard from one of Mrs Mkhize's neighbours who had witnessed the macabre spectacle from her room.

'When will the bloodshed stop?' cried John Nofomela angrily, banging his hardened fist on the rickety table around which they were seated. 'For years we were persecuted and driven from our country by the whites, like diseased animals, killed by the police, hanged on their gallows. Now, when apartheid is dead we are hunted by our own people.' He laughed at the irony of his words. 'For years Inkatha's jackals refused to support us in our fight for democracy. Why?'

'Inkatha is as racist as the Afrikaners,' said Paul Ngwenya, sneeringly. 'They want their own state, distinct from their ancient tribal enemy the Xhosa. They're unable to see that when the black people have the real foundations of political power, they can take the riches that rightfully belong to them and have been denied them for generations. Instead they sanction the murderous forays exacted against helpless people by their gangsters, men like Shozi.'

'Again we must go on the offensive,' said Nofomela. 'We obeyed the old men and laid down arms against the whites. But the Inkatha warlords have to be contained and destroyed. They are killing our children.'

The third man, Elijah Ngubane, watched the other two for a moment and stretched out his long legs under the table, folding his arms on his sunken chest. He was older than the others by two years and was generally accepted as the leader when they were together.

'I agree,' he said, his tone as hard as newly forged steel. 'But we can't go warring against Inkatha for everyone to see. The warlords are free men. We aren't and we'd be hunted down, leaving our young leaders open to criticism they can do without.'

As he spoke a large cockroach, its shiny wings laid flat like fine silk, streaked across the floor, twitching the inch-long feelers protruding from its head. Ngubane saw it out of the corner of his eye and with the speed of a snake retracted his foot from under the table and slammed it on the insect, squashing it with a crunch, spreading it thinly on the cheap linoleum. He viewed it distastefully and resumed.

'After a little planning we can conduct a campaign of elimination, beginning with Moses Shozi. Inkatha sees the ANC as an undisciplined, disorganized rabble and it'll be the last thing they expect.'

'He's well guarded,' said Ngwenya. 'His men never leave him.'

'There is always an opportunity,' countered Ngubane. 'We must take it. When he's dead we'll concentrate on the others. We'll always be on the move. No one will be able to pin it on us or the ANC.'

The room was owned by Joshua Dhlamini and the three Xhosas were his guests, sleeping at night on the solid floor, their bedding and spare clothing stacked during the day against the wall. The accommodation, with an external toilet and shower behind, was a few hundred metres from Dhlamini's house. It was situated on the road running through the township and surrounded by a pigmentation of banana trees and a thick convolution of Natal bush. In addition to his duties as mayor, Dhlamini ran a general store on the outskirts of the settlement. He had purchased the room for storing sacks of meal, canned food and dried meat, but the extra storage had never been required and he now used the room for housing guests who passed through, like the three guerillas. It suited him because he feared Inkatha and playing host to their arch-enemy in his house would have placed his life and the lives of his family at great risk.

When Ngubane finished speaking Dhlamini went to the table. He had heard the conversation and was worried, the furrows on his brow deeply engraved. 'Inkatha will seek the most terrible revenge,' he said tremulously. 'They have informers everywhere and will quickly find you. My family will be destroyed.'

Ngubane soothed him. 'We'll leave this place,' he said quietly. 'While we're at work we won't come near you or anyone else. We'll live in the bush as we've been taught to do.'

Dhlamini gave a watery smile, a little reassured, but Inkatha atrocities were still an ugly scar. He was weak at heart and admired the three men, wishing he had their nerve. 'Thank you,' he said. 'I'd rather die than see my children dismembered and put to death in front of me.'

Ngubane smiled. 'They'll never find us.' He knew Dhlamini had little courage, but the man was loyal and he had his purpose. He addressed the other two. 'Tomorrow we'll visit Shozi. Now let's sleep.'

Chapter 14

Near Moses Shozi's house

When the first hint of dawn revealed the disarray of ramshackle dwellings that formed Malakazi township the three guerillas left Dhlamini's room for the undergrowth that bordered the settlement. In fifteen minutes they reached Mrs Mkhize's house and passed quietly, noting the broken door and blackened earth around which the killings had occurred two evenings before. Even at the early hour they saw others pushing along the narrow paths of the grassland to the nearest road where they could pick up the bus to the city.

After three kilometres Ngubane, his round shoulders like those of a roosting crow, went off the path, calling a halt.

'The house is in the next valley,' he said adjusting a ten-inch knife he carried at his waist. 'Meet here at noon.'

They were a third of the way up a hill on a path that soon descended through grey head-high boulders and thorn trees. About to split up Nofomela and Ngwenya inched forwards then stopped as Ngubane spoke again. 'We're being followed. Keep to the path.' Casually he ambled off, winding down to where the track disappeared.

When they passed the bend the guerillas went from the trail into the grass among the rocks. For a while no one appeared, then with infinite care a figure emerged, a black youth, barefooted and clad in a dirty shirt and shorts to his knees. In his hand he held a stick and a thin bush knife poked from his belt, the blade crudely fashioned out of a piece of mild steel, ground so it was cardboard thin.

For a while the youth concentrated ahead then turned his attention to the immediate trail, combing for tracks. Unsure, he slid out the knife, the movements of his head sharp and truncated, apprehensive.

Ngubane came from the grass, a black spider, and the youth pivoted pathetically, waving the blade like a twig. But he was too late and the guerilla deflected the metal, jerking the youth round and embracing his neck, forcing his arm against his windpipe until he choked.

'Who're you from?' said Ngubane. He reduced the grip and waited, then again took up the slack, unsheathing his blade and resting the edge on the scrawny neck.

'I was told to follow you.' The youth spat onto the track, scowling as Nofomela and Ngwenya came from the rocks. He was a Zulu and though unnerved by the blade on his jugular he reminded himself that Xhosas, especially men of the ANC, were beneath contempt. He stretched his neck to ease some of the pressure caused by the guerilla's arm but Ngubane drew him closer, the first drops of blood smearing the steel. 'Who's your master?' he said.

The youth spluttered, gritting his teeth and arching his swollen lips over his gums. 'He'll kill me,' he gurgled, watching the others advance.

'Then you must leave the area,' chipped in Nofomela, his pupils like cannon holes. 'It's your master or us.'

The youth considered his options. If he refused he was convinced he'd be destroyed. 'I work for Moses Shozi,' he said faintly. 'He told me to follow you, find out where you go.'

'How long have you been tailing us?' Ngubane altered the position of the knife.

'Since yesterday morning in Malakazi,' said the youth.

Ngubane thought over the previous day. Most had been spent in Dhlamini's room. The youth couldn't have learned anything but he would have seen the mayor. Dropping his arm he shunted the knife to his other hand, clasping it cleanly and switching the blade back to the neck.

The youth jumped vigorously against the weak hold, pulling strongly as the tip of the knife nicked him below the ear. Like a hare running for its life he dodged to the side of Nofomela and into the grass, his knees pumping high, hurdling rocks in his path.

Dispelling amazement at the youth's boldness Ngubane chased after him, cursing loudly at his carelessness and jostling his comrades to make way. He held the knife like a sword, pointing it ahead, the curved Bowie blade glinting as it reflected rays from the rising sun. In several giant strides he had caught up and he lunged repeatedly, feeling a thrill as the tip drew blots of blood that were absorbed by the youth's shirt. The Zulu shook each time the steel punctured his skin, his spent breath a shrill whistle and he leaned his body over as he ran, trying to evade the incisions that were slowly bringing him down.

Metres from the track Ngubane came abreast, finding his victim's collar with his long fingers. The youth cried as Ngubane yanked him to a stop, rotating the weapon and slipping it under his neck. With a rising jerk Ngubane sliced it in, navigating the tempered steel through arteries and thin muscle, noting how the young arms flailed insipidly as the blood spurted out in a jet.

Ngubane held him as he died then dropped him onto the hill. Flaring his mouth he turned victoriously as his colleagues came up. 'Hide the corpse,' he said, wiping sweat from his brow. 'He chose the wrong master.' He poked the knife into the earth and cleaned the blade, removing the final traces of blood with tufts of grass.

They took the body further from the trail and laid it between the rocks, rearranging the grass to form a grave. They left the scene, losing one another as they went on their different routes to Shozi's house.

Chapter 15

Moses Shozi's house

Ngubane's route to their destination was the shortest and he arrived first, approaching through thick bush that lay alongside the stream. The house was nearly 300 metres away on level ground, and he peered at the curtained window of the upstairs room where he expected Shozi to be fast asleep.

For an hour he rested on the bank of the stream, every now and again checking the buildings. Then like an alien in a deserted land a tall man left the rear quarters and strolled to the house. He disappeared and a little later Ngubane saw the curtains of the room drawn and a man appear. He had never seen Shozi before but the heavy figure could only be the gangster and he craned his neck to get a better view. For a while Shozi stretched in the window, luxuriating in the tender warmth of dawn and then he had gone.

Ngubane leant on a tree, the picture of the man he had come to hate fuelling his resolve to see him dead. He had what he wanted, confirmation that Shozi was at home.

Over the next half-hour other men emerged from the quarters. Ngubane counted twelve and they sat on mats in a circle round a big pot of porridge one of them had carried from a detached outhouse, chatting noisily as they helped themselves. When they finished they were joined by the tall man, who came from the house. For a few minutes he spoke rapidly, periodically pointing over the hills in the direction of Umbali, a large township further up the Edendale Valley. After clearing their remains they returned to their rooms and a little later five of them headed for the grass.

For most of the morning Ngubane watched the house from his position on the bank. The remaining guards stayed in their quarters and there was no sign of Shozi or the tall man, who he assumed was the gangster's lieutenant. At a quarter to twelve he left the bank and took a circuitous route round the *kopje* and between the rocks that bordered the stream further up. He finally rejoined the path from Malakazi and steadily made his way to the spot where he had agreed to meet the others. He stayed near the track until they arrived then the three hid themselves in the bush, eating a meal of dried meat and bread, stuffing the food into their mouths between brief accounts of the morning's work. From their vantage points behind the outhouse Nofomela and Ngwenya had not seen Shozi and became exited when they heard of his presence.

'We must take a chance he is still there and kill him tonight.' Ngubane scratched the bristle on his cheek, his belly full. 'There isn't time to get the guns from Umbali and we don't need them.' He went to a small sapling and urinated against it, grossly splashing the yellow liquid up and down the thin stem.

Startled by the statement Nofomela and Ngwenya appraised his narrow back. Ngwenya was the first to speak. 'How can we kill him without guns?' he asked, frowning. 'His men are never far.'

Nofomela nodded. 'We can have Kalashnikovs by tomorrow. We must wait.'

Ngubane fastened the buttons on his fly, shaking his head. 'We might have to wait hours, days, for a decent shot. When Shozi doesn't hear from the youth he'll go crazy and come looking for us. He'll take in Dhlamini, torture his family and then kill them. It would've been different if he didn't know about us but he does.'

'We'll have to enter the house,' said Nofomela, mindful of the way Zulus treated their captives. 'It's too dangerous.'

'There's no alternative,' said Ngubane grimly. He gazed down the hill to the valley, welcoming the unremitting breeze. 'I'll do it alone. I'm the only one with a knife.' He grinned, a straight line. 'But first we must get our things from Dhlamini's room. From now on we live in the bush. The flames of hell will seek vengeance when Shozi dies.'

Chapter 16

Moses Shozi's house

As the three guerillas left for Malakazi, Moses Shozi reclined contentedly in the lounge of his house, replenished by a fill of low-grade stewing steak and a vegetable mash. Setlaba, his large angular frame equally recharged by the meal, lingered dutifully nearby.

'The boy should've shown by now,' said Shozi irritably. 'It was a simple job.' He scowled, bowing his head in thought.

Setlaba was pleased when Shozi's anger was elsewhere, when an accusing finger could not be directed at him. 'He'll be back,' he said sagely. 'Movements of men like that are as unpredictable as a woman's love.'

Shozi propped a cushion behind him, clearing phlegm with an angry cough. 'Where're the men?'

'I sent some to Umbali. The rest are cleaning the rooms.'

'During the night I want one of them behind the house,' said Shozi after a while. 'Not knowing exactly where these guerillas are makes me nervous. Their type never lies down.'

'They're scum,' said Setlaba. 'The ANC military arm, Umkhonto we Sizwe, is finished.'

'Not yet,' replied Shozi. 'Some of them haven't got what they want. Mass conflict on our natural territory between us and the Xhosa has subsided from the exchanges a year ago, but elements in their military are as virulent as ever. If these men succeed they'll have what is ours by birth.'

55

Chapter 17

Moses Shozi's house

In the early afternoon with the sun past its peak the three guerillas reached the room in Malakazi. They gathered their bedrolls and spare clothing and were again in the bush retracing their steps to Shozi's house. When they reached a point near where the youth lay in his grave they left the trail and settled.

'After Shozi's dead we'll hole up here,' said Ngubane, lying on a bed he had shaped for himself. 'When the dust is no more, we'll go to Umbali for the guns.'

Nofomela and Ngwenya also spread themselves out on the earth after clearing patches in the grass and they were soon asleep, shaded from the sun by the leafy branches of a tree. They slept soundly until the late evening then built a low fire from dry sticks and roasted a chicken they had caught in the township.

Shortly after eleven o'clock they cleared the site, scattering the fire and stuffing their belongings under the rocks. They resumed their journey, keeping to the track for most of the way until they began their descent into the gangster's valley.

There were no lights on in the house and quarters as they came from beyond the *kopje* and to the bank of the stream. Ngubane studied the house while he toyed idly with the hilt of his knife. Then he went into the grass followed shortly by the others at intervals. When he was in line with the house he parted from his comrades and ran up to the end wall, stopping flat on the roughened surface. He held back a minute before feeling himself along to the corner. Diagonally across the yard he saw Ngwenya appear from the bush next to the quarters and then closer, over a bit, Nofomela.

56

Cautiously he looked round, squinting to penetrate the dark more easily, and could see the outline of a porch. He was about to move when Nofomela waved urgently, pointing ahead. Signalling that he had seen him Ngubane looked into the shadow, meticulously taking in every inch. He saw nothing and went carefully down the wall. He was beginning to think Nofomela had gone mad when he saw a man squatting next to a voluminous earthen pot, his head hanging so his chin touched his chest.

Ngubane watched the figure for a while. He thought about trying elsewhere but decided the guard was still a threat. He was five metres away and he judged how quickly he could cover the distance. For seconds he stood poised then he went in, unsheathing the knife. He was nearly on the squatting figure when the man came awake, reflexively grabbing for a stick leaning on the wall. But the Zulu was not fast enough and Ngubane bowled the weapon to the ground, stabbing with his knife, the steel sinking unhindered into the soft gut.

The guard's eyes bulged as the knife went in to the hilt. His expression was vacant, staring helplessly at the quarters, mutely calling his friends to his aid. Ngubane sliced the knife through the stomach wall, smothering his hand hard over the mouth to stifle sound. He drew out the knife and stabbed again, rotating the blade, then quickly extracted it as the dying man collapsed at his feet, the blood flowing from the mutilation onto the stone slabs.

Wiping the knife on the man's shirt Ngubane studied the door. When the steel was clean he moved to it, testing the handle on the varnished wood. It held fast. There was a lock and he wondered if there was an internal latch. He went to the corpse and dug into the pockets of the baggy shorts. Stifling a triumphant cry he removed a key and went to the door, eagerly inserting it. It went in unhindered and was the right one.

As if walking on broken glass, he went through the kitchen and into the lounge. Visibility was poor, external

57

light mostly shut out by heavy drapes on the windows. The luminous hands of his watch showed twenty to twelve and he thought of the dead man. At some point the guard would be changed.

He saw the stairs and after assimilating the dark went to them and began his ascent. On the first floor he calmed himself before going to the room that was sure to harbour the gangster. There was only quiet and he eased the door inwards, slipping through until he was just inside. Near the window he made out a wide bed and he listened, hoping to catch the breathing of Shozi deep in sleep. His heart pounded and he pulled up the knife, changing his grip, certain now that the gangster was there for he could see the shape of a body lying on the bed.

Ngubane went nearer and then the room was bathed in the light of a table lamp. Standing, encased in a sneer, was Shozi, his Webley pointed at Ngubane's heart. 'You took your time,' he said, lazily. 'I saw you killing my guard. He must have been asleep.'

The taunt penetrated Ngubane like the sting from a wasp but he kept his attention on the gangster.

'You're one of the guerillas,' continued Shozi, looking at Ngubane as if he was a leper. 'I thought you'd come sooner or later. You must have killed the youth.' He removed the sheet from a pile of blankets and grinned wickedly. 'I knew you'd use a knife. That must have looked tempting. I suppose your comrades are outside. They'll die as well.'

'No' said Ngubane. 'You will die. It will be the end of a heinous reign. The house is surrounded.'

Shozi blinked, a hint of doubt, and Ngubane took his chance. Lifting the knife with the craft of a juggler and taking the end of the blade he threw it with a scream. 'Die you monster.'

The knife spun lethally in the crisp air and for a second Ngubane felt victory was his. But Shozi was already going down, all the while keeping the gun unerringly on his foe.

The knife flew by and certain of the guerilla's death he fired. The slug hit Ngubane above the heart, driving him back like a stickman caught in a wind, his body corkscrewing in a contortion of flying arms and gangling legs. He landed on his hip, expecting the second shot and acutely conscious he had to keep moving. He rolled and came to his feet.

At the second shot Ngubane leapt like a running deer as the bullet cut into his calf. He got to the door, projecting himself through onto the landing. Excited voices out the back spurred him on and he hopped and skipped to the stairs, blood inseminating his clothes, a powerful dye.

Incensed that the guerilla did not go down, Shozi shouted with rage, the thought of his enemy escaping too much to bear. He sprinted through the door, yelling for his men, threatening them with a cruel death if they failed to stop the man who had dared think he could take his life.

Ngubane half-fell half-slid down the narrow flight of stairs, clutching the balustrade for support, expecting Shozi's men to burst through the kitchen at any second and block his path. He felt naked without a weapon and longed for a cold Kalashnikov in his hands. When he reached the ground floor he turned from the kitchen hoping he could get out through the front. In several hops he was at the curtain covering the French windows and he drew it aside, relieved when he saw the dark night. Grabbing an iron ornamental cow he smashed it into the glass, breaking the membrane into shards that rocketed away. Behind him he heard the guards enter the kitchen, driven on by the screeching gangster above and he lurched through the glass onto the porch. Partly crippled he went across the slate into the grass that came up to the house, doubling over, knowing the men would soon be on him if they could get sight of him.

Moments later Shozi appeared on the porch firing wildly at a figure he could not see, cajoling like a trooper and commanding the men behind him to take to the grass.

Motivated by the thought of a slow death at the gangster's hands Ngubane kept going until he came to the *kopje*, gulping for air, the blood on his shirt expanding concentrically, the petals of a morning rose. The ache in his shoulder was growing and he felt himself getting weaker as he lost blood. Behind him he heard Shozi's men brushing through the grass in pursuit and at times he glimpsed them against the white house. He thought of his friends and was sure they had escaped. To tackle superior numbers when they did not know how he had fared would have been folly. He huddled amongst the rocks, concentrating his senses to determine the whereabouts of his pursuers and trying to stem the flow of blood from his wounds. A few of the lights downstairs in the house came on and after a while there was no sign of Shozi or his hoard. He did not think the gangster had joined his guards in the chase and he mourned the loss of his knife.

After twenty minutes squatting amongst the rocks, his wounds urgently needing to be dressed and bound, Ngubane moved to the stream, desperate to reach his hideout in the valley beyond. His progress was dogged and slow and on occasion he picked up the voices of the men, but he passed through the night undetected, finally coming to the crest of the hill. He breathed more easily, confident he had shaken them off.

Within 100 metres of the hideout, Ngubane left the track and dropped into the grass. His strength was near its end but he lifted himself on his elbows and cupping his hands together mimicked the hooping call of a night owl, calling four times. There was only the murmuring of the gentle breeze and he called again, this time grateful as an answering cry came to him from a little up the hill.

In minutes Nofomela and Ngwenya were by him and they carried him the last stage down the slope to their resting place. With nimble fingers they sliced the cloth from the wounds and used a kit they always carried in the bush to treat ruptured tissue. When at last they laid him on his makeshift bed Ngwenya spoke.

'If only we'd had weapons,' he lamented. 'They'd have fallen and choked on their own blood.'

'We're not wanton killers. Shozi was the target.' Ngubane breathed deeply, arranging his frame into a more comfortable position. 'I failed. The Zulu saw me killing his guard.' He sighed weakly. 'Tomorrow his men will be all over this area.' He spoke to Nofomela. 'Before dawn go to Umbali and get the guns. We can't save Dhlamini but we can still kill Shozi.'

Chapter 18

Moses Shozi's house

Less than two hours after the attempt on his life the gangster's men returned to the house and assembled in the yard, expecting their failure to evoke another rabid outburst. But with a disgusted shake of his head Shozi sent them to their quarters, instructing only Setlaba to stay.

'The guard was incompetent,' said Shozi going back and forth on the porch. 'If I hadn't seen the Xhosa I might now be a corpse.'

Setlaba held himself abjectly. 'He'll not escape,' he said defensively. 'At first light we'll scour the valleys. He was badly hurt.'

Shozi chuckled scornfully. 'He was one of those guerillas. His friends would've been nearby. By now they'll be far from here.'

Chapter 19

Malakazi township, KwaZulu

Ngubane was still asleep when his comrades rose half-an-hour before first light and rolled up their bedding. His breathing was deep and harsh as his body fought valiantly against the damage inflicted on it and waged war on incipient infection. They cleaned and dressed the wounds, liberally applying antiseptic lotion and binding the tissue in a casing of white bandage.

'He needs a doctor,' said Nofomela soberly, poignantly reminding himself of the slow deaths of his friends, long since deceased, the victims of lesser wounds incurred in the bush.

'Dhlamini.' Ngwenya buttoned his shirt, his thoughts jumping ahead to the mayor in Malakazi. 'His brother's a doctor.'

Nofomela frowned. 'We gave our word we wouldn't go to him again.'

'The Zulu's life is already under threat,' intoned Ngwenya without feeling. 'The true test of his loyalty is now.'

'Yes,' agreed Nofomela, finding no fault with his comrade's reasoning. 'Besides, Ngubane's in urgent need of help and we don't know of anyone else in these valleys.'

They ate some stale food from their bag, then hoisted their drowsy friend and began the trip to Malakazi, along the path they'd taken earlier. It was an arduous journey and they traveled slowly, most of the time bearing Ngubane's full weight and finding it difficult walking three abreast on what was strictly a single track. Ngubane stirred periodically and they noticed with alarm his rapidly worsening condition. At mid-morning they reached the outskirts of the township and laid Ngubane in the long grass.

'I will go to Dhlamini.' Ngwenya surveyed the shacks imperiously. 'If he doesn't help us I'll kill him.'

'Be patient,' said Nofomela. 'Although he is a weak man he was a friend when we wanted one. Ngubane can't travel much further before he needs attention. He has to be seen by a doctor.'

Ngwenya set off through the grass, going in a circle before coming up to Dhlamini's house from behind. He knocked on the kitchen door hoping the mayor wasn't at the store. Dhlamini's wife answered and wrung her hands when she saw the guerilla.

'What do you want?' she asked in Zulu, her posture unwelcoming. Her husband had told her the three were about to move on and she hadn't expected to see them again. As far as she was concerned they would only bring death.

'I want to see your husband,' Ngwenya replied. 'It's a matter of urgency.'

She was going to lie, but she changed her mind, guiltily reminding herself that men like Ngwenya were allies, part of the black consciousness movement of which she'd been a member since a child.

'I'll get him,' she said, leaving him on the doorstep.

Dhlamini was soon there and he drew the Xhosa into the kitchen, closing the door conspiratorially.

'It's not good that you come here to my house,' he said fearfully. 'I can't be associated with you. Inkatha's spies are everywhere in the townships.'

Ngwenya held him on the arm. He detested the mayor's lack of spunk but did not show it. 'I must speak to you privately,' he said, irritated by the presence of Dhlamini's wife.

Without addressing the woman directly Dhlamini told her to leave and didn't speak until he and Ngwenya were by themselves. 'Why are you here?'

'Early this morning Ngubane entered Shozi's house and tried to kill him. He failed and in the process was wounded. The shoulder needs attention. He's lost a lot of blood and the wound is already infected.'

Dhlamini ground his worn teeth, reluctant to implicate himself, thinking about the rage of Inkatha, in particular that of Moses Shozi. 'I am not a doctor,' he said, hoping to drive Ngwenya away.

'But your brother,' said the guerilla persistently. 'He's the man who can help us.'

Dhlamini twitched uneasily. 'I have medicine here and bandages. Take this.' He shot eagerly over the linoleum to a cupboard above the fridge.

'No.' Ngwenya was insistent. 'He has to have professional care. Nothing less will do.'

Dhlamini was already poking in the cabinet. He closed it. 'Is he so bad?'

'He will die unless the bullet is removed. He is our brother, one who has sacrificed years of his life for the struggle. No wife, no children, no home. Everything was done for people who've suffered years under oppression. Are you so selfish that you can't give this little bit of help?'

Dhlamini knew the guerilla wouldn't back off. 'Tell me where you are and return. I'll do what I can to get the doctor. But he's a busy man.'

'We're up on the hill in the grass. We'll see you. I'm sure you won't let us down.' Ngwenya left the house and was soon lost among the shacks.

Dhlamini saw him go then joined his wife in the living room, where she sat stone-faced, playing with a string of beads round her neck.

'Ngubane tried to kill Shozi and was badly hurt,' he said from the doorway. 'He's in the grass. They want my brother to help him.'

'Is Shozi dead?' she asked, voicing her main concern.

'The attempt was unsuccessful. The man was unscathed. He's still alive.'

She beat her hands together. 'How can they make a mistake like that,' she cried. 'Why couldn't they have made sure? He'll destroy the township looking for them. You'll die.' She wept.

'Shozi won't associate us with Ngubane,' said Dhlamini, trying to be positive. 'No one knew they were staying in my room.'

'No one?' she replied incredulously. 'You yourself have said that his spies are everywhere. There're few ANC guerillas in these valleys, men with the audacity to break into an Inkatha warlord's house and try and kill him.'

'You're being pessimistic,' he said. 'When Ngubane's shoulder is patched up they'll be gone. I'm going to my brother.' Dhlamini let himself out and headed for the north of the township, keen to see his brother and finish with the three Xhosas.

The doctor lived in a house similar in design and construction to Dhlamini's, in keeping with his elevated status in the township. Attached and set back from the dirt road was his surgery, a plain brick building comprising a consultation room and a compact four-bed wing for critically ill patients.

As it was a Sunday, Dhlamini went to the house and rang the bell. The doctor opened it, shabbily dressed and not prepared for visitors, but inviting his brother and friend to pass inside. Dhlamini stayed where he was.

'I've an emergency. A colleague needs urgent medical attention. He's up on the hill.'

'What's wrong with him?' asked the doctor. 'Is it serious? Was he in a fight?' Many of his patients were the victims of knife and gun wounds.

Dhlamini took his brother and led him into the hall. 'The man's an ANC guerilla and he's been shot. You're the only doctor in these parts loyal to the ANC.'

66

The doctor spewed out the first question that came to him. 'Who shot him?'

'Inkatha,' said Dhlamini, not wanting to scare the doctor off by saying it was the result of an attempt to assassinate Moses Shozi.

'Stay here,' said the doctor. 'I'll get my bag.'

A minute later the doctor joined the mayor, holding a small case. 'Come,' he said. 'We'll go through the kitchen. Lead me to him.'

They went from the house and amongst the breeze-block dwellings, with their corrugated iron roofs and meagre vegetable patches ravaged by the drought. There were only a few people about, mostly women and children, going about the daily chores of carrying water and wood to their homes while the men were at work in the city. Some greeted the two men, but others, members of Inkatha, showed their disgust for those who had refused to join them even though they were Zulus.

In the grass on the hill Dhlamini and his brother found Ngwenya and Nofomela crouching next to their sick comrade. The doctor knelt beside Ngubane, releasing the clasp of his bag and drawing out his stethoscope. He felt the man's chest and examined the dressings without removing them, prodding carefully.

'He's lost a lot of blood. That's the cause of his weakness. The bullet must be removed and the wounds cleaned. They should heal. He's young, strong and will recover. For a few days he needs plenty of rest and regular treatment.'

'That means you, doctor,' said Nofomela. 'We don't want to take any risks with his life.'

'I'll replace the bandages,' said the doctor. 'Find a place in the township where he can stay.'

Ngwenya rubbed his growth of stubble. 'We can't use Dhlamini's room. You're the only one left, doctor. He can stay in your surgery. Anyone else will have to go.'

The doctor leapt angrily to his feet. 'There are two old people there. They're critically ill.'

'Do they have relatives, visitors?' said Nofomela.

'There are a few who visit infrequently.' The doctor blanched under his mottled skin. 'But he can't go to the surgery. Inkatha will go there first.'

Ngwenya sprang over Ngubane and slapped the doctor's face. 'You swine,' he cried. 'We're fighting for you and you treat us as if we're diseased.'

Nofomela went between them. 'This will not help Ngubane.' He confronted the doctor. 'Where else?' he demanded.

The doctor shuddered, wishing he was somewhere else. 'Who shot him? Inkatha is a band of cut-throats, disorganized. It may give us a day or two.'

'No,' said Dhlamini, unapologetically. 'They'll come to us before anyone else. Ngubane tried to kill Moses Shozi.'

Heaving his stomach as if he was about to vomit the doctor screamed: 'They'll be here in hours. He knows you'll need a doctor.'

'Ngubane can't lie in the bush,' said Nofomela, despising the man's cowardice. 'Find a place where he can be treated.'

The doctor trembled like a man facing a death squad. 'My sister-in-law lives further up the valley from me,' he said. 'I'll speak to her.'

'Arrange it,' said Nofomela bluntly. 'You've an hour. We'll be here with Dhlamini.'

Slinking off, the doctor went from sight and the two guerillas squatted next to their friend. For forty minutes they waited, Ngwenya tugging impatiently at stems of grass, breaking them into small pieces, and Nofomela gazing vacuously into the distance. Dhlamini sat obediently, keeping himself apart, silent, hoping the doctor would come up with something.

Quite suddenly the doctor was on them. 'There's a room in the house,' he whispered, his lined features tense. 'He'll not be disturbed.'

'Lead us to it,' said Ngwenya, rising and dusting his shorts. 'It's in your interest to make sure we're not seen by the wrong people.'

Chapter 20

Edendale Valley, KwaZulu-Natal

Leaving Pretoria, Krige and Dalton travelled to Pietermaritzburg and then the Edendale Valley. They bought food and canned drinks at a general store and it was mid-afternoon when they came to the turn-off to Umbali township. There was little sign of other life, only a few aging American sedans used as black taxis and the occasional small groups at the side of the road, the children waving in welcome.

'Where's the Zulu's house?' said Dalton, looking at what to him was a green wasteland. 'I don't like this place. It's only grass and hills. There're no cars. We stand out like pimples on a baby's arse.'

'KwaZulu's fragmented, broken up by white farms,' said Krige. 'It's not unusual to see whites on these roads.' He glanced at Dalton. 'Keep to this road. We'll see the gangster's house.' He uncased a pair of binoculars and held them on his lap.

Before long they saw Shozi's residence on the undulating land below them, the quarters in its shadow. 'Stick to a crawl,' said Krige, focusing the lenses on the complex. He studied it for a while then gradually took in the *kopje* that lay close to the bank of a meandering stream and a compact wild growth of trees and other natural vegetation. 'The rocks are perfect,' he said sinking into the seat. 'The notes I have are accurate.'

'And if you don't get a shot at him?' Dalton angled himself, studying Krige.

'I'll go closer,' said Krige. 'What do you expect? You've been in this business as long as I have.'

'You're forgetting the guards,' said Dalton. 'How do they fit into your plans?'

'I want to be back here by four o'clock,' said Krige, as if he hadn't heard. 'That gives us three hours of light.' He put down the glasses. 'Before then I want to see Malakazi where we should find the guerillas. We need to find a place for the car in that area so we can get out quickly after we have finished with the guerillas.'

Dalton released the clutch sharply and speeded up. 'What do we say if the Zulu police find the car?'

'The vegetation is a lot thicker round Malakazi than here and leaving the car there gives us a better chance of it not being detected,' said Krige.

Gradually the terrain changed from the predominant grass to a mix of scrub and flat-headed trees. After two valleys the township of Malakazi was visible from the road and marked by a corroded sign at the end of a graded track.

'Go on a bit and let us get out,' said Krige. 'We won't take long and I want a closer view.'

Further on Dalton pulled up the car, parked and the two men entered the bush. They walked until they reached higher ground and saw below them the dispersed amalgam of housing, an insignificance compared to the expanse of Soweto, the south western townships of the Transvaal, or Gauteng as it was now called.

'The path from Umbali comes in from the other side,' said Krige, going under a tree. 'It's to the east of the room the guerillas are apparently using.'

'Where is it?' Dalton looked at the map, scanning the shaded part of the settlement. 'How do you know?'

'The intelligence I've been given.' said Krige. 'That's about the end of the path.' He touched a spot on the map. 'The mayor's house is a few hundred metres to the west and the same again south. On a hypotenuse that's 700 metres. On this scale it's about there.' He moved his finger slightly.

'Very clever,' said Dalton. He expanded his broad chest and frowned. Mathematics had never been his strong subject.

Krige looked through the binoculars. 'Dhlamini's house is obvious,' he said after a while. 'It's twice the size of the others, which is what I'd expect.' He shifted the glasses a little. 'I've got the room. It's set alone with nothing beyond it except bush. It couldn't be better for us when we come back after killing the Zulu.'

'If they're there,' said Dalton. 'I'll be happy when they get some lead and we can get out of here.'

'They'll be there and you'll get your wish,' said Krige, his jaw line taut. 'You really hate them. Some will say they were fighting for human rights.'

Dalton' bronzed skin drained of colour. 'You astonish me Major. Life means nothing to them. They're savages, professional killers. Your children will die on their stakes. Is that what you want?'

'I want peace,' said Krige, baulking at the irony. 'Ultimately we must live together. There's enough here for all of us.'

Dalton shrugged in disgust. 'That's what I want, peace. These animals don't make it possible.'

'They do,' said Krige. 'Many of them want peace. Unless you and others like you change, you'll be the hunted, erased from this earth until you become a forgotten tribe.'

'Never,' said Dalton, stroking his gun.

'You can't stop it,' said Krige softly. 'But we digress.' He examined the area around the room. Finally he fed the glasses into their case. 'No sign of anyone at the house or the room. There is nothing else we can do here. Let's hide the car and go for the Zulu.'

They drove the vehicle down a deserted track that led further into thick vegetation. It was out of sight to anyone who wasn't deliberately looking for it. They took their weapons, the rifle in its scabbard to avoid attention, and started along the path to Shozi's residence.

Chapter 21

Malakazi township

Shortly after the doctor showed the guerillas to his sister-in-law's house he removed the bullet in Ngubane's shoulder and wrapped him in a bandage that all but hid his chest. He promised to return the next morning and for the remainder of the day Nofomela and Ngwenya stayed alongside their friend as he slept. The house was only of three rooms but the woman had no children and her husband was in prison for burglary. She gave them a room at the back, her manner curt and formal and she made it clear she was housing them under sufferance.

'I want to be amongst our own people,' said Ngwenya, standing at the window that overlooked the encroaching bush. It was early evening and they had been out to get something to eat. 'I hate having to watch my trail constantly.'

'We'll soon be out of KwaZulu,' said Nofomela. 'The ANC is at last in central government and that's where we will go. Inkatha will die like a cancerous limb.'

'They'll never relinquish their warring instinct,' said Ngwenya. 'Look at scum like Shozi . He reviles the Xhosa, calls them cowards, pigs.' He rolled a globule of saliva with his tongue and spat it onto the concrete. 'If only we had the men to take him and put a necklace over his head.'

'Forget Shozi,' said Nofomela. 'We didn't kill him. He's too well protected. We must be calm and now that we are back in this country wait for the call to help the objectives of our comrades.'

Ngwenya squinted at Ngubane, lying as still as a board under the grey blankets, breathing noisily. 'We're bound by him,' he said coldly. 'For days we'll be harboured in this miserable room, with Inkatha gangsters digging into every crevice. Our safety lies in the bush. How do we know the doctor and Dhlamini can be trusted? They might be leading them to us now.'

Nofomela moved wraith-like over the floor and patted his colleague. 'These thoughts will destroy you,' he said philosophically. 'Ngubane will recover and in a day or two we'll be gone from here. Patience, my friend, he needs us.'

Chapter 22

Near Moses Shozi's house

Before four, Krige and Dalton reached Shozi's valley, out of sight of the house and 100 metres from the path that joined Umbali and Malakazi. The wind that had fanned the feathery-green grassland through the day had abated, giving in to solitary silence. When Krige, walking ahead, reached the path he crossed it and steered for higher ground, climbing to the crest of a hill.

'There's the target,' said Krige, coming to a halt and turning to Dalton. 'This would've been perfect but the range is too great. I want to be sure of a shot through the head.' They shielded themselves behind some scrub and 800 metres below them they had a bird's eye view of the house and the guards' quarters at the rear. There was no one in sight.

They concentrated on the buildings for a while longer then left their spot, finally going over the path to the bottom of the valley below the road. Neither one spoke, each with his private thoughts. For a while they followed the narrow stream, occasionally driving speckled partridges from their nests in the bank and exciting a lone steel-blue kingfisher that flew up and down its domain.

'Up here,' said Krige at last, stepping agilely through the shallow waters and making for the *kopje* between them and the house. They positioned themselves amongst the rocks, close to where Ngubane had rested the previous night.

'This is too close,' said Dalton. 'We might as well sit in his house.'

'I told you this is where we'd come,' said Krige, unsheathing the rifle and laying it on the bag. 'When their master dies at their feet they'll be dumbstruck. We'll be in the next valley before they start looking.'

'Very clever Major,' said Dalton. 'And when is he supposed to appear?'

'His men spend hours around the pot every evening,' said Krige, getting annoyed at Dalton's constant sarcasm and beginning to wish he was alone. 'If he's there he'll join them.'

'Thanks for telling me,' said Dalton. 'I thought you were pushing your luck, hoping to get a shot at him. You knew all the time that he eats with his guard. You're not one for sharing information. I suppose you know precisely how you're going to kill the guerillas. What if they're not there? We'll be left standing in the dirt with our dicks in our hands.'

If ever he had been close to annihilating someone physically, Krige knew it was now and the person was Dalton. He remembered the acrimony he had felt towards Richter and Koch on the Cartwright job and he wondered if the group could ever find men of class, the breed needed for this type of operation. His training in the police had taught him the importance of staying calm and not reacting to puerile comments however much they fuelled his native instincts. But sometimes he failed and he wondered if this was going to be one such failure. He was so close.

'The guerillas have been there for a month,' said Krige. 'It would be too much of a coincidence if they've gone when we're about to strike.' He checked the mount underneath the scope, fighting his impulse. 'You sound as it you're about to crack,' he said. 'You can leave. I told you I can do this job alone.'

'Like hell you can, not all of them,' said Dalton. 'I'm interested in seeing a full score. It makes sense to keep me informed.'

'For what reason? I'm doing the work,' said Krige. 'Perhaps you think I'll get killed. Do you really think you can go it alone?'

'Yes,' said Dalton, annoyed at Krige's superior intelligence.

'And now you know everything,' said Krige coolly. 'It's as much as I do. There's no certainty in this game until the corpses are at your feet in a line, going hard.'

Krige turned then suddenly bent lower. 'Get down. The place is coming to life.' He held the binoculars on the yard between the house and the quarters. 'There're twelve of them and no sign of Shozi.' He gave the glasses to Dalton and took the magazine from a pocket in the bag. He inserted it into the rifle and, rotating the bolt, shunted one of the cartridges into the breech. Making himself comfortable, he poked the weapon through a V in the rocks and placed his eye to the lens.

For over an hour they silently watched the activities in the yard and long shadows were beginning to disfigure the valley when Krige inched his trigger finger forwards. 'Our man's arrived,' he said in a monotone. 'He's just come out of the house with someone else.'

Dalton lifted himself carefully. 'Which one is he?'

'I showed you his picture.' Krige stabbed at the safety catch with his thumb. 'He's the one on the left. Do you still want him to die? He hates the ANC.'

'He's a kaffir,' said Darlton defiantly.

Krige lined up the crosshairs, the flow of adrenalin pumping through his veins like an opiate. 'The waiting is over,' he murmured, firming up on the gun.

Chapter 23

Moses Shozi's house

Moses Shozi was restless, drinking from the stock of bottled beer he kept in the fridge, at times sitting, then prowling around the house. He was angry that only by sheer chance he had been able to avert death and repel the Xhosa guerilla, a man he had come to detest from the depths of his soul. For hours he pondered on suitable retribution, bitter that the men employed to defend him had failed. That he had hurt the guerilla was certain. The solid impact of the first bullet and the agony on his face was evidence. At dawn his men had searched the valley and those to the east and west but by early afternoon they had found no trace, not even a drop of blood.

After a nap to ward off the effects of the beer, Shozi began to prepare himself for a march on Malakazi where the Xhosas had first been seen. He ordered Setlaba to be ready with the men to move out when the evening meal was over, a ritual he enjoyed as it helped him keep in tune with what was going on in the valleys.

When the cooking fire had reduced to an orange glow and the rich stew was simmering in the pots, Shozi clad his hefty body in the long shorts and loose-fitting shirt he favoured when not formally on parade before his superiors in Inkatha. Setlaba waited for him in the lounge, annoyed at the slow deliberations of the man to whom he was inextricably bound.

At last Shozi came down the stairs, routinely suspending his belt and revolver on the balustrade. He was still in a dark mood. Setlaba, above the others, was responsible for his security and therefore he was primarily to blame for the ease with which the guerilla had got into the house. Perhaps

Setlaba was only capable when the enemy was as weak as Mrs Mkhize's sons and he had the others behind him.

The lieutenant sensed his master's mood and warned himself to be careful. He did not want to end his days prematurely, left to decay in some hastily dug grave. Shozi held no compunction in quartering the bodies of his opponents and those of his own men who did not meet his standards.

'The men are ready,' he ventured. 'Will you kill Dhlamini?'

Shozi gave a rude belch. 'Dhlamini's of little consequence, a puppet. The man I want is the one who was here last night, the guerilla. Only his death and the deaths of his friends will satisfy me.' He walked to the shattered glass door, the jagged hole temporarily covered by a piece of wood, and gazed out over the veld. 'It is time to add firearms to our traditional weapons. The Xhosa wasn't armed but these men have access to Kalashnikovs. If we don't kill them they'll come with their guns and we must be adequately prepared.'

'What about tonight?' Setlaba was unnerved by the thought of going against guns with only a *panga*.

'There is no time,' said Shozi, flecks of saliva shooting from his mouth. 'Tonight we'll rely on the steel of our blades. If we find them, they're dead.' He left the doors and went over the carpet on his raft-like feet. Setlaba followed him through the kitchen onto the porch where the guard had been killed, the reddish-brown stain from the large pool of blood still evident.

For a moment Shozi stood on the porch, absorbing the aroma from the pots. Then he went onto the brushed earth that stretched between the house and the guard's quarters, feeling the first pangs of hunger. Thick African mats had been laid round the fire and he sat cross-legged facing the house, waiting while one of the men spooned a generous helping of stew onto an enamel plate put before him. Setlaba sat opposite and the guards helped themselves, hungrily

79

piling the food onto their dishes and breaking off chunks of bread on the mat. The men chattered amongst themselves, keeping nothing from the warlord's ears. They were all Zulus and members of Inkatha and the traditional tribal bond of loyalty was never stronger.

The bullet came with a sharp supersonic clap in its wake and skimmed through the fat on Shozi's neck, administering pain, the bite from a cat's fangs. His left hand flew to the incision, releasing the plate to disgorge the contents onto his lap and he rubbed his neck vigorously, spreading the blood in the gory impression of an aspiring artist's first work. He scrambled up and went over the fire, landing between Setlaba and a guard and then towards the house. 'I've been shot,' he shouted. In a few strides he was on the porch and then into the lounge. His men dropped their plates in alarm and with Setlaba in the lead ran to the wall of the house.

'It came from over there,' cried Setlaba, trying to work out the direction from the sound. 'Spread out and encircle him. We cannot fail.' He formed his arms into the shape of a pair of buffalo horns then marshaled his men, splitting them into two groups. They went off, running for the protection offered by the grass.

The lieutenant waited until they had gone then went into the house in search of Shozi, fearful of his master's rage and regretting the warlord had not been killed.

Chapter 24

Moses Shozi's house

In the rocks Krige pulled in the rifle. 'He's still alive. I was certain it was his last meal. It means going in to get him.'

'I thought you could use that thing,' said Dalton acidly, training the glasses on the house. 'You screwed it. He's disappeared and the others have left the fire. You could've made sure.'

Krige wrapped the cloth round the scope and unzipped the bag. The weapon was now of no value.

'They're coming in this direction,' said Dalton. 'You can pick them off.'

Krige bagged the rifle and assessed the threat posed by the guards as they deployed themselves in a pincer movement. 'Let's go,' he said. 'I'm not going to stand here like a psychopath and gun them down unnecessarily. Shozi's the target.'

'What's the problem?' said Dalton. 'The more we get the better. We can wipe them out and then get Shozi. What a collection. Imagine the press headlines - warlord and his guard destroyed.'

'Forget it,' said Krige, wishing he had killed Shozi when the chance was there. 'We're moving out until later. You're coming with me.'

Dalton got up, keeping his head beneath the top of the rocks. 'That was a wasted opportunity if ever I saw one.' He followed Krige as the farmer ran towards the stream.

Relentlessly the guards closed in on the *kopje*, chanting as they ran each one eager to be the one who brought in the man who had fired the shot. Their noise spurred the whites on between the thickets and they accelerated and swerved in bursts. When they reached the stream Krige turned at ninety degrees away from Malakazi and followed the bed as it wound through rushes and the adjacent plantation. In seconds they had disappeared, devoured by the natural landscape, leaving no sign of their passing except to the finest tracker.

Once into the trees Krige stopped, listening for sounds of the chase. 'Take cover,' he said. 'Don't use your gun unless I say so.'

They slithered separately into the undergrowth, choosing clumps of bush and hiding amongst the leaves. Overhead a mynah bird emitted an angry shriek, ruffling its feathers indignantly and piercing the air with its yellow beak. Then there was silence.

The minutes ticked by without sign of the guards and Krige checked his watch. It was twenty minutes after they had fled the rocks. He left the bush he was behind and moved to Dalton, leaving the rifle on the ground. 'Looks as if we've lost them,' he said.

'What's the plan Major?' Dalton removed pieces of vegetation from his shirt. 'I hope it's more successful.'

Krige fell, taking Dalton by the sleeve and to his knees.

'What are you doing?' Dalton removed his hand angrily. 'You're going mad. Let's get out of here.' He was about to vacate the bush when Krige cautioned him roughly. 'Keep still.' His mouth parted narrowly. 'There are two of them. I'm not sure if they saw us.'

'These are mine,' said Dalton, reaching for his gun. 'I'll show you how to shoot.'

'Put it away,' said Krige. He took the Beretta from his jacket. 'Use this. It can fire in bursts of three. Now I'll see how good you are.'

Dalton glowed. He had what he wanted. He took the weapon. 'You'll not be disappointed.'

Krige's sighting materialized into two of Shozi's guards, each carrying a *panga* in one hand and a stick clasped in the middle by the other. They were advancing warily, apart. The crack of the rifle bullet was still an unpleasant memory and they had no wish to die without at least a chance to fight.

Dalton poked the pistol carefully through the leaves, aware of how easily bullets could be deflected by the merest twig. He aligned the sights and waited patiently as the men came to him, his palate as dry as scorched earth and the skin on his cheeks and round his jaw like dried hide. Krige watched him, wondering what drove people on in their hatred, their souls scarred by the insatiable longing to destroy. He saw the guards get nearer, half-hoping they would change their minds and leave. But they did not and at twenty-five metres Dalton fired.

Disgusted by his feelings of fascination Krige saw one guard and then the other rocked like Japanese Daruma dolls, dancing soundlessly under the shock and then falling as if lowered on a winch. In seconds they were warm corpses in the lush green, their lives dissipating on a red tide.

The whites kept low, checking into the trees for friends of the dead men. 'The others must have gone towards Malakazi,' said Dalton. He gave Krige the pistol. 'It is a pity. I can handle more of them.'

Krige went to the guards. He had seldom seen bullets kill so cleanly. Dalton was an exceptional shot. He examined the bodies then retraced his steps. 'It's too light now for Shozi. We need a couple of hours until it gets dark.' He stuffed the Beretta into his belt. 'My guess is we can catch him by surprise. He won't expect another attack so soon.'

'You're doing the job.' Dalton brushed himself briskly. 'My gut feel tells me he'll be sitting up all night thinking of you, his men crawling all over the place like greenflies round a pile of shit.'

'If I fail,' retorted Krige, 'you're next and it won't only be Shozi. You'll have to kill them all.'

'I imagine you're pretty good with a gun and I have every confidence you'll take it in your stride,' said Dalton. 'You should've brought an SMG. We're not here for fun.'

'Aren't you?' said Krige. He went to the rifle bag. 'Shozi will die tonight and I'll be the one who kills him. You're safe.'

83

Krige and Dalton were in the trees until it was dark then they returned to the rocks. Lights were on downstairs in the house and in the quarters but there was no sign of anyone and no way of knowing if the guards had come back from their search. Krige touched the Beretta behind his belt, the cold steel kept from his skin by the shirt and he welcomed the strength it gave him. He did not have a specific plan except that he wanted to be finished with the Zulu and heading for Malakazi. In the poor light he could just make out Dalton three metres from him, wedged between the rocks. He looked at the house, noting the curtains across the French windows. He got up, placing the binoculars on top of the rifle bag. 'I'm going in,' he said. 'No point in sitting here any longer. I'm leaving the rifle.' He added drily. 'If I don't return you might eventually get a long shot at him.'

Krige loped along the stream, changing course for the grass when he was clear of the rocks. He went in a circle until he was on the other side of the house then he moved in, stopping when he was near the front porch. From his angle the doors were giant mirrors and he was puzzled to see the gaping hole through which the guerilla had escaped. It was covered by a board, the surface starkly matt next to the shining glass.

Chapter 25

Moses Shozi's house

Setlaba had never seen Shozi in such a rage.

'You let them get so close they nearly killed me,' ranted the warlord. 'It happened last night and again today.' It was shortly after his lieutenant had ordered his men into the grass and the two of them were in the lounge.

'It was a rifle bullet, fired from a distance,' said Setlaba. 'I haven't enough men to station all over the place away from the house.'

'You only need a few to cover the main points,' returned Shozi. He touched the plaster on his neck, remembering how near he had come to death. 'The enemy is getting stronger and more organized. Yesterday they were persecuted by the whites, today they have the freedom and the vote to behave as they wish. If you can't accept these changes I must replace you.'

Setlaba bowed, the words shaming him. 'I misjudged them,' he said, 'their determination to kill you.'

Shozi took pleasure in seeing his subordinates squirm as they begged for life. Sympathy was not one of his virtues.

'Your men won't catch them,' he said emphatically. 'When they return, I want two men to be placed in the *kopje*. That's where the shot came from.'

Setlaba lifted his head a little. He was glad the warlord had come to the same conclusion. He couldn't then be faulted on where he had sent the guards.

'There must also be a man patrolling round the house,' continued Shozi, 'with two men at the front.' He went into the kitchen, observing the empty yard. 'Bring me some food,' he said, his appetite returning. He hitched up his trousers. 'The visit to Malakazi will be tomorrow. Dhlamini must also die, alongside those he has harboured on our land,

85

knowing who they are and the evil scheming that peppers their hearts.' His hand went to his waist and drew the knife Ngubane had used to try and kill him. He held the weapon at chest height, the beautifully honed edge uppermost, and stroked the metal with his thumb. 'The guerilla's got good taste. I wonder where he got it.' He slashed it through the air, admiring the magnificent Bowie shape and the texture of the high-quality stainless steel. 'He would like this returned and I'll take satisfaction burying it into him.' He put the knife on a shelf above the fridge as Setlaba walked off into the yard. The lieutenant could imagine the look on his master's face when he embedded the blade in the Xhosa.

Shozi ate alone in the kitchen, intent on the men he wanted to kill. A few of the guards came back and he saw them go to Setlaba before helping themselves to food from the pots. He hadn't expected them to be successful. The man who had fired the rifle was skilled, whoever he was. It could have been any one of his enemies, from the ANC or even from the other the group, the Pan Africanist Congress or PAC. He slid the plate from him and went into the lounge eager to get a report from Setlaba, whatever it was worth.

When it was dark Shozi switched on the lights downstairs and pulled the curtains over the French doors and the temporary plywood he had stuck on with tape. The cast iron figurine was back on the table, the thin horns undamaged by the blow. As the curtains came together he glimpsed the plantation of trees and wondered who was out there, if the rifleman had returned and if he was even now planning another attack. He moved quickly away and went into the yard. Most of the guards had ventured in and they were talking amongst themselves.

Setlaba saw his master and ran to him. 'There's no sign of the marksman. The men searched the grounds and the rocks and the valleys towards Umbali and Malakazi.' The stress of having to please Shozi in circumstances that were out of his depth was beginning to tell.

'Have all the men returned?' asked Shozi.

'Two are still out there. They must have gone further afield.'

'Perhaps,' said Shozi, his eyes darting daggers. 'Let the men eat then give them their orders.' He wished it was full moon. 'I hold you personally responsible.'

He went indoors his instinct telling him the gunman wouldn't give up. He picked up the knife and took it into the lounge, placing it on the cushion next to his gun. Setlaba's ignorance and inability to perform as required under pressure worried him, especially now when animosity between Xhosa and Zulu was at its most volatile since the legendary kaffir wars of the nineteenth century. He sat on the sofa, switching on his prized sound system and tuning in to the deep chanting of Ipi Tombi.

The music lulled him into a doze and he woke with a start when the machine automatically cut itself out at the end of the tape. He turned off the power, angered by the uncertainty and scratched his crotch thinking it a while since he had last had a woman. They held his interest for only days and he had contacts in Umbali who kept him informed of the pretty girls, young ones in their late teens, preferably virgins. It was never difficult persuading them to come to the house and he did what he liked with them, frequently humiliating them and resorting to depraved acts until he was sexually drained.

He went up to his bedroom and languished in the dark next to the window thinking of the two guards, if they had come up with anything. He doubted it.

Chapter 26

Moses Shozi's house

Krige prepared himself in the shadows of the house, the safety on his pistol showing off. Faint voices from the quarters carried to him and he went to the porch. But before he could go further a man appeared from the yard wide of the house, first visible and then masked by a tree.

Krige froze, hugging the wall. He laid the pistol on his stomach, lining it to where the guard would emerge. The man reappeared, his *knobkerrie* resting on his shoulder like a rifle. He kept coming, his bearing relaxed. Then he stopped, taking the stick down so it jutted out like a horn.

Ahead of him, the guard saw the amorphous shape of Krige obscuring the line of brick.

He was not sure. He told himself to be cautious and he wanted to call for assistance but the disgrace of a false alarm made him do otherwise and he went on, crackling parched leaves and hoisting the weapon above his head.

With little separating them Krige came from the wall, landing off-balance. He regained his posture rapidly and raised the gun high to get the best aim. He fired and as the guard received the bullets in his chest he came in low, grabbing the body and controlling its descent. He listened for a moment then took the corpse into longer grass. He moved back and onto the porch where he could see between the curtains. He pressed the board from the glass on the hinge of tape until it touched the fabric. His view covered most of the room, the empty sofa and chairs. He opened the curtains and went in, taping the board loosely on the glass. He considered the stairs and was about to go to them when he heard someone coming through the kitchen. He had just made it behind a chair when Setlaba marched in and called up the stairs.

Almost immediately Shozi showed, bare to the waist. He prompted Setlaba to speak and began to descend.

'The two men have not returned.' said Setlaba, putting his heels together to improve his bearing.

'I knew they wouldn't,' said Shozi. 'They're probably dead. Have you posted the others?'

'Yes, they're in position now. The house is secure.' He remembered the rocks and rebuked himself for forgetting them.

'The curtains are not together,' said Shozi, only half-listening. 'Anyone can see in here.' He went to the French doors and took the cloth. With a cry he let go, back pedaling hurriedly, a swell of paranoia throttling him. 'Someone's freed the tape,' he shouted, snatching the pistol and fanning the hammer.

As Shozi took the gun, Krige came out, alternating the Beretta between the two men. 'Leave it,' he said.

Shozi kept the revolver vertical, calming himself now that the intruder had exposed himself. 'Who are you?' he asked in English. 'Why have you broken into my house like a common thief? You're white.'

'Makes no difference,' said Krige. 'Your rule of terror is over. You got away with it.

Welcome to hell.' He hesitated fractionally then pulled the trigger.

But Shozi's native reactions were untarnished and he was already ducking when the pin on the Beretta detonated the first charge. The bullets pierced the balustrade, decelerating as they tore at the grain. Like the canny fighter he was he weaved to avoid the succeeding shots, getting closer to Krige all the time.

Seizing a chance to kill Setlaba, Krige fired at the lieutenant before leaping out of Shozi's path. The lead blew Setlaba's head apart, sending him nervelessly into one of his master's speakers, speckling the box with blood.

Heckling crazily Shozi changed his line and lunged. The two men collided, wrestlers, the gangster immediately

89

feeling the power of his extra weight. He threw away the Webley in a fit of confidence, enjoying the combat and wanting to see the white subdued before a prisoner's death. Artfully he trapped the Beretta between them and got hold of it, then letting it go as he swept Krige's feet from under him.

They fell as one, the black on top, emptying Krige's lungs like a punctured balloon.

For long seconds Krige lay still, his mind wandering in a maze, his mouth open, ready for his lungs to pull in precious air. It came like a charge of new life and then Krige saw the gloating black. With a Herculean effort, his spirit suddenly inflamed, he came up, driving his fist at the grizzled skull.

Taken by the blow Shozi howled like a dog, his head feeling as if it had been split by an axe. He fell near the chair where he had left Ngubane's knife. Then he remembered it. Through half-shut eyes he saw the hilt overlapping the edge. The guns were somewhere else and the knife was a weapon he loved, if he could get it. Reaching out, he was nearly there when his arm was kicked aside, unrewarded. Towering over him was Krige. 'You nearly got it,' said Krige. 'But that against this is no match. You should've made sure I couldn't get it.' He revealed the Beretta, removing himself from the Zulu with the chilled articulations of a judge in a barbarian court about to pronounce sentence.

'Why does a white want to kill a Zulu?' said Shozi, recovering. 'We have a common enemy. Unkhonto we Sizwe will never give up until Zulu and white lick the filth from their boots. Chris Hani was their supreme commander, a folk hero, a communist to his bones. His followers want revenge and nothing less than absolute control of this country. Being part of a new government is trivial.'

'I have orders,' said Krige tersely. 'Your death is one of them.'

Shozi wrinkled his nose. 'For what cause do you say that white man? I'll call off my men and let you go in peace. We are brothers.'

'You're a murderer,' said Krige quietly, as if trying to justify taking the Zulu's life. 'You should have been hanged.'

'Without Inkatha you'll be destroyed by ANC militants,' said Shozi, noting how Krige hesitated and feeling a vestige of hope. 'They're your killers. You haven't told me who you work for.'

'It's not important,' said Krige. 'This is the end.' A bullet ran with the words. For a terrifying infinitesimal moment Shozi knew it was coming but he couldn't avoid it and he collapsed onto his chest, his nose reconfigured by the green pile, the tiniest secretion of blood innocently irrigating his skin from behind his ear onto his neck.

Krige moved from the corpse, still carrying his Beretta as he went to the stairs. He climbed them to Shozi's room and studied the view from the window, delving into the recesses for Setlaba's guards. There were two he could see, each near the corners. A third man walked up and, after talking to the other two, went on his circular path.

Krige turned the light on and returned to the lounge. He could hear the men out the back, getting nearer and he extinguished the overhead beam and lamps. He shifted one of the curtains, millimetres, looking for the guards he had seen. One was visible, the other blanked out by the end of the porch. He thought it unlikely they were carrying guns, if the three he had encountered were typical. He was surprised Shozi hadn't provided his men with arms; AK47s were easily procured. They might have saved his life.

Krige gave the third man he had seen time to walk around the building but he did not appear. He parted the centre of the curtains and opened the board, going onto the grey slate. He thought of picking off the two guards with the silenced gun but the light and range were against him and he left the porch at a run, bisecting the distance between the two men. He was almost through the gap before they saw him. They hesitated under the inertia of surprise then shouted and set off in pursuit, waving their long knives, their powerful

91

legs driving them on swiftly. They were ten years younger, used to arduous journeys on foot and he could feel them gaining on him. Their cries aroused others, who also joined in the chase, coming in a swathe past the house with the noise of an infantry charge.

Near the *kopje*, with the two men closing in, Krige stopped, realizing he wouldn't make it into the rocks, and whipped up the gun, steadying himself. But he had left it late and they were quickly within striking range, scything the blades in large circles. Miraculously he evaded the steel and with the others arrowing in he danced out of reach. The gun popped, spewing out a fusillade that brought them down. Going low, he prepared for the attack from behind. There were five, three bunched together and the others to his left. Choosing the group of three he fired again, intermittently spraying their bare bodies with the bullets, killing them as they tumbled, skittles in an alley. He turned on the last two. They were nearly on him, their *pangas* poised in readiness. His finger tensed again but before he could fire there were two shots behind him, fusing together to be almost one and they threw their arms into the air, harmlessly releasing their *pangas* and sticks as they fell. Stunned, Krige saw Dalton appear from the rocks, as calm as if he had just come in from an afternoon stroll.

'They nearly had you Major.'

Krige got up. 'Two more to your score,' he gritted acidly. That Dalton had possibly saved his life angered him and there was no place for gratitude.

Shouts came from the house and the lights went on downstairs. The verandah doors were opened and the remaining men came out. Krige started running from the scene. 'Get the rifle. Our work here is finished. Shozi's dead.' He followed Dalton through the rocks and after retrieving the rifle they went along the stream for Malakazi, finding their way without difficulty in the dark.

They took the trail used by the guerillas and pushed hard over the rough terrain, alternately walking and running for

92

thirty metres at a time. Behind them the voices of the guards slowly died as they lost their quarries and after an hour they stopped, leaving the trail and taking refuge in the grass.

Chapter 27

Malakazi township

'We're twenty minutes from Malakazi,' said Krige, his head between his legs as he rested.

'How did you kill him?' asked Dalton. He lay down, pulling his holstered pistol away from the ground.

'He got a bullet in the head,' said Krige without emotion. 'Teichmann will get his headlines.'

Dalton howled with mirth, the noise breaking randomly into a cackle. 'Well done. I wish I'd been there.' He pulled the Browning from its sheath, cocking and then releasing the hammer monotonously. 'At least I've the guerillas to look forward to.'

Krige vented his shirt to let the breeze dry the sweat. Killing Shozi hadn't gone as planned but he had achieved his objective and the Zulu was dead. He was drained, from the exertion and the mental strain. He hoped the Xhosas would be easier to kill. He had already had a fair share of luck.

Dalton angrily holstered the weapon. 'Are you ready? We don't want the guerillas to run for it. These niggers move so fast on the veld Shozi's death will be common knowledge before we arrive and anyone not an Inkatha supporter will go to ground fearing revenge.'

'We're ahead of the pack,' said Krige without interest. He wished Dalton would shut up. He went down to the path. Dalton kept up and they were soon at the steady half-run of before.

An hour later they reached the edge of Malakazi and left the trail, moving on the perimeter to where they expected to find the room. There were few people about, the four o'clock rise in the morning and the journey to the cities demanding early nights, and the lamps in the main dirt street provided most of the illumination.

'I can't see it,' said Krige coming to a halt. 'I'm going in a bit. You stay here.'

Dalton glanced at him. 'Don't leave me out of it. I might have to save you again.'

Before Krige came to the first buildings he saw it, hidden by bush and further over than he had been able to see through the glasses earlier. He couldn't tell if anyone was inside and he went to fetch Dalton.

In a minute both men were at the room and Krige went to the front. He took one look at the door and banged it with his fist. 'They're not here.' He stared at the heavy-duty lock, nailed through a galvanized fitting to the wood, conscious of the smile on Dalton's face.

'So we wait,' said Dalton contemplating the lock. 'I knew we'd be lucky to find them.'

Krige leant on the wall. 'The mayor will know if they're still sleeping here,' he said. 'If they've gone we've lost them. Then it's up to you and the others in your party to start again.'

Dalton flexed his fists. 'They're still here somewhere. I can feel them.'

Krige went to the back. The grey paint on the small window panes had been hastily applied and there were vacant strips a few centimetres wide. But the external light was insufficient to give him any clue to the contents of the room and he returned to Dalton. 'I'm going for Dhlamini. Stay here, they might still be using it. But don't have a go at them without me.'

'You're still hogging all the action,' said Dalton scanning Krige. Then he said acquiescently. 'Well you never can tell. They might be dead when you get back, all wrapped up ready for body bags. I'm sure you'll see it as self-defence.' He went into the bush.

Krige watched him then set off. He found Dhlamini's house easily, in a large plot of its own. There was light downstairs and he approached the kitchen door. It was of the stable type, the top open and he heard voices, a man's and a woman's, hers louder than his. He understood some Zulu and tried to catch the words. The woman was admonishing the man, her harsh tone rising and falling cadentially. She referred to men she wanted him to have nothing to do with. To her they would only bring trouble. Krige went in.

The voices carried on and he quickened his pace down the passage. At the end he came to a lounge and saw a man on a chair and a woman standing near the windows. They stared at him in disbelief.

'Dhlamini,' said Krige walking in. The man did not reply and he continued: 'I want the three men, the guerillas. You know where they are.' He spoke in English, unwavering.

Dhlamini was quiet, signalling his wife to be still. He exhaled, a pair of bellows. 'They've gone,' he said. 'I refused to help them.' He left the chair and made a revolting noise to show disgust. 'Men like that are of the past, poisoned by hatred for whites and Zulus. I got rid of them.'

Krige grinned wolfishly. The mayor was scared and he was lying.

'They were in that room of yours. They were seen there a few days ago and you were giving them a bed.'

'No.' Dhlamini came nearer, holding up his hands, as delicate as a concert pianist's. 'It's a mistake. The room is used as a storehouse. I ordered them to go.' He was cringing, fear constricting his throat.

'I want them.' Krige went up to the mayor. 'Where are they?'

Dhlamini's wife ran over and dropped to the floor. 'Stop,' she cried. 'They are murderers. He had no choice.' She looked at her husband. 'He was threatened. You don't know what they're like.'

'I do.' Krige loaded a cartridge into the breech.

Dhlamini gauged the man before him, the wide shoulders and lean pride, the coldness as if he had just emerged from an ice-box. He was too strong; and he had the gun. 'Their leader was seriously hurt, near death,' he said at last. 'They came to me begging for assistance, as human brothers. I abhor what they represent but I couldn't ignore their suffering.' He scraped his feet, hoping what he had said was acceptable. 'I took the sick man and his comrades to a woman in the township. The local doctor treated him.'

Krige released the safety on the gun, the long silencer casting it like a sniper's rifle. 'How was he hurt, how badly?'

'The woman didn't want him,' said Dhlamini. 'She's a good person. I forced her to provide for him.'

'Answer me,' Krige grated. 'What's wrong with the guerilla?'

Dhlamini heaved his chest, contracting his limp stomach to where it should have been. 'He tried to kill Shozi, the Inkatha warlord. Something went wrong and he was shot. He'd lost a lot of blood and the wound was becoming septic.' He presented another look of revulsion.

Krige hid his astonishment at the coincidence, swinging the gun nonchalantly. The mayor would have to guide him to the woman. Why did the fat woman have to be there? She couldn't be trusted to keep quiet. And neither could he trust Dhlamini, the squirming mayor who would babble as soon as he was released. A link would be made with the gunmen who had slaughtered Shozi and his guards.

With a plea Dhlamini's wife bowed low, placing her hands on the floor. '*Nkosi*,' she said using the term for a chief. 'We are innocent. Don't harm us.'

Krige viewed the pathetic figure. Life or death, it was up to him, he had control. For several seconds he paused then raising the weapon shot her once, then again in the head. She collapsed without ceremony, dead. Dhlamini blubbered, holding his stomach and falling next to her.

The Afrikaner took his jacket. 'Show me to the woman.' He led him to the door and shoved him through.

Dhlamini was incoherent, powerless to resist, numbed by the brutal suddenness of his wife's death. He could feel the long-barreled pistol digging into him. At first he hadn't noticed the fitted silencer, but it was all too obvious when the white pulled the trigger, making only the little popping noise as the lead was expelled. It was terrifying seeing life destroyed so cleanly without a sound. And he would be next. He bemoaned his own limitations wishing he had been wrought in the mould of the traditional Zulu warriors, their fighting spirit, their disregard for death and commitment to survival whatever the price, their beautiful physiques. It had not been.

Outside, Dhlamini curved from the room where Dalton waited. Krige, placing the gun in his pocket, wavered between summoning him or going on alone. Dalton was a powerful force in close combat, his ability with the pistol unquestioned, but he was impulsive and his lust for pure destruction potentially dangerous. And the guerillas might return to the room.

'Keep walking.' Krige closed on Dhlamini. 'No mistakes or you'll go before them.'

They moved on, Dhlamini, his shoulders set defensively, and Krige, suspicious, his senses as taut as the string on an archer's bow. After a few minutes Dhlamini changed course for a group of isolated houses. Fifty metres from them he lifted an unsteady arm. 'The one at the end,' he said tremulously. 'She's a good woman.'

Like the other houses in the row the woman's was a grey shadow. But unlike the others it had an add-on at the rear, a long passage of new brick leading to a room with a vegetable patch that couldn't have yielded much tagged on at the end.

'Where's the guerilla?' Krige came up to Dhlamini.

'At the back,' said Dhlamini. 'He was in a poor state. I know he's there.' The mayor's thinking was becoming more ordered and he was sure Krige would kill him when he had confirmation the Xhosas were there. Somehow he had to get away.

Krige studied the place, begrudgingly conscious of the help Dalton could have given him. 'Where does that lead to?' he asked the black, pointing at the only door they could see.

98

'It gives access to the kitchen and the passage that also comes from the front and goes to the rear bedroom.'

Krige nodded acceptingly. He wanted Dhlamini alive until he found the men but inevitably the mayor would try and escape or, if the opportunity was there, alert them.

'Check the door,' said Krige drawing the pistol. Dhlamini led the way, Krige watching him like a hawk. The door opened onto a small kitchen fitted out with a stainless steel sink and a cooker and fridge crammed together, the glossy enamel scratched and worn in places down to the raw metal.

'Go in.' Krige dug Dhlamini in the ribs and they entered. The inner door was a little ajar and he cautioned the mayor as he went to it. The passage was black and quiet, resembling a tomb. He turned, deliberating for a second, then exploded aggressively, striking for Dhlamini's head. The mayor reacted courageously but he could not fend off such an assault. As his legs went Krige tried to hold him but Dhlamini was heavy and he hit the floor, his arm careering into the oven. The noise was enough to carry through the house.

Running from the unconscious man, Krige made for the room he believed sheltered the guerilla. He passed a vacant room and then was as far as he could go. All was still, claustrophobic. He went in. The switch was in the usual place and he gave the room light from a bulb on the ceiling. There was only a single bed along the wall and two piles of clothes stacked under the window with military care. A man was in the bed, his body covered by a thin sheet and he mumbled something, restless. Krige checked the passage and went to the bed, recognizing the haggard countenance of the guerilla leader, Ngubane. The man was sleeping deeply, as if in a coma, and Krige peeled the sheet to his navel. A clean bandage was strapped in overlapping layers around the Xhosa's chest, from the solar plexus to underneath the arms, a professionally applied wall of white. Krige exalted at seeing one of the men he sought lying powerlessly before him but the others were out there somewhere. They could

99

return at any minute and Dhlamini would regain consciousness. Suppressing his conscience he touched the end of the silencer to Ngubane's temple and fired, allowing the weapon only the slightest recoil in his hand. He used one bullet, sure of the effect and felt for the pulse under the jaw. It ceased and he left the room as he had found it.

In the kitchen Dhlamini was regaining consciousness, shifting his body on the hard linoleum for more comfort. He had served his purpose. Krige straddled him, ejecting the near-empty clip from his gun. He inserted another and knelt next to the mayor.

Chapter 28

Malakazi township

Several rows west of Ngubane's death bed Nofomela and Ngwenya weaved their way to their colleague. They had spent little time in the dingy, cell-like room at the woman's house, where the closeness and smell of Ngubane's sick body carried the premonition of death. The flow of blood had been stemmed but he was extremely weak, most of the time asleep, only taking a little broth made by the woman that they had managed to get into him. Before noon they had gone to find food for themselves.

On the main thoroughfare of the township they had eaten at a small cafe, dried *mielie* porridge and thick slices of bread and jam washed down by strong sweet tea. For the remaining daylight hours and into the night they had rested in the grass on the hill, grieving over the failure of the previous evening and the inevitable revenge that Shozi was sure to want. Ngubane was a problem. A week or more could pass before he had the strength to walk, to rough it in the bush before they dared make contact with compatriots in a neighbouring township, Umbali or Venter's Hoek further east with its unpalatable Afrikaans name. If, that is, Ngubane survived. The thought that it would be better if he died, naturally or by their hands, had also entered their thoughts.

As they came in sight of their temporary place of abode Nofomela touched Ngwenya on the arm. 'The foolish woman has left the door open,' he growled, 'inviting the beggars who roam these streets to enter. Where are her brains?'

'She'll bring trouble on us,' agreed Ngwenya, angrily increasing his pace. They were ten metres from the door when Ngwenya stopped and urgently beckoned Nofomela to do the same. 'Someone's on the floor,' he whispered. 'I can see his boots.'

But Nofomela carried on past his comrade up to the door. He took one look and bolted into the kitchen.

Krige, the pistol wrapped in his fist, was lining up the muzzle on Dhlamini's head. His back was to the door and he was about to do the job when the minimal change in shadow caused by Nofomela's long frame, alerted him and he came round as the Xhosa launched into a dive. Swinging the gun from Dhlamini to his assailant Krige fired.

The bullets missed Nofomela's cheek by a small fraction and the two men locked, each fighting for control, knowing that the least error could mean death. They rocked back and forth, banging into the fridge and stove, the sour stench from the black's unwashed body overwhelming in the humidly confined space and Krige breathed harshly through his mouth as he tried to get the Beretta that Nofomela held as if it was the only thing he wanted in life.

All at once another shadow filled the kitchen as Ngwenya came in. Krige saw him and increased his bid to get the weapon. Strong as he was his arms began to tire against the rangy power of Nofomela who, like Ngwenya, had the lean exercised muscles of men who had experienced hardship for most of their lives without the lavish excesses of the privileged.

Like a racing horse coming out of the starter's gate Ngwenya sprang into the fray, instantly going behind Krige and getting his forearm across his neck. He yanked and then yelled: 'White man, you've come for us.' His triumph was obvious in the small enclosure. 'Now let's see what you can do.' He tightened his hold, using his strength and weight to take Krige to the floor.

Krige's valiant efforts grew weaker as he was strangled by the pressure on his throat. He fought for air, a fish stranded on a beach, the denied need for life-giving oxygen intolerable. He released the pistol and with a strange sense of relief felt the weapon removed, to what end he couldn't care.

His family spun dizzily, his beautiful wife Kirsty, their sons. What would happen to them, he loved them so much. Nofomela stood over him, a look of contentment as he held up the Beretta, briefly admiring the solid workmanship of the famous Italian gunmaker.

'Don't kill him,' he said to Ngwenya, 'just make him rest until I've seen Ngubane. Then he'll crow like a cockerel.'

In a last go at breaking the grip Krige flopped weakly onto his side, taking Ngwenya's arm and enveloping the long muscles that stood out like snakes on a branch. He tried to pry the arm loose but his waning strength was as feeble as a baby's and he relented. He saw Dhlamini lift himself up onto his elbows, shaking his head as he tried to clear it. Then, immersed in a black tide, he lost consciousness and fell against Ngwenya.

The black lay out the body, looking at Nofomela and then Dhlamini.

'You led him here,' Ngwenya accused the mayor. 'If Ngubane is hurt you will die.'

'He killed my wife,' pleaded Dhlamini. 'There was nothing I could do.'

'Get up,' ordered Ngwenya. 'Bring the white by the feet and follow us.' The guerilla stood aside as Nofomela marched off, waiting for Dhlamini to obey.

The Zulu took Krige by the ankles and into the passage, knowing he was in grave trouble if Krige had already killed Ngubane. In seconds his worst fears were confirmed as he heard Nofomela hysterically proclaim the death of the Xhosa leader.

In the room Ngwenya went for the mayor and beat him with his fist. 'You betrayed us. You're as guilty of this foul murder as the white. Your death will be most sweet.' He challenged Dhlamini: 'Who else was with him? Where are they?'

'No one,' said Dhlamini. 'He's working alone. Whites still hate the ANC.'

On a quarter turn Ngwenya nodded to Nofomela then slammed his knee into the mayor's groin, hard against the pubic bone, lifting him off the floor. The pain robbed Dhlamini of any resistance and he doubled over helplessly. Taking a stride Nofomela sighted the pistol and fired into the mayor's head.

The bullets lodged in Dhlamini's brain and he was dead before he collapsed at Nofomela's feet. 'We should never have trusted him. He's always been weak.' Nofomela stamped on the mayor's face, still etched in the agony he had suffered before death. 'Now it is time for the white.'

Chapter 29

Malakazi township

When the doctor's sister-in-law, sitting alone in the front of the house, heard Dhlamini fall she shuddered fearfully and listened, with her ear to the wall. Ever since her brother-in-law had told her who they were and that the wounded one had made a hit on Moses Shozi she was afraid. The warlord was the devil's henchman. He would search every inch of KwaZulu for the assassin and be merciless with anyone who gave them succour or a roof.

For a couple of minutes she heard no more and relaxed. It must have been the two returning. She sat on the newly covered sofa, in its bright floral print and continued mending the frock on her lap.

The noise came again but now it was much louder as if a drunk was loose in the kitchen. Again she listened at the wall and instantly withdrew in alarm. It was fighting, by whom she didn't know, in deadly earnest. The room doubled as her bedroom and she hurriedly packed a carrier bag with basic items. She switched out the bulb and let herself out, vowing not to return until the guerillas had gone.

Chapter 30

Malakazi township

Dalton was certain the guerillas had gone from the room for good and he waited for Krige to disappear before going after him. As he went through the undergrowth he picked him up ahead. He followed slowly, the vegetation thinning and then he saw it, the house of the mayor that Krige had located earlier through the binoculars. He kept down as Krige paused before going inside.

For a few minutes Dalton waited then Krige left with a black he assumed was Dhlamini. The pair headed for the north, the mayor appearing to cooperate. After 200 metres by his reckoning Dalton saw Dhlamini point out a house.

Dalton viewed it sceptically. Why would the guerillas leave the relative isolation of the room for here? When the two went into the kitchen he moved until he was behind the window in the extension and sank next to a tree.

Dalton was beginning to wonder what Krige was doing when the light in the room came on and he saw the farmer. The window was too high to see what was happening without going closer but he kept in the grass. Krige again showed and the light went out. He was puzzled.

As he thought about going nearer he was startled by the emergence of Nofomela and Ngwenya further along, making for the house. They were at nearly fifty metres and he saw Ngwenya stop and Nofomela run to the door. Then Nofomela dived through like a man possessed.

Dalton left his position at a run, just as he saw Ngwenya also go into the house and shut the door. He was low as he moved to the kitchen wall. There was scuffling and he braced himself to go in. But before he could act he heard Ngwenya cry out. He did not understand the language but he felt he had more time. It came again and then quiet.

Dalton waited a moment and then went in. As he came to the passage he was brought up as Nofomela cried out. He looked out and saw Dhlamini pulling Krige into the room. The door was banged shut and with a strange feeling of loyalty to Krige he went to it. When he neared it he heard shouting and someone being beaten and then the distinctive noise of a silenced pistol.

With full power Dalton went through the door, counting on surprise and his ability in close combat of any kind. He landed down the wall and pivoted rapidly to face the centre of the room, readying himself like a fighting tom. Almost touching him was Dhlamini's corpse and diagonally from him was Krige, alone as if he carried a plague. In front, a metre apart, stood the two guerillas, both watching him as if they had known he would show.

Aiming the pistol, Dalton fired at the black on his left then altered to the other and fired again. The noise shook the brick, as if trying to bring the dead to life. To his disbelief the blacks kept on, their arms reaching out for him like a net. He felt the wall, a third force set against him. With a cry he found the gap between them, a forward flip that took him across the room. He crashed into the bed and fell, just missing Krige's outstretched legs and hitting his gun hand on the iron bed. Like a man reawakening from a journey into Neverland Krige opened his eyes, slowly taking in the spectacle before him.

When Nofomela saw Dalton lying on the concrete, his gun diverted and Krige conscious, he halted.

'No, white boy, keep still or you'll die like this miserable coward.' Without taking his eyes off the whites he kicked at the corpse. Dalton and Krige were motionless.

'Slide your gun from you, white boy,' continued Nofomela. 'Do it slow and easy and then stand next to your friend.'

Without the gun Dalton knew the odds were reduced. The kaffirs had been taught to fight and with a firearm they were formidable. That the one had not used it when he was against the wall meant they preferred a brawl, which was in his favour.

'Where do you want it?' he inquired looking up at Nofomela. He kept his gun still and cautiously drew in his legs.

'Under the bed,' said Nofomela. 'Do it now.'

Krige watched Dalton carefully, ready, knowing he was the type who would never give up his gun unless forced into submission.

'Come and get it black man.' The contempt lashed Nofomela like a rider's crop and Dalton moved, leaping for Ngwenya. The black ducked, his fists wild. He shouted as Dalton swerved and held him, his body between him and Nofomela. Dalton kept on, gathering his strength and throwing Ngwenya at his comrade, all the while firm on the gun. Nofomela tried to avoid the body and bring in the Beretta. In a flourish he grabbed Ngwenya, taking him in and then pushing him off, concentrating on the white. But before he could assemble himself, Dalton cut his pistol onto his arm, callously destroying his grip on the gun.

Halting, Dalton lifted his pistol and cried: 'You're finished kaffir.'

Krige got up, mostly recovered, his eyes on the blacks, Ngwenya on his knees and Nofomela not far from him.

'You've been saved again Major. One day you'll learn to take me along.' Dalton grinned, keeping the pistol on the two guerillas. He glanced at Ngubane. 'What did you do to him?'

'I put a bullet through his head. He'd already been shot after making a hit on Shozi.'

Dalton looked at the corpse on the bed. 'Well, well. What a small world,' he said phlegmatically. 'Now we will deal with these two.'

Krige ambled over and retrieved the Beretta from next to the bed. There was a round in the chamber and he covered Nofomela. 'You nearly had me. In this game each mistake can be fatal. I was lucky, you're not.'

108

The two guerillas watched the whites closely. Two metres separated Nofomela from Dalton, with nearly three to Krige. He could reach either white in a second but to be successful in his attack and prevent being gunned down he would need a distraction and it would have to come quickly. He thought of the woman and wondered where she was, why she hadn't come to investigate. There was enough sound to alert her.

Then like a repentant monk Nofomela bowed his head. 'The mayor of this town was an enemy of peace between our peoples,' he began. 'It was necessary to take his life.' He gave the whites an impartial stare. 'We have always cooperated with the security in this area. We didn't know you were working for them.'

Dalton inched a pace forward, dangling his pistol. 'You still don't. We're of no name and you're killers. There's nothing in this country for you. You shouldn't have come back.'

Nofomela launched himself at Dalton, seeking the barrel of the pistol and striking for the jaw with a right hook that came from below his waist. 'Pigs,' he bellowed. 'You'll never take me. Burn in hell.'

Behind him Ngwenya took what he guessed was his last hope, going along the wall to put Dalton and Nofomela between himself and Krige. He steered for the exit and accelerated down the passage.

Krige leapt past Dalton, landing square on to the departing figure. With the gun at his hip he aimed at Ngwenya's back and pulled the trigger. But to his disgust the guerilla disappeared through the door and ran like a buck into the dark.

Nofomela and Dalton were prancing under the bulb, each on the gun. They were starting to sweat, the salty excretion accumulating rapidly on their faces as it left their pores, amplified by the exertion and their generated heat.

Krige watched them, a strange look, as if contemplating something other than the safe release of his colleague.

'Get him Major,' shouted Dalton, 'the smell is killing me. What are you waiting for?'

Nofomela was working hard to wrest the gun loose, hustling with the enthusiasm of a vulture stripping meat. The white's hand was hooked in his belt, drawing his trousers up into his crotch and squeezing his testicles. He knew Ngwenya had escaped and couldn't understand why the other white took his time. At last Krige came in and he released the barrel, springing like an animal on heat, bursting forth. At first he stumbled then he plunged into the passage.

The whites ran after him, jostling as they came together. 'Leave him to me,' said Krige. 'Get back.' He fired at the running black.

But Nofomela was well ahead and in another second went unscathed into the kitchen. In an enormous leap he flew into the dark, vanishing like the magic man in a circus.

Krige emerged outside. Angrily he sank to the earth. 'We had the bastard and let him go.' He knew they were both to blame for being careless and he was angry with himself. He couldn't admonish Dalton. He might be dead now if it had not been for him.

Dalton appeared, replacing the empty magazine in his pistol with a spare. He was also angry, with himself for giving Nofomela a break and with Krige for thinking he could take on three adept fighters one-handed. 'I hope you've learnt your lesson,' he said cuttingly. 'This sort of mission is like scuba diving - don't do it alone. Teichmann will tear your guts out when he hears that two of the guerillas escaped. It doesn't help that they know we're white.'

'Teichmann can go to hell,' said Krige. 'He's safe in Pretoria. Anything can happen in the field and there're no hard and fast rules of engagement. The black's are no threat to us. They're criminals and will go for shelter.'

'I hope so, for your sake,' said Dalton.

Krige reacted angrily. 'Get this straight. I'm doing your party's dirty work because you bastards are incompetent. I'm not answerable to anyone.'

Dalton eyed him provocatively. 'What's next?' he said, smiling thinly. 'We can discuss our performance at the debriefing. I'm sure there'll be one.' He changed the subject. 'Who lives in this place?'

'She's a friend of Dhlamini's and not important.'

'She's keeping pretty quiet.'

'Wouldn't you keep quiet with grown men running round killing each other?' said Krige. 'My guess is she's not here.'

Dalton started to go into the house.

'Leave it,' said Krige curtly. 'She's out of it. The work here is done.'

The two whites went north, before crossing the township and going up the opposite hill. In seven minutes they were at the road they had come down in the late afternoon and using it as a guide started walking to where they had parked the car.

When they saw it, Krige marched up to the driver's door. 'Get in. I don't want to drag this shit out any more than I can help.'

Chapter 31

Durban, Republic of South Africa

Peter Smith was incensed that someone he trusted in the DSO must have taken the copy of the file from his office and that he had no chance of getting another copy from David Staples, Jan Krige's lawyer, who had the original.

Only three men had access to Smith's office when he was not there. They went through the latest deliveries and opened anything that was clearly urgent. Smith's secretary went through the other mail later. Of the three, two had been in the DSO for a long spell. The third, John Kallis, was fairly new, young and intelligent.

Smith cut to the chase. It was the kind of thing he wanted over and done with. He spoke first to his secretary and she said she had accepted a package marked Urgent, Addressee only. Next, Smith called in the two older men separately. One said he had been away on the Thursday and that he had not seen anything that drew his attention on the remaining two days. With a feeling of despair Smith summoned the other man.

After a while the man said: 'When I went into your office I found Kallis there; it didn't surprise me because he had access. He was standing next to the mail tray and was reading a bound document with a black cover and a gold, embossed title. I asked him if it was a good read. He said yes and that he would have to contact you. At that point I left.'

'Thank you,' said Smith. 'You have been a great help. Keep this to yourself.'

The man went from the office and Smith felt he was about to get his prey. He phoned through to Kallis and said he wanted to speak to him. Kallis appeared immediately and seated himself, a little curious.

'John, did you find a package on my desk last Thursday marked Urgent, Addressee only. If you did, what were the contents and where is it now. Jacobs said you were reading it.'

Kallis could feel the noose tightening. 'I put it back on your desk. It was not that important and I knew you would see it the next day.'

'What was it about?' asked Smith, prepared to be patient.

Kallis knew the game was up. He stared arrogantly at Smith and said: 'It was entitled State Security 1960 to Present, File A.'

'What did you do with it?' asked Smith, controlling the desire to eliminate him.

Kallis spoke confidently. He knew he was out of the DSO and that Smith might have him prosecuted. But that was something he would have to bear. 'I sent it to people I know in the group of no name.'

'Who are your contacts,' demanded Smith.

'I can't tell you,' said Kallis.

Smith knew he was not going to get anything from him and he had no hard evidence of what had happened, except admission.

'Get your things,' said Smith. 'I'll call security to escort you from the premises. I never want to see or hear of you again.'

That afternoon, Smith phoned James Steiner at his flat.

'I found out what happened to the file,' said Smith. 'I now have confirmation that it did reach this office. After enquiries the finger pointed to an agent, John Kallis He knew I had him and he confessed. The file was sent to contacts he has in the group. I threw him out of the DSO and he was led from the building.'

Steiner did not say he had met Kallis. It was of no importance. 'What are you going to do now about the file?' he said.

'Well at least I know where it is now,' said Smith. 'As I said before, it is only a copy and I want the original. For the time being I just have to wait until I get my chance.'

'You will get it,' said Steiner.

Kallis was born in Pretoria. His mother was Afrikaans, his father English. He grew up in a happy, disciplined environment and did well at school. He was accepted by Pretoria University, one of the prime academic institutions in the country. He was very clever and graduated with a first class degree in political science. He later went through two years of compulsory military training and in the last eighteen months gained his wings as a paratrooper. During his training he won prestigious awards for use of a pistol and survival. He was made an officer and in the next ten years attended the monthly parade of his regiment, a pre-requisite for non-permanent personnel. At one stage he thought of joining a special forces regiment, but it was full-time and he decided he did not want the army as a career, as interested as he was in the military. During the formative years of his twenties he worked in an attorneys' office. The work held no interest for him and his passion was boxing. He trained at a gymnasium in Pretoria and at one time was thinking of becoming a professional.

At the age of twenty-eight, when he thought he wasn't going anywhere in life, he joined the group of no name, a fairly new political party. It was primarily set up to supersede the weak Nationalist Party, which was the governing party during the apartheid years, and provide a political voice for Afrikaners. Kallis found the group intellectually stimulating and he formed a bond with Johan Teichmann. Teichmann was rising rapidly in the party and impressed Kallis by his progressive attitude, unlike some of the right-wing members who were still locked in the past.

Teichmann saw an active political life for Kallis and he wanted him to join the party full time. But, as involved in

114

the group as Kallis was, he wanted to see more of South Africa and when he was twenty-nine, went to Durban. He immediately took to the city, with its attractive women and exciting lifestyle.

When he was having a drink with a few others in a local hotel, he mentioned that he was interested in getting work in the country's security services. One of the others casually referred to the Directorate: Special Operations, a newly established organization designed to investigate and prosecute national priority crime. Kallis contacted the DSO and was taken on as a field operative.

The work captivated Kallis and he formed an active social life with work colleagues. He kept in touch with friends in the group, particularly Johan Teichmann. Kallis soon found out that Teichmann wanted information on DSO operations and contacts. Kallis's strong allegiance to the group, which had developed since leaving Pretoria and joining the group, led him to comply with Teichmann's requests.

Kallis had been employed by the DSO for five years and was annoyed that Peter Smith had found out he had taken the file. After leaving the DSO building in central Durban, he went to his flat, his seemingly innate stupidity still preying on him. He stood at the main window and looked out over the city. He knew he would not be seeing it for some time. After a few minutes he turned from the window. He was not going to let this setback interfere with the plans he was formulating for his future.

After spending a few hours in a nearby bar, Kallis decided to contact Johan Teichmann. First thing the next morning he phoned Teichmann in Pretoria. After the usual greetings, he told Teichmann what had occurred at the DSO.

'Why don't you come back to Pretoria,' said Teichmann. You have been away long enough. We need men of your calibre and I think I have something that would be just right for you.'

'I won't ask you what that is over the phone,' said Kallis. 'It sounds very interesting. When can I see you?'

'Be here on the first flight tomorrow morning,' said Teichmann. 'I'll meet you at the airport.'

Chapter 32

Pretoria

Kallis met Teichmann as planned. They did not go to the group offices, and instead went to Teichmann's grand Dutch-style house outside town. When they got there, Teichmann asked the servant to bring a pitcher of lemonade and they were soon seated on the spacious front lawn.

'It was interesting to hear what you had to say on the phone,' said Teichmann. 'I thank you for sending us the file and I can assure you it has been appreciated.'

'Thank you,' said Kallis. 'It was a pleasure.'

Teichmann poured lemonade into Kallis's glass and his own before going on.

'Your background and credentials are excellent and you are suited for a specialist job I have in mind. You will concentrate on work that for now plays an important part in the life of the group.'

Teichmann got up and walked around his chair, exercise he badly needed. 'The last statement is extremely important. It means that any threat to the success of the group will be identified and nullified by you, to the best of your ability. The work might entail killing our opponents. These are the people you and I decide undermine the objectives of the group.'

Teichmann stood in front of Kallis. 'After lunch I will give you the job description and the terms and conditions. If you find them satisfactory and have no queries you can start as soon as possible after signing the contract. I hope you accept because your first job is highly dangerous. Let's go and have lunch. I know of an excellent Italian restaurant near the office.'

At one-thirty, Teichmann and Kallis, after an excellent fillet steak, walked to the group offices. The building had been acquired recently and, like Teichmann's house, was designed and built in the Dutch style. The two men went to Teichmann's office, palatial with grand views of the old city and beyond.

Once seated, Teichmann didn't waste time. 'I will fill you in on this job from the beginning to where we are now. When you hear what I have to say you will realize that to some extent you have already been involved.' Teichmann lit a cigarette, coughing wretchedly when he first inhaled. 'Three weeks ago, a man who was leading a team in the group on the development of a file, secretly removed it from its safe. This file and another file I will refer to later are two of the most important documents ever to be conceived and developed by the group. At this stage, we believe the work on the files is complete and they are entitled State Security 1960 to Present, File A and File B.' A few days ago you sent me a copy of File A, the original of which was taken by the man.' Teichmann inhaled again, digging deeper for his fix, half the cigarette already devoured. 'The man took the file and sent it by courier to a prominent Durban lawyer, Andrew Cartwright. When this was found out by our security people, the few who had access to the file were subjected to intense interrogation. You can imagine what that must have been like and it was not difficult to make the man responsible admit his guilt. We could not release him onto the street for fear of him divulging the details of his work to people in authority. With his detailed involvement in the creation of the file, he would have been able to present an extremely convincing story that would have brought the group leadership to its knees and caused irreparable damage from which we would never have recovered.'

'What happened to the guy who was responsible for taking the file?' asked Kallis. 'Somehow I don't think things went too well for him after he was found out.'

118

'Under the circumstances there was only one way of shutting him up,' said Teichmann. 'We had him killed.'

Kallis expected the reply. 'Do you know what happened to the file after it was sent to Cartwrght?'

'We do not know where Cartwright put it and we had to assume it was at his house. We sent three men to Durban to break into the house and find the file. They agreed that our appointed leader of the operation would do it alone and meet the other two later. His name is Jan Krige. As things worked out Cartwright was killed by Krige but Krige could not find the file. He had to get out without it. When he got to the meeting point the others weren't there and he had to return to Pretoria on the night train.'

'That was not very friendly of them,' said Kallis. 'Trust is everything and they don't appear to have it.'

'You are right,' said Teichmann. 'They are dead now but I will come to that later. In answer to your question on what happened to the file, I can only say this. I believe that Krige is telling the truth when he says he has not got the file, and that means someone else got hold of it. We do not know who took the file but a copy was made and you came across it.' He stubbed out his cigarette and lit another. 'There is something that might be of value to you concerning this someone. After leaving Cartwright's house, a person has systematically and with clinical precision killed four of our people. Two were the ones who went to Durban with Krige, one was our man in Pretoria who organized the operation and the fourth was a DSO informer. He told his boss, Peter Smith, in the Scorpions about the job, who we believe was your boss. The story does not end there. A stranger was at Krige's farm when Gerrit Viljoen of the group arrived. For whatever reason this person spared Krige's life and escaped even though he had just been shot by one of Viljoen's men. We believe he is the one to whom I refer and we want him.'

'Whether or not we get hold of this man is, in real terms, of no consequence,' said Kallis. 'The prime aim in all this is to find and obtain the original file.'

'Exactly,' said Teichmann. 'But I would still take great pleasure in catching this stranger.'

'What exactly is in the file that makes it so important?' said Kallis. 'I only read a couple of pages. The title got me going. How does one identify the original?'

Teichmann smiled. 'The second question is very important and I'm glad you asked it. The original has a small Oriental seal heavily stamped on the inside of the back cover and under the synthetic backing. You have to peel away part of the backing to find it. The seal is virtually undetectable unless you know exactly what to look for and where it is located. Only six men, now seven, are privy to what I have just told you. The six, including me, have always worked on copies but the system I have just described was created in case the original fell into the wrong hands, which it did. An agent of ours might then need the capability to identify it quickly without having to resort to a time-consuming process. In answer to your first question, the file names the leaders appointed by the state during the apartheid period who were in the police, security forces, the government, the state security council and those who held positions of influence. The file is a detailed composition of activities executed and directed by those listed and the evidence that would convict them if they were ever prosecuted and brought to trial,' Teichmann drew deeply on his cigarette then went on. 'The file also makes reference to original signed minutes, memoranda, written orders and reports. This information was kept separately from the file. Revelation of the contents of the file would convict many of the most powerful and prominent people in the country and achieve the catharsis that the Truth and Reconciliation Commission wanted but never got.'

120

'I'm not sure I understand the reason for compiling the file,' said Kallis.

'It is designed to protect those who gave us so much in the past and, if necessary, provide a way out for them. Each person listed has a second set of identity documents for them and their family, names of contacts overseas and immediate access to travel documents. In short, everything is there for a quick exit if things get to hot.'

'All very clever,' said Kallis. 'I can see why you want it retrieved. In effect it is the most powerful form of protection. You mentioned another file, File B.'

'I did,' said Teichmann. 'The other file lists only blacks. The two were created simultaneously and are identical in terms of design. But there is a clear distinction between the two. File A is to protect, while File B is to persecute and eliminate.'

Teichmann's secretary came into the office with some papers and gave them to her boss. Teichmann glanced at them and gave them to Kallis. 'Sign the contract after you have read this stuff and return it to me,' he said. 'You can start now. I have some papers for you to read that might be of interest. You will have to find out everything you can about the missing file, including details of all those involved with it. You are the only one on this work and you will do it alone.'

Chapter 33

Durban

After seeing Peter Smith and hearing his account of the conversation with Jan Krige's lawyer, James Steiner wanted to get away for a break. He thought of Sophie, and her wish to go to Japan. He phoned her at work.

'How are you?' said Steiner when she took the call. 'I thought you might be with John Kallis.'

'I can't be with him even if I wanted to,' she said. 'He left the school and someone said he had also left Durban.'

Steiner made no comment. 'You said when I last saw you that you wanted to go to Japan. Well I'm not doing anything at the moment and I thought I might take you up on that.'

She went silent and he could hear her breathing. 'Are you still there?' he asked.

'Of course I am,' she said. 'And yes, I would love to go.'

'Great. I was thinking of going for about a week. When can we leave? I'm available now.'

'Let me see out this week,' she said. 'It's only another couple of days. How does that suit you?'

'I'll get tickets on JAL for Saturday morning,' he said. 'Enjoy your class and I'll ring you tonight.'

That afternoon Steiner booked tickets on the early Saturday flight to Narita, Tokyo's international airport.

Chapter 34

Tokyo, Japan

Steiner and Sophie Carswell arrived at Narita Airport, Tokyo, late on the Sunday afternoon. They caught the limousine bus to the Shinjuku area in the centre of the city, an area adorned with class department stores and hotels that dominated the landscape. Steiner booked them into separate rooms that had good views, particularly of Mt Fuji in the far distance, the highest and most symmetrical mountain in Japan.

'Why two bedrooms?' asked Sophie. 'I was looking forward to some passion. You have been there before.'

'Patience,' said Steiner, a smile on his lips. 'I moved too quickly last time and got your boyfriend going, remember? My desire got the better of me and this time I am going to be more careful.'

'I obviously hurt your pride,' she said and changed the subject. 'Let's have a drink before dinner. There is plenty of time and this is such a fantastic hotel. I can be ready in thirty minutes. How does that sound?'

'I'll come to your door,' said Steiner.

They ordered drinks in the main lounge and relaxed in the sumptuous seats. For a while they drank in silence and then Sophie said: 'You must know Japan really well. Where are we going tomorrow?'

'We are going to a national reserve called Nikko,' he said. 'Whatever you have heard about the mountains, forests and lakes in this country, all are insignificant when it comes to Nikko and when you have been there you will rank it as one the most beautiful places you have seen. By all accounts it has the finest examples of architecture in Japan, in the form of shrines, temples and mausoleums. This includes the Toshogu shrine dedicated to Ieyasu

123

Tokugawa, founder of the Tokugawa *shogunate*. You must have heard of the great *shoguns*.'

'You're mocking me,' she said.

'No,' he said. 'I wouldn't do that to someone as lovely as you.'

She was a little embarrassed by the compliment but still liked it. 'When do we get to Nikko?' she asked. 'I can hardly wait.'

'Now you are mocking me,' he said. 'Early tomorrow morning I want to go to the Tokyo *dojo* of my teacher, Chinen *sensei*. It's in Yoyogi, one stop on the JNR train from here. That shouldn't take more than an hour and then we'll get the train to Nikko.'

'I would like to see where you spent so much time training,' she said. 'Let's have dinner. You can show me some typical Japanese dishes.'

After an early breakfast Steiner and Sophie set out for the *goju-ryu dojo*. She knew little about the traditional martial arts, except that they were very different from the Japanese styles that had been copied and distorted by the west, in terms of technique, principles and philosophy. She had picked up most of her understanding listening to Paul Adams, who held a high black belt grade in *aikido*.

They went to Shinjuku station and caught a train the one stop to Yoyogi. At the station they walked half a mile to the *dojo*, a relatively old one-storey building constructed in the Japanese style. Steiner slid back the panelled door and they replaced their shoes in the foot-well at the entrance with slippers.

The training area comprised a large space with a sprung timber floor. Japanese scrolls hung on the wall and wooden swords and other similar weapons used in training were supported upright in racks. An old shrine was in one corner.

They went towards the small office at the side of the hall. When they approached a girl came out.

124

'James *san*,' she said, clearly pleased to see him. 'What are you doing here? You were only here two weeks ago and only for a short time.'

'I had to leave,' said Steiner. 'I went back to South Africa. I came over with Sophie for a few days.' He turned to Sophie. 'This is Michiko Tanaka the irreplaceable office girl. We spent many hours drinking *sake* at the local eating house and enjoying their fat eels.' He addressed Michiko. 'Where is Chinen *sensei*?'

'I am so sorry,' said Michiko. 'He is in Okinawa until the end of the month. He will be so sorry he missed you.' She smiled. 'You are his favourite and always have been.'

Steiner looked down, a little embarrassed. He and Chinen had a very special relationship.

'Where are you going on this trip?' asked Michiko. 'Last time you went to Nikko. Now, it is the start of autumn and you will find it at its most beautiful.'

'We are going to Nikko this morning,' said Steiner. 'It's a place I love. We'll be staying at the Yumoto Spa *ryokan* on the shores of Lake Yunoko.'

Michiko studied him. 'Did you ever meet the blond man and his Japanese friend who were looking for you last time?' she asked. 'The Westerner really wanted to see you. He is in Tokyo now and yesterday he came in with two other men and asked me if you were here. I said no. I think they will come back.'

Steiner looked at Sophie. She had gone deathly pale and he put his arm round her.

'Who were the other men?' he said.

'I do not know them,' she said. 'They were foreigners and one of them was striking the *makiwara*. He was very strong and has had a lot of practice.'

Steiner looked away, thinking. If the men returned he did not want Michiko to lie for him and deny having seen him. Michiko would also be asked where he had gone and again he would not want her to lie. He started to worry about Sophie and knew they had to go somewhere and talk. The blond man was certainly Paul Adams.

He faced Michiko. 'It is very nice to see you and I am sorry I missed Chinen *sensei*. Please tell him I was here and give him my best wishes. Goodbye.' He took Sophie's hand and led her round to the exit. After putting on their shoes they left the hall.

Steiner and Sophie did not speak to one another until they were seated in a café near the station.

'So Paul Adams is still after me,' said Steiner. 'He doesn't like to lose. What interests me is that he must be confident I'll appear. He doesn't even know what I look like.' He took a sip of coffee. 'Someone must have told him I would be here and I think he knows you are also here. He might hold a grudge against you for ditching him and think I had something to do with it. To me that means two things. He still wants revenge for what I did to you in London and he is not happy that we are together.'

'But who could have told him we were here?' asked Sophie. 'I know he comes to Japan fairly frequently but the coincidence of him being here at the same time as us is virtually impossible.'

'Think of anyone who knows we are here together,' said Steiner.

Sophie held her head in her hands, deep in thought. Then she looked up with satisfaction in her eyes and said: 'Paul Adams knows my father and they speak to one another on the phone.'

'Why would he tell Adams I was here with you?' asked Steiner.

'I think he phoned my father and during the conversation asked about me,' she said. 'I had told my father I had met you again and that we were going to Japan for a break.'

'It all adds up,' said Steiner.

'What do we do now?' asked Sophie.

'I don't believe we should change our plans because of him,' said Steiner calmly. 'We must just be careful. Grab your things; we have to go to Ueno to pick up the train to Nikko.'

Chapter 35

Tokyo, Japan

That same morning, Paul Adams rolled out of his *futon* in a small business hotel in Shinjuku. He dressed casually and after a wash and soak in the hotel bathhouse, went to the dining room where he met his two friends. They too were highly trained in *budo*, the Japanese martial arts, and both men, like Adams, were English.

'What have you got lined up today?' asked one man, Adrian Peters. He spoke to Adams.

'I think I'll spend a couple of hours at the *dojo* and then go and see if James Steiner and Sophie Carswell have arrived. Her father said they would be here now.'

'Why don't you forget about them,' said the other man, David Brown. 'They're not worth it. I didn't know you were so obsessed by them.'

Peters and Brown were already in Tokyo when Adams appeared and contacted them. They were both very powerful individuals and the art of their preference had always been *karatedo*. They were trained in *kyokushinkai*, a different style from the *goju-ryu* that Steiner was heavily involved in and one in which emphasis in training was often given to full body contact, an approach Steiner found meaningless.

'You would also be obsessed if someone raped your girlfriend, killed a very good friend of yours here in Japan and who has now got hold of her. For all I know she had started a relationship with James Steiner before she and I split up. Talk about deceit.'

'What will you do to them when you find them?' asked Peters. 'You can't touch the girl.'

'She's a whore,' said Adams. 'But I know I can't harm her. Above anything else I want him to pay for killing my friend.'

'I think you are throwing the girl into this as well,' said Brown. 'If you harm her the police here and in England will hunt you down. Your desire for revenge in this sordid case must only be satisfied by what you do to Steiner and that means finding him.' Brown could sense death, a macabre fusion of excitement that some unfortunately developed after years on the mat. 'We will help you. The quicker the job is done the better. I don't want this Steiner business to spoil my holiday.'

Adams appreciated what Brown had said. He wolfed down the last morsel of food. 'I'll see you guys here at eleven after a spell on the mat.' He turned for the door and left.

At eleven precisely Adams returned to the hotel. He met Peters and Brown in the lobby and the three of them set out for Yoyogi. When they left the station Peters touched Adams on the arm. 'It's just come to mind. Do you and Steiner know what one another looks like?'

'No,' said Adams. 'I'll ask the girl if he is there.'

'You're not thinking,' said Peters. 'This is only surveillance. The action comes later. If he is there with the girl, she will see you. You don't want that.'

'You are right,' said Adams. 'What do you suggest?'

'I will have a look from the entrance, alone,' said Peters. 'It is highly unlikely Sophie Carswell is in there without Steiner and if I see a young white woman and a white male we will sit out here and be patient. You will know you have struck gold if Carswell later comes out with a white man. We will then follow them. If there is no white girl in there and no white male, I will go in and ask the office girl if they have arrived. I can't do that if there are any white guys in there – one might be Steiner and she would call him. If there are white guys in there and no white female we will wait until we can get positive

129

identification that one of them is Steiner. If he is not here, we are back to square one.'

'Very clever,' said Adams. 'Let's get going on this. Go and have a look. We'll stay out of sight.'

Peters quickly crossed the road and went to the dojo. He opened the door and scanned the space inside. He saw only a few Japanese men. Without hesitation he went to the office. The girl appeared, with no sign of recognition.

'I'm a close friend of James Steiner,' he said, disarmingly. 'I heard he was coming over and was hoping to find him here. I have no address for him. Can you help me?'

His manner brought an immediate response. James had not told her to keep his plans to herself. 'James *san* and the girl he was with are going to Nikko for a few days. They will be staying in the *ryokan* at Yomoto Spa on the north shore of Lake Yunoko. I do not know when he will return to Tokyo.'

'Does he have an address in Tokyo,' asked Peters.

'No,' she said. 'He used to have a flat when he was here for long periods, but he cancelled the lease. Can I give him your address in Tokyo and your name?'

'I do not have an address and I want to surprise him. Thank you. I might see you again.'

Peters left the *dojo* and rejoined Adams and Brown. 'We've cracked it,' he said, clearly pleased. 'Steiner and Carswell are going to the Nikko Reserve and staying at the Yumoto Spa *ryokan* on the north shore of Lake Yunoko.'

'Good work,' said Adams. 'Let's go back to the hotel and get our bags. We can also have some lunch before we head for Nikko. I would like to be there by early evening.'

Chapter 36

KwaZulu-Natal, Republic of South Africa

When the two guerillas, John Nofomela and Paul
Ngwenya, escaped from Krige and Dalton in the house
they ran swiftly and separately through the grass. Each
knew where the other one would go and soon they met up
in a small gully.

'We can't stay here for long,' said Ngwenya. 'They
won't give up on us.'

'They don't know the bush around here as well as we
do,' said Nofomela. 'I think they will give up and go back
to their masters but we can't take the risk and we must
move into the forest.'

They moved out of the gully and walked for a while
along a well-worn footpath. Then they left the path and
entered the dense forest, ideal concealment except from
sniffer dogs. They found a bare patch of ground near some
boulders and settled down to rest.

For two hours the guerillas slept and then Nofomela
woke up and nudged his friend. 'We must discuss our
plans,' he said. 'The whites killed Shozi and then came
after us. They were working from detailed information
about our whereabouts and it was a well organized
operation. You said earlier that they will not give up
hunting us and I think you are right. That means we must
leave KwaZulu.'

'Where will we go?' urged Ngwenya. 'We have spent
much of our life in this area and hardly know anywhere
else.'

'Think carefully,' said Nofomela. 'We can quickly get
used to any place we choose and organize ourselves.
Clearly we must be careful because we might be found by
others. But we have evaded the best of them before and we

will do it again, as we proved tonight.' He thought for a moment then said: 'One thing is certain, we must make contact with people we know and use them to establish our base.'

'Who do we know?' asked Ngwenya, a little apprehensive.

'There is someone I've known for years,' said Nofomela. 'He is white but we have a lot in common and share one another's political beliefs. I knew him for a while in Angola when he was also on the run and we have kept in contact ever since. He is in Pretoria. He is a member of the ANC and they wanted a plant in the offices of an outfit known as the group of no name. Because of the internal bickering and bitterness in the ANC between the security forces, police and government bodies, the plant had to be independent and not aligned to any of the factions. This guy, Rupert Bosch, was selected.' Nofomela got up and stretched his legs. 'There is something I haven't told you. I am virtually certain that one of the whites, who the other one called Major, was a man named Jan Krige and ex-head of the now defunct Johannesburg murder and robbery squad. His photograph has at times appeared in the press. I want to find out more about Jan Krige, why he came to kill us and who he is working for. He and the other guy weren't doing that job alone.' He looked around him and then resumed. 'I think Rupert Bosch can shed some light on this and that is another very good reason for seeing him. Let's start moving. We can pick up one of the night taxis and get to the station in Pietermaritzburg. After that it is Pretoria.'

Chapter 37

Nikko Reserve

James Steiner and Sophie Carswell arrived at Nikko Station early in the afternoon, a couple of hours before Adams and the two men were due at the same destination.

'That is one of the most famous places in Nikko,' said Steiner, pointing to the entrance to a complex of mausoleums, temples and shrines a little further down the road. I told you the Toshogu Shrine, dedicated to Ieyasu Tokugawa the first *shogun* and the mausoleums of Ieyasu and his grandson, Iemitsu, are in Nikko. The complex over there is where they are entombed.'

They walked closer and admired the famous architecture and artwork of the buildings, regarded by many as the finest in Asia. 'If you like, we can make time to visit this place when we leave,' said Steiner. 'I can assure you that it is worth it.'

Sophie marvelled at what she saw. 'Let's do that,' she said. 'How do we get to the hotel? I feel tired and would like to lie down for a while.'

Steiner put his arm around her and said: 'Buses to the top of the reserve are fairly frequent and the ride will take about thirty minutes. There is a stop on the other side of this road.'

When the bus came there were only a few others on it, and after buying tickets seated themselves at the rear. The bus followed a steep, winding road and at times they had magnificent views of mountains shrouded in forest of different shades of gold, red and orange. The region comprised several lakes, spread out and rising with the terrain from the town to Lake Yunoko and the Yumoto Spa. Two rivers joined the middle lakes, each with its own waterfall, the Ryuzu Cascade, north of Lake Chuzenji and

133

known as Ryuzu-no-Taki or Dragon's Head Cascade, and the Kegon Falls.

When Steiner and Sophie reached the Yumoto Spa *ryokan*, they disembarked and confirmed their reservation. They were shown to two rooms placed near one of the well-known bath houses, cut into the rock and always covered in a sulphurous mist that emanated from the spa.

'These are lovely,' said Sophie when they were shown the rooms, each with traditional ta*tami* on the floor, and *futons* already laid out. 'I have heard *futons* are hard when you sleep on them.'

'I am sure you will cope,' said Steiner. 'By Friday you will never want to give them up and you will have become true Japanese. Now have a rest. Give a knock on my door when you get up, or buzz me on the phone.'

Steiner closed her door and went to his room. He sat in a chair near the window and looked out over the lake. His mind had been on Adams and the two men since leaving the *dojo* in Yoyogi. After their brief talk in the coffee house he had not spoken to Sophie again about Adams and neither had she. He thought it unlikely that Adams had gone back to the *dojo* today, found out from Michiko where he and Sophie were going and started out for Nikko. But if they had, they could be in Nikko now. He lay on the futon and closed his eyes.

A little over two hours later at eight, Sophie rang him on the phone.

'I feel great,' she said. 'That was exactly what I needed. Do you want to go now for something to eat? I feel like some *sushi*.'

'There are a number of other typical dishes,' said Steiner. 'I'll go through them with you. Before we go and eat, would you like a soak in the bath house?'

'I would love that,' she said. 'I'll be ready in five minutes.'

A few minutes later Steiner knocked on her door and they went along the passage to the bath house. There was

134

no one else there. 'Take one of these,' he said He gave her a small flannel towel he took off a shelf. 'When you have taken your clothes off you cover yourself with that. You then wash yourself at one of the taps over there against the wall and when you are finished you rinse yourself and get into the pool. It is very hot.'

'Do I have to take the towel into the pool?' she asked.

'Yes,' he said. He pointed to a one-person cubicle. 'You change in there.'

They spent an hour in the bath house, most of it in the pool. When they finally got out, Sophie said: 'Don't you want me. You never show any interest.'

You're a great girl,' said Steiner. 'You have to be patient.'

She could not understand him. She knew she was one of the most alluring girls around and most men found her hard to resist. But James Steiner was different, in an unknown, exciting way.

They ate in the main dining room and had several dishes, some of which they shared. They then went for a walk along the shore of the lake, marvelling at the sulphurous vapour emitted by the subterranean pools through fissures in the rock.

At nine they went back to their rooms. 'Tomorrow we'll go down the road to Lake Chuzenji and perhaps climb the foothills of Mt Nantai, the highest peak in Nikko' said Steiner. 'It is so beautiful and isolated you won't see anyone for miles. Except for me, you will be alone in your own little world.'

'I look forward to that,' she said. She stepped closer and kissed him on the lips. 'It's really nice being here with you.' She could only guess how appealing she was to him. She turned to go to her room.

'Hang on,' said Steiner. 'Get your bag. You are sleeping in my room tonight'

'Why?' she asked, surprised. She could see he wasn't asking her to sleep with him.

'I sense we are in danger from Adams and his friends,' he said. 'We must sleep together. I think they are closer than we think.'

She went quickly into her room, collected her belongings and joined him.

Inside his room he closed the door and locked it. 'Sleep over there,' he said, indicating the *futon* near the window.

She was scared of what might happen. She went to him and said: 'James, I am so glad you are with me.'

'They're not after you,' said Steiner. 'I am the one they want. Now get some sleep.'

Chapter 38

Yunoko Spa, Nikko Reserve

Adams and the two men arrived in Nikko at nine in the evening, later than Adams expected. They left the station and went to a nearby coffee house.

Once seated, Adams said: 'I think we should give it another hour and then go up to the *ryokan*. Buses are less frequent at this time but they run into the early hours. Before we go this is what I have in mind.' He drank some coffee.

'When we get there, Brown will ask at the desk for Steiner and Carswell. If they are not in the main areas and booked in, the receptionist will check the key rack. If the keys are gone, it is a near certainty they are in their room and the receptionist will probably reach for the phone to call them.' Adams hesitated and then continued. 'Before he does, ask for the room numbers and tell the receptionist you can find the room. On your signal, we'll move. If they are pointed out downstairs, we'll decide then what to do.'

'A clever plan,' said Brown. 'I hope it works.'

'It will,' said Adams. 'Let's go and wait for the bus.'

At ten they disembarked from the bus at the Yumoto Spa *ryokan*. They looked at the one-storey building, wondering what it held in store for them.

Adams turned to Brown 'It looks pretty quiet, which is good for us.' He nodded towards the doors. 'See what you can find out.'

Brown went over to the hotel and into the small lobby. He looked at some pamphlets on the wall and glanced around the large restaurant and bar that extended beyond the reception desk. There were only two people having dinner, a Japanese couple, and there was no one at the bar.

He sauntered over to the male receptionist who was bent over some hotel records.

'I believe James Steiner and Sophie Carswell are booked in here tonight,' he said. 'I would like to see them if they are in.'

As predicted by Adams, the receptionist looked in his register and then at the rack of keys. 'They are booked in and I think they are in their rooms, 311 and 312,' he said. 'I'll phone them and tell them you are here.'

'I have two friends with me,' said Brown. 'We can find the rooms. We would like to surprise them. Steiner's a close friend of ours from England.'

The receptionist smiled but something about the man unsettled him. He bowed his head in welcome.

Brown went through the main doors and to the front steps, disappearing from sight. In an instant the receptionist reached for the phone and punched in 311. At the reply he said: 'There are men here and they are coming to your room.' He quickly replaced the receiver.

After a brief wave with his hand, Brown waited for Adams and Peters. When they joined him the three men entered the *ryokan*, went past the receptionist and set off for the rooms.

Chapter 39

Nikko Reserve

James Steiner was half asleep when the phone gave a subdued ring. He reached for the receiver and took it to his ear. What he heard was enough to wake the dead and he replaced the receiver as he came to his feet. He knew the visitors were Adams and his two friends and he had half expected them to come for him in the hotel in the night hours. He quickly put on a pair of dark blue chinos and pulled on his soft shoes. He grabbed his bag and went across the floor to Sophie, who had not been disturbed by the phone.

'Get up,' said Steiner in a whisper. 'There are men coming to the room and we have to leave. They are not friends.'

Sophie was awake instantly. She took a look at Steiner, got to her feet and put on her jeans and shoes. 'Where are we going?' she urged. 'Can't we face them here?'

'No,' said Steiner, going quickly to the window and opening it. 'We'll have a greater chance outside. I want to head for the marsh.'

She swept up her bag and followed him. Together they went through the window and down a fire escape to the flat ground that separated the hotel from Lake Yunoko.

'This way,' said Steiner, taking her hand and leading her to the corner of the lake where the road to Nikko town started. He took the footpath that skirted the shore.

They slowly disappeared from sight of the hotel and once or twice Steiner looked behind them as they ran down the path. No one was in sight and he felt they were ahead of the men. The road lights were still on and provided relief from the darkness of the night. But the light soon went when they reached the south shore and Steiner

139

led the way along a footpath into the seclusion of the forest. After a few hundred metres on a narrow track, he stopped.

'I think we are ahead of them,' he said. 'When they try the door to the room and we don't answer, they will smash the lock. The empty futons, which will clearly have been slept on, will tell them we have gone through the window. They will follow and know we have taken this way out. We must keep moving and hope they think we have stuck to the road. There is a footpath not far from here which leads across Senjogahara Marsh to the Ryuzu Cascade, on the north shore of Lake Chuzenji.'

'And what then?' said Sophie in a low voice.

'We will find a small hotel for the rest of the night,' he said. 'We'll decide our movements in the morning. Let's go.'

After another few minutes they came to the marsh. In the faint moonlight it resembled a seething cauldron that threatened death to anyone sucked under the mass. The footpath was two metres wide and firmly constructed of wooden planks a centimetre apart. It wound like a snake and swept first to the right and then to the left until it reached the opposite shore 400 metres in the distance. To Steiner and Sophie it was a welcome sight that seemed to offer final escape from their pursuers.

They stepped onto the planks and started across the marsh. For all its atmosphere of the surreal, it was strangely beautiful and so silent. Their progress was steady and in minutes they disembarked on the far shore, and went quickly into the forest that in places came close to the water's edge.

'We'll wait here for a moment,' said Steiner. 'I want to see if they are following.'

From their position there was no sign of Adams and the other two and they carried on in the direction of the Ryuzu Cascade.

'You know this area well,' said Sophie in admiration. 'It's as if you were brought up here.'

'I used to come here a lot,' said Steiner. 'I was usually alone and I enjoyed the quiet.'

Ryuzu Cascade was to Steiner one of the wonders of the world, and when they reached it they sat on a rock at the top, taking in the sight. The road they were on when they left the Yumoto Spa *ryokan* passed nearby, hidden by dense vegetation.

Steiner lent back, spreading himself on a flat part of the rock. 'It often amazes me,' he said, 'how something so hard can feel so soft when you need it.'

Sophie smiled and started to lie down next to him. She was on her elbow, with her head held sideways, when she gasped and drew herself to him. He instantly knew Adams and his friends had caught up with them. He turned on the rock and pushed himself to his feet.

The three men were only metres from them, confident, grinning. Adams took a step forward. 'We got you at last. Did you think you could evade us?'

'What do you want?' asked Steiner, well aware that the men were slowly encircling them. 'We are here on holiday.'

'I'll tell you what I want,' said Adams. 'Three weeks ago you killed one of my best friends in this reserve. You also killed two acquaintances of mine in Takamiyama. They were brutal killings of innocent men and you are going to pay.'

Sophie gasped, the raw accusations stinging her to the core. 'I led him on in London and never admitted that to you,' she said. 'You chased him to Japan. He was only defending himself.'

'You're lying,' said Adams. 'I've never seen anyone as upset as you were then, after he had raped you. If you're telling the truth it doesn't change anything as far as I'm concerned. But my friends will find you satisfying after we

141

have dealt with Steiner. They will find that only a whore can make love with unashamed desire.'

Adams waved his hand forwards and moved for Steiner. Sophie cried out and ran at him, hitting his chest with her fists. Callously, he threw her aside and she fell onto her back, a spent force.

Steiner was silent, showing no feeling and when Adams was just over an arm's length from him he went in. The strike came from nowhere and Adams fell between two rocks, his arms and legs assuming the surreal. His movement fluid and continuous, Steiner closed swiftly on the others, taking the first down with a ruthless kick to the groin. As the second came in, he swept the man's front foot away in a classical execution of *ashi-barai*, and took him heavily to the ground with the edge of his leading hand. The man collapsed, his control gone.

The three men remained where they had fallen, each partially concussed by the vicious, clinical assault. Sophie, mesmerized by what had taken place in front of her, ran to Steiner and embraced him. She didn't smile and again wondered what had happened to the three men who had gone for Steiner three weeks before.

'Thank you,' she said. 'I find it hard to believe how anyone can move as you do. You are quite something, tall, dark and so dangerous.' She looked at Adams and his friends. 'What happens to them?'

'They'll recover,' said Steiner, his breathing as silent as the way he moved. 'They might try again. How are you?'

'I feel great now,' she said. 'But, I didn't when I first saw them.'

'The town is not far and we can make it in ten minutes by skirting the far side of Lake Chuzenji. Get your bag and let's go.'

A little later they reached Nikko Town. There were a number of hotels in the main street and down side roads. They chose one that was suitably discreet and got a room for the rest of the night.

When Sophie woke the next morning, she found Steiner already up and seated near the *shoji* overlooking the street. She got up and walked over to him. 'This is one morning I feared would never come,' she said. 'Did I tell you how scared I was last night when those brutes descended on us out of nowhere?' She smiled and sat down next to him.

'No,' said Steiner, taking her hand. 'But that is over and I think we have to change our plans. Who knows what those men will do next. I don't relish the idea of spending the remainder of this visit looking over my shoulder.'

'What do you have in mind?' she asked.

'I think we should go back to Tokyo on the next available train and when we get there find a room in one of those hotels in Shinjuku. We can use it as a base and visit areas like Mt Fuji, which is inspiring to say the least. There are also some very interesting places to see in Tokyo. One thing is for sure. I won't go near the *dojo* again on this trip. It seems to bring bad luck'

She laughed. 'I agree,' she said. 'Let's have breakfast and go.'

Steiner and Sophie reached Tokyo three hours after leaving Nikko Town. They booked in at the Hilton Hotel in Shinjuku, which like the other sky-scraper hotels in the area offered everything that anyone could want. For three days they went to Mt Fuji where they spent the night in the Fuji Hotel and visited the temples, other ancient buildings and, later, the parks in Tokyo. On the Saturday they flew back to Durban and arrived early on the Sunday morning. They passed through immigration and went straight to the house where she was staying.

'You won't forget a trip like that in a hurry,' said Steiner, when he was leaving. 'I don't think you will hear of Adams again. You did incredibly well.'

Sophie embraced him and kissed him full on the lips. 'I can't thank you enough for such a marvellous time. It helped me purge things from the past. I hope to see you in a day or so.'

'Yes,' said Steiner, turning to go to his car. 'I also got rid of some things I wanted to forget.'

Chapter 40

Jan Krige's farm, near the Kruger Reserve

Four hours after leaving Malakazi township, Krige and Dalton reached Pretoria and took the road to White River. When Dalton dropped him off at his Land Rover, Krige said: 'I will never do anything like that again. We were lucky to get out alive.'

Dalton concurred. 'Yes,' he said. 'It was a close call as they say and the group will not get me to do their dirty work again.' He then added, cryptically. 'The only thing I want to remember is the two of us working together.'

They parted and half-an-hour later Krige reached his farm. He hadn't phoned Kirsty while he was away and he expected a deluge of questions, something he could do without after what he had been through.

Kirsty was drinking coffee on the verandah when he pulled up in the yard. She watched him leave the Land Rover and did not leave her seat to greet him.

'Hi,' he said. 'I missed you.'

'I don't believe you,' she said. 'It's not difficult for someone of your intelligence to find a phone box in Pretoria. Were you really there, or were you somewhere else.'

Her words cut through him like a scythe in full swing and the saying the truth hurts passed through his mind. 'I was there,' he lied. 'It was extremely hectic, but my thoughts were often of you. I'll tell you what it was all about.'

'Surely you must have known the gist of it before you went,' she said, without emotion.

'I did,' said Krige. 'But it was not clear. That is why I didn't tell you. I would have looked a fool.' He poured some coffee and sat down in his beloved rocking chair. He

145

could see she was not impressed and knew he had a real job if he was to convince her that it was a genuine business proposition.

'Did you go in those clothes?' she said, looking at his khaki shorts and shirt.

'I took a change of clothing with me,' he said. 'It is in the back of the Land Rover. The spirit of the whole thing was informal.'

She didn't say anything and knew in her heart that he was spewing out lie after lie. All she could feel at the moment was that something was up, and she had to find out what it was for her own protection.

Krige looked at her and gave his story. 'They phoned me before I received the papers by courier. They are a group of wealthy business men who want to acquire some of the best land in this area and develop it. This farm is perfect for them and the meeting was to establish the framework for negotiations if we were prepared to sell a reasonable acreage. There offer at this stage is 750 000 rand for 1000 acres on the west range.'

'That is an insult,' she said. 'It is worth double that. Did you know the price they were talking about before you went?'

'I did, but I wanted to see how serious they were and how far they would go,' said Krige. 'I know it is very low but in all business deals you have to meet the players in person.'

'What did you say?' she asked, still not believing him but preferring to listen to his lies, wondering what would come next.

'I did not think they would go much higher,' said Krige. 'I rejected the offer.'

'And it took you three days to say that,' she said, finding the story so fictitious it nearly made her laugh. 'Where are the papers? I would like to read them.'

'I got rid of them,' said Krige, a last effort to get his head off the block.

146

She got up and put her cup on the table. 'I bet you did,' she said sarcastically. 'I'm going to see Maria this morning and I might stay for lunch.' Maria and her husband owned a neighbouring farm. 'I'll see you when I get back. I need time to think.'

She left him with a lot on his mind. He sat on the verandah until he heard her car and then went inside. He phoned Teichmann.

'You must have seen the news,' said Krige.

'Yes,' said Teichmann. 'We later contributed an article on the types of men they were and their crimes that have until now gone unpunished. You did a great job.'

'I'm afraid we only got one of the guerillas,' said Krige. 'The others escaped and they could be anywhere now.'

'We will find them,' said Teichmann, emphatically. 'They will then get the same treatment.'

'As long as it's not me who has to do the job,' said Krige.

'You're out of it, as I promised,' said Teichmann. 'We will get someone else.' He terminated the call.

Krige knew that any dealings with the group had to be taken as it came, despite Teichmann's assurances to the contrary. He knew in his heart that they had him in chains.

147

Chapter 41

Pretoria

After catching the last night train in Pietermaritzburg, the two guerillas, Nofomela and Ngwenya, reached Pretoria the next day at noon. They had something to eat in a station cafeteria and then found the nearest phone box. Nofomela pulled his dog-eared diary from his pocket and after finding Rupert Bosch's number made the call.

When Bosch answered, Nofomela said: 'Rupert, it's a voice from the past. Do you want to know who it is?'

'Tell me,' said Bosch. 'The suspense is killing me.'

'It's John Nofomela. Paul Ngwenys's also here. Does that ring any bells?'

'It certainly does,' said Bosch. 'I still remember the great times we had together. Where are you now?'

'We're at the station,' said Nofomela. 'We've just arrived from Pietermaritzburg.'

'I normally break for lunch about now,' said Bosch. 'How about meeting me?'

'Where do you suggest?' said Nofomela.

'When you come out of the station you will see the main street,' said Bosch. 'Walk down it on the right side and you will soon come across a restaurant named Strada. It's Italian and very good. I can meet you there in a few minutes. We are just around the corner.'

'That's fine,' said Nofomela. 'We'll see you then.'

Rupert Bosch was born in Cape Town of Afrikaans parents. He went to the prestigious private school Bishops and excelled academically. He was an outstanding athlete at school and in his last three years was awarded the most coveted honour for athletic prowess. After school he went to Stellenbosch University, regarded by many as one of the finest in the country and read political science. Military service followed university and again he excelled, particularly in the use of weapons. He was very interested in joining one of South Africa's elite special forces regiments, but he was becoming inexorably drawn to politics. The party to which he gave his support and allegiance was the governing Nationalist Party of the apartheid era, now a shell of its former self. With no real opposition he joined the African National Congress in 1988, which later in 1994 formed a black government under Nelson Mandela. To Bosch, the ANC had the diversity and potential to be one of the strongest political forces in Africa. It was during the late apartheid period that Bosch got to know some of the activists who were fighting for black rule and it was then that he met John Nofomela and Paul Ngwenya. After two years, he became an operative in the security wing of the ANC. Unlike some of his colleagues he avoided any alliance with the developing factions and for that reason and his intelligence, was favoured by the head of security. In the early 1990s, Bosch was asked to infiltrate the higher echelons of the group of no name because the party was suspected of being a seditious power that craved the previous Afrikaner state with whites in control.

The three men met at the Strada as planned and took a table at the rear. It was obviously not a cheap restaurant.

'Well, tell me what you two guys are doing in Pretoria,' said Bosch. 'I thought you were forever captivated by life in KwaZulu-Natal.'

'This might sound strange, but two whites came to kill us,' said Ngwenya, speaking for the first time. 'We were lucky to escape. Earlier they had killed Moses Shozi, a leading member of Inkatha and the provincial government.'

'Do you have any idea who they were and who they are working for?' said Bosch. 'It sounds as if these men had you two earmarked for extermination. To me, that means they were working for someone or, alternatively, an organization.'

'Agreed,' said Nofomela. 'We all know there are mavericks running around with a grudge killing at random, but these guys were highly trained professionals.'

'That means there is an organization of some sort behind them,' said Bosch. 'Leave this with me and I'll see what I can find out. This organization, if there is one, might be on my doorstep.' He glanced knowingly at the two guerillas. 'Where are you guys staying?'

'We were hoping you might be able to suggest something,' said Ngwenya.

'I will see what I can do,' said Bosch. 'It will have to be a hotel for a couple of nights. There are plenty of reasonably priced ones in this area. See what you find this afternoon and give me a ring at the office. This is my home number in case you need it.'

'Thank you,' said Nofomela. 'I knew we could rely on an old comrade.'

Bosch left, followed shortly afterwards by the two blacks. 'Let's work our way down some of these side roads and get a hotel,' said Nofomela. 'We'll also have to buy some clothes.'

Chapter 42

Pretoria

Nofomela and Ngwenya soon found a small hotel down a side street and then went and bought casual clothes, denim jeans, cotton shirts and soft shoes at a department store. They were both tall, handsome, powerful men and the clothes were ideal for showing off their physiques. When they got back to their room in the hotel, Nofomela phoned Bosch.

'We've got a place,' said Nofomela. 'It's near the restaurant.'

'Great,' said Bosch. 'I have been thinking about what you told me at lunch and I might have something that sheds a lot of light on this business in Natal.'

'When can we meet?' said Nofomela, ice in his voice. He wanted nothing except to find the men who tried to kill them in Malakazi township. 'We're available.'

'I can meet you tomorrow night,' said Bosch. 'It gives me time to find out as much as I can. There is a bar, the Voortrekker, on the other side of the station and down the second road on the left. It is quiet. How about meeting me there at eight?'

'We'll see you then,' said Nofomela. He replaced the receiver.

The next evening after a meal in the hotel, the two blacks went to the bar suggested by Bosch. He was already there, a pint of lager in a long glass on the table. Nofomela and Ngwenya joined him and he ordered two beers for them. Once seated, Bosch went to the point.

'I'll describe a sequence of events that I am sure are connected in some way with the attempt to kill you. About three weeks ago a file, File A, was removed from a safe in the offices of the group of no name where I work. It was

151

sent to an eminent trial lawyer in Durban, Andrew Cartwright. I am sure you have heard of him. He has always been an ardent supporter of the ANC and funded them heavily in their fight against white rule. He has continued to pour money into their coffers.' Bosch swallowed the last of his beer, relishing the bitter taste, and ordered three more from a passing waiter.

'The group found the man who took the file. He was one of those who had played a central part in compiling it. He then vanished.'

'Where's the file now and what's in it?' said Nofomela, already transfixed by the little they had been told so far.

'This is where the fun starts,' said Bosch, delighting in the attention he was getting. 'I'll answer the second question first. The file is a compilation of those whites who were in positions of power and influence during the apartheid period. This covers government leaders, members of the state security council, the senior commanders in the security forces and police and other prominent organizations. The file contains minute details of the private and public lives of these men including documents of significance that were authorized and signed by them and orders they gave in writing, all of which could result in their prosecution if found. A by-product of the information compiled was a complete set of false identities and contacts, here and overseas, which they might need for protection against intense scrutiny of past actions. For your interest the white file, as it is sometimes called, is entitled State Security 1960 to Present, File A. I add that a similar file, File B, containing the names and details of prominent blacks has also been created, but it is still secure in its safe. The difference between this black file and the white file is not only that one is for blacks and the other for whites, but that the former is for persecution and execution and the latter for protection. Now, I will answer your other question.' He paused and Nofomela immediately interrupted.

'Are our names in the black file?' he asked.

'I knew that was coming,' said Bosch. 'Yes, they are and with high priority.'

'That explains the other night,' said Ngwenya.

Bosch continued. 'The group sent three men to Cartwright's home to retrieve the file, which they were guessing was there. Two of the men fled and the leader of the operation in the field, Jan Krige, killed Cartwright.'

'So he works for the group,' said Ngwenya, startled by what he had heard.

Bosch went on. 'Krige says that he never found the file and the group believes him. Now this convoluted plot gets heavy. An outsider or unknown man appears to be involved in all this. The deaths of the two who fled from the action in Durban, the group leader of the operation based in Pretoria, and an informer for the Directorate: Special Operations, the Scorpions, were all killed by, it is believed, this outsider. It is not known if this guy got hold of the file. But, an agent of ours, John Kallis, who was working inside the DSO, intercepted a copy of the file sent anomalously to the DSO. John Kallis was caught after he sent it to the group, dismissed and he now works for us in Pretoria. The stark reality in all this is that nobody knows where the original of this file is, except those who have it. And, the group wants it back'

'What a story,' said Nofomela. 'It is almost unbelievable. What does Kallis do?'

'No one seems to know,' said Bosch. 'To me that indicates undercover work' Bosch looked hard at the two men. 'By the way all this stuff is highly confidential. If anyone found out that I had told you, I would end up like the guy who removed the white file.'

'You know you can trust us,' said Nofomela. 'We would like to know more.'

'I will help you in any way I can,' said Bosch. 'But, we must never be seen together and any progress you make must be given to me. You will in essence be working alone.'

'Thank you,' said Ngwenya. 'We will write up everything we know and don't know. The first thing we want is Krige's contact details and anything else you have on him.'

'I will get that for you,' said Bosch. 'Ring me tomorrow. But, if you contact him you must find a way of surreptitiously extracting from him anything of relevance that he has not revealed. Remember that if he sees you in the flesh he will recognize you. That would initiate an intensive enquiry that could blow us all apart.'

'We accept that,' said Ngwenya. 'One of us will ring you tomorrow.'

Chapter 43

Pretoria

When Rupert Bosch met the two guerillas in the Voortrekker bar and told them that when he left they must never be seen with him again, he did not realize that it was too late. John Kallis was seated in a corner behind an oak pillar and he saw Bosch when he entered the bar and sat down with the blacks.

Kallis had not been introduced to Bosch, but Teichmann had on one occasion pointed him out across the office floor. When Kallis casually asked Teichmann what Bosch did, the older man said he was involved in security. Kallis doubted Bosch knew who he was and he thought no more of it. He would meet him sometime.

With nothing to do except drink, Kallis idly watched the three men. He was curious when he noticed that they were deeply involved in a conversation without a smile ever touching their lips and that Bosch appeared to do all the talking. After they had finished their beers, Bosch got up and left. The more Kallis thought about what he had seen the more interested he became. He knew he could easily find out where Bosch lived and that left the other two men.

When Nofomela and Ngwenya left the bar, Kallis waited a short while and then followed them. He did not have to keep on their tail for any distance. He saw them go down a side road and then disappear into a small hotel, the name of which Kallis noted.

On the way to his flat, Kallis, deep in thought, went into the group building and up to his office. He opened a cabinet and extracted a list of all those who had unrestricted access to the safe where the original files were

155

kept. Rupert Bosch's name was on the list. Kallis replaced the list and left the block. A plan was evolving in his mind.

The next morning Kallis was in his office early and immediately continued working on the notes concerning the missing file. He was only too aware that retrieval of the file rested on who had taken it and what they had done with it. He knew the answer to the second question effectively meant the case had been solved, but the first could provide a valuable link in the chain.

At nine Kallis picked up his receiver and phoned a close university friend. The man worked for the main telephone company in the district.

'Piet, it is John Kallis. I haven't spoken to you for a while. I was working in Durban until recently and now I'm in Pretoria.'

The man, Piet Joubert, was pleased to hear his friend's voice. 'We must meet up. Where are you?'

'I'll ring you as soon as I have a permanent residence,' said Kallis. 'I would like you to do a big favour for me.'

'Just ask,' said Joubert.

'I would like you to tap someone's line for me. It's extremely confidential and is to do with the operations of the company for which I work. I would like the tap to be on two phone numbers, one in an office and the other in a private flat, and to be working round the clock for a week to start with.'

'Give me the numbers and the name,' said Joubert. 'I'll set it up today.'

'Great,' said Kallis. 'The numbers are all in Pretoria.' He read them out, for the flat and the office. 'The man's name is Rupert Bosch. Please ring me if you come up with anything, which I believe you will. I would also like a tape.'

Chapter 44

Durban

One evening, James Steiner had a phone call from Peter Smith of the Scorpions.

'Would you like to go for a drink?' said Smith. 'I know of a good bar opposite the town hall in West Street. It is new and reasonably quiet.'

Steiner had spent the few days since his return from Japan training and conducting classes. He had contacted Sophie Carswell once, but she had been unable to see him.

'I would like that,' said Steiner. 'I can meet you there at eight.'

'I'll see you then,' said Smith and cut the call.

The two men met in the bar as arranged, ordered beers and found seats.

'How are things at work?' asked Steiner. 'Have you found the missing file?' He smiled, knowing Smith wouldn't find the questions amusing.

'I won't answer that,' said Smith. He took a mouthful of beer and lit a cigarette. He exhaled and spoke at the same time. 'There is a lot going on, some of which leaves a particularly nasty taste in my mouth. It is the kind of stuff that excites tension and hatred and never seems to end.'

'To what are you referring?' asked Steiner, interested.

'I'm talking about deliberate, organized killings between whites and blacks,' said Smith. 'In many respects this means that there are still people in this country who have never accepted that apartheid is over.'

'We know that,' said Steiner patiently.

'I am specifically talking about serious crime organized by powerful groups,' said Smith. 'Some years ago the British set up SOCA, the Serious Organized Crime

Agency, to counter this sort of thing. Our equivalent is the DSO or Scorpions, but sometimes I feel we are getting nowhere in our fight.' He shrugged. 'Perhaps the British feel the same way. I hope they do.'

'Something's bugging you,' said Steiner. 'What is it?'

'It preys on me incessantly,' said Smith, 'and I don't know who's behind it all. Two days ago, a well known Zulu member of the KwaZulu-Natal provincial government, Moses Shozi, was executed inside his house by a highly trained white male. Shortly afterwards, three black ex-guerillas were attacked in Malakazi township, which is not far from the Zulu's house. One was killed and the other two escaped. The mayor of the township and his wife were also killed. The killers were whites, probably the same men who visited Shozi. Other than the fact that the killers were white, I have no idea who they were or where they came from.'

'It sounds like the missing file except that I am the one the group wants to find.' said Steiner.' He grinned. 'But they don't know who I am or where I came from.'

'They should have a better relationship with Jan Krige,' said Smith, at last releasing a smile. 'He could tell them everything. Anyway, the missing file is also one of my problems, or should I say my real problem. Thinking of it drives me insane. Let's have another beer and split.'

Chapter 45

Pretoria

After Krige had phoned Teichmann and closed the job in KwaZulu-Natal, he sat in the lounge with a drink. The deeds of murder, whatever the guerillas and Shozi were guilty of, and the lies he had told his wife Kirsty, tore at him. Kirsty did not believe him and he could not blame her considering his antics of the past. He had no doubt that she was in turmoil, and he felt there was little else he could do except tell her he loved her.

Kirsty returned to the farm after lunch. After she had parked her car in the garage round the back and turned off the engine, she knew what she was going to do. She went through the kitchen and down the passage to the lounge. She saw Krige in a chair on one side, his face drawn. But that did not deter her.

'I am going away,' she said, walking into the room. 'I need more time to think. I am certain you didn't go to Pretoria and I think you are still tied up with the group. I don't love you anymore and I can't stand your lies. You must think little of me to do this.'

The words struck him hard and he felt empty inside, a dry well. He had no response. 'Where will you go?' he said limply.

'I am not sure at the moment,' she said, finding satisfaction in his look of despair. 'I will phone you and tell you what I intend to do.' She turned and walked down the passage.

Krige soon heard her car and he watched it as it headed for the main gate. He was devastated.

Chapter 46

Pretoria

Rupert Bosch left the office at the usual time of seven and returned to his house on the outskirts of Pretoria. The house was architecturally a fairly modern concept and set in two acres of verdant lawn, shrubs, flower beds and deciduous trees. He loved the place and regarded it as the finest acquisition he had ever made. The house was single-storeyed and the extensive living room in the front opened onto the gardens through large glass doors that offered an unhindered view.

After parking his Mercedes in one of the garages at the rear, he entered the building and went through to the living room. He had just poured a liberal Scotch and soda when the phone went. He sat down and picked it up.

'Bosch,' he said, taking a mouthful of the spirit.

'Rupert,' said the voice on the other end of the line. 'It is John Nofomela. Paul Ngwenya is here as well. Is it convenient for you to speak?'

'Yes,' said Bosch. 'I planned to phone you later. How are things going?'

'Pretty good, although I would like to get out of this hotel and the city.' said Nofomela. 'We like grass and trees not concrete.'

Bosch laughed. 'You need a place like mine. It offers the best of both worlds, easy access to the city and the bush.'

'You told us to phone you to get Jan Krige's contact details, and anything you might have found out about the two cases involving the murder of Cartwright and the attacks on us in Malakazi.'

'I haven't found out much more but I am working on it,' said Bosch. 'I have Krige's details here.'

'Fire away,' said Nofomela, feeling he was getting closer to the man he despised.

'Krige left the police force several years ago after attaining the rank of major in the Johannesburg murder and robbery squad,' said Bosch. 'He inherited his father's farm half-an-hour north of a one-horse town called White River. It's on the road to the Kruger Reserve.' He read out the phone number and area code. 'Krige has a wife, Kirsty, and two sons who are at boarding school in the Cape. Someone who might be of use to you is Krige's lawyer, David Staples. His practice is in Pretoria under his name.' Bosch took a swig from his glass and then continued. 'Krige was definitely the leader of the two-man operation that ended in the deaths of Moses Shozi, your comrade Elijah Ngubane and the Malakazi mayor and his wife. The names and details of Shozi, you, and your two friends are certainly prominent in the black file. Even though the others are dead they will remain in the file, marked deceased.'

'Do you have anything else?' asked Nofomela.

'No,' said Bosch, wanting to pour another Scotch.

'Ngwenya and I have been thinking of how we can get Krige to reveal what he knows about the white file, which we believe he has, and his involvement in the operation in KwaZulu-Natal,' said Nofomela. 'Cartwright's death and the deaths of those to whom we have just referred, rank as cold blooded murder. He certainly wouldn't like us to expose him to the National Prosecuting Authority. We could act as witnesses and we would be immune from prosecution, assuming there is no evidence against us for past deeds. But that is a chance we would be prepared to take. From what you say, virtually all the potentially incriminating stuff on us is in the black file and at the moment it is held by the group. We would like to get hold of it as well as the white file, but that will have to wait until we know how we can do it. The plan I have outlined will have to be enough at this stage and it should enough to make Krige reveal what he knows.'

'It could work,' said Bosch, 'even though you didn't actually see him kill Shozi, the mayor, the mayor's wife, and your friend. As you say, coming out in the open like this is a very good reason for getting hold of the black file for your own protection, knowing that what it has on you is extremely comprehensive. Remember that if you try this on Krige and he resists or denies any involvement in the disappearance of the white file and the murders, you must control yourselves and not harm him. If you do harm him the group will hunt you down mercilessly. They have a soft spot for him.'

'Thanks,' said Nofomela. 'I know what you mean.'

Chapter 47

Pretoria

The day after Bosch's telephone conversation with Nofomela, John Kallis had a phone call from Piet Joubert.

'Bosch last night received a call from a guy named Nofomela,' said Joubert, concealing his excitement. He, like many people, was always gripped by listening secretly to the conversations of others. This particularly applied to what he was about to tell Kallis. 'I recorded the call as we discussed and even though I know nothing about what is going on, I think you will be extremely interested.'

'Excellent,' said Kallis. 'I can meet you at your flat after work.'

'Fine,' said Joubert. 'You know the address. I look forward to seeing you.'

At around six that evening Kallis drove to Joubert's flat. He was let in immediately. His friend led him to the sitting room he had seen before and it crossed his mind that Joubert was poorly paid. Joubert pointed to a seat and extracted a computer disc from his bag. He inserted it into a new CD player and started the machine.

Kallis listened intently to every word and the more he heard the more satisfied he became. When the recording had finished he said: 'You have done a first class job. It's exactly what I expected and wanted to hear.'

'I only pushed a few buttons,' said Joubert. 'Take the disc and I will keep at it. Anything else and I'll ring you.'

'You are doing me a big favour,' said Kallis. 'One day I'll tell you what this is all about.'

The two men parted and Kallis went down the steps to his car. He could not believe his good fortune and he was looking forward to proceeding with his plan.

After a quick meal in his flat, John Kallis changed into casual clothes. He left the flat and drove to the area where Rupert Bosch lived alone. Kallis easily found the quiet, winding road and when he saw the magnificent houses he reluctantly admitted that Bosch had very good taste. He drove past the house, saw the lights at the front were on and then parked further along the road. He was 100 metres from the house and when he neared the gates, he vaulted over the fence into a bed of ubiquitous shrubs. He waited for a moment then skirted the lawn towards the front of the building. When he was close to the lounge, he stopped in the shadows and scanned the room through sliding glass doors. Bosch was not in sight and he went quickly onto the verandah. He tried one of the sliding doors and it yielded readily in his hands on well-oiled runners. He slipped into the room and listened, aware that if Bosch did not come to him he would have to go and find him. He was not sure Bosch was in the house and if he was alone. They were uncertainties he had to live with and he would have to assess his options when he knew more.

The lounge was sunken and he had just reached the steps leading to the bowels of the house when he heard someone walking towards him down the passage. It disappeared at an angle and he guessed it served the bedrooms. He stood as if carved in stone and then Bosch appeared, still dressed in his office suit.

At the sight of Kallis, Bosch stopped dead. When he had recovered from the shock, he said: 'What the hell are you doing in my house. Isn't there such a thing as privacy?' He spat out the words, wondering what Kallis wanted.

'I came for a talk,' said Kallis. 'It will interest you.'

'Why can't it wait until we get to the office in the morning?' said Bosch, assertively.

'I want to get this out of the way before then,' said Kallis, taking a step backwards, allowing Bosch to enter

164

the room. Bosch came down from the landing and lowered his weight into the nearest chair.

'Last night you received a phone call from a man named Nofomela. His friend Ngwenya was with him. You obviously know these guys. The conversation described a way of getting Krige to tell these two men that he alone had taken the white file, File A, from Cartwright's house, which he now had in his possession, and extracting a confession that he is guilty of killing some blacks in KwaZulu-Natal.' Kallis smiled. He enjoyed seeing guilt written on Bosch's face. He went on. 'I really don't have to tell you that if the group leadership knew you were divulging secret information to ex-guerillas, they would hang you by your balls from the tallest skyscraper in Pretoria.'

Bosch sagged in his chair. He knew Kallis had him on a skewer and he knew he would have to pay a heavy price for his actions. He wished he had never heard of the guerillas. They were disturbing the easy life he had got used to.

'I know you recently spoke to these guys because I saw you drinking with them in the Voortrekker bar,' said Kallis. 'I can imagine now that the conversation would have covered everything about group operations in Durban and KwaZulu-Natal. You had also told them about the black file, which must have mortified them because they're in it.'

'What do want of me?' asked Bosch, feeling powerless under the weight of evidence against him. 'You must have had my phones tapped.'

'I did,' said Kallis. 'It is not difficult when you have contacts in the right places. Now, I'll answer your question. You are one of the chosen few who have access to the room and safe where the files are kept. That means only the black file because the white file has gone.' Kallis moved a little closer to Bosch. 'I want you, with this access, to remove the black file. I will meet you

165

somewhere and you will give the file to me. After that you must disappear. That is primarily for your benefit, because when it is discovered that the file has gone, you and the others with access will be subjected to the most severe interrogation. I have heard that even if you have a water tight alibi, the slightest suspicion on their part will mean your summary execution. I had thought of killing you myself but that is too untidy and I would run the risk of being found out. You will therefore have your freedom instead. I add that if you decide to run now and not comply with my request, I will reveal your conversation with the guerrillas to the group. They will hunt you down far more assiduously than if you were suspected of stealing the file. They hate traitors more than anything and you would spend the remainder of your life in fear.'

Bosch knew he had no way out. Kallis held all the cards. At least he would escape with his life. 'When do you want the file?' he asked quietly.

'There is a bar called Fontein a few kilometres out of the city on the Kruger road through White River,' said Kallis. 'It is in the middle of nowhere. I'll be there in the car park at eight tomorrow night. Don't keep me waiting or I might think something has happened to you.' Kallis turned towards the verandah doors. 'I will expect to see you then. Sweet dreams.' He went like a phantom through the doors and then he was gone.

For an hour after Kallis had gone, Bosch thought about the visit. He recognized he had been caught red handed by a relative newcomer in the group and he did not even know Kallis's function. In some ways he was grateful that he had been let off the hook rather than be killed, but he was not sure why Kallis wanted the file.

As he sat in the chair, Bosch thought about the next day. It was a foregone conclusion that after removing the file and giving it to Kallis, he would not be able to return to the house he loved for a very long time. He would become the hunted one and it could mean eventually selling the place. Getting the file was not a problem. He would go to work at the usual time and, using his own set of keys to get into the room and safe, remove the file late in the day at around seven-thirty. Most of the people would have left by then and no one would want to work on the file now that it was effectively complete. After he had taken the file he was aware that it would be too much of a risk to come back to the house and he would have to pack the clothing and important items he wanted tonight.

Bosch packed his things and loaded the car. He was tired, mentally and physically, and he finally fell asleep on the sofa in the lounge.

Chapter 48

Near Pretoria

Rupert Bosch was up early the next morning and he sat on the verandah, absorbing the vista. He was there for an hour and then cooked a plain breakfast of eggs and bacon. Replenished, he washed the plates and went to bath and dress for work.

He was in the office at nine and it took time for him to build up the vestige of enthusiasm that he needed to clear the desk of most of the papers he was working on. A completely cleared desk would have drawn comments he could not face.

For the rest of the day, when he kept largely to himself, he saw no sign of John Kallis and he wondered if he had come in to work. They were on the same floor and it was surprising because he usually saw him at least once during the day.

At seven-thirty Bosch picked up his worn leather brief case and nonchalantly went down the stairs to the floor where the file was held. No one was around and when he came to the room he wanted, he inserted the key and entered. In a matter of seconds he was in the man-sized safe and his eyes focussed immediately on the black file that was lying on the nearest table, its usual place. The white file was noticeable by its absence.

Bosch picked up the document he had seen many times and slipped it into his case. He locked the safe and external door and went swiftly to the nearest fire escape. The room he had just left was on the third floor and he increased his pace down the iron stairs until he reached ground level. There was one man on duty and he nodded briefly as Bosch went to the door that led to the car park. Once in his car he sped up the exit ramp out of the garage and accelerated in the direction of the Fontein public house where he was to meet John Kallis.

Chapter 49

Near Pretoria

John Kallis had spent the day in his flat, having decided he deserved a day off and not wanting to see Bosch in the office. He felt hugely satisfied knowing that very soon the black file would be in his hands. The way matters had fortuitously converged, for him to be presented the file on a plate, was to him nothing short of a miracle. What he wanted now was the white file and the conversation between Bosch and Nofomela could well guide him in the right direction. With both original files in his possession, he believed he had extensive leverage and choice in who he contacted about them. By far the most important thing to him was the sum of money that interested parties would pay him for getting sole ownership of the files. At this stage he had the time at his disposal to plan his next moves and keep his job in the group without being under any suspicion of taking the files. The group would now beg him to retrieve what he already had.

When Kallis pulled into the car park at the rear of the Fontein bar, he saw that Bosch was already there sitting in his Mercedes. He parked a few cars away and, leaving his door open, approached him. He didn't expect the delivery to take long.

As Kallis neared the car, Bosch rolled down the window. 'Here's the file. I want to get out of this place.' He held up a nondescript package and poked it through the window.

Kallis took the package and opened the envelope. He slid out a bulky black folder and read the inscription on the front. It said State Security 1960 to Present, File B. He turned from Bosch and partly peeled away the synthetic sheet attached to the back cover. The seal was there and that was enough for him. He closed the envelope and fastened it with the metal catch. He was confident Bosch knew what he would get if he betrayed him. He looked at him and grinned. 'I'm sure you are packed. I don't want to see you again.'

Bosch said nothing and ignited the engine. With tyres screeching he drove to the exit and turned right, in the opposite direction of Pretoria. Kallis watched him go and then headed for Pretoria. He could not wait to read what lay so innocently on the seat next to him.

Chapter 50

Pretoria

At nine the next morning, a man in the group offices went to the safe where the black file was kept. He needed to pick up some important documents connected to the work in which he was involved As soon as he stepped into the safe he was amazed to see the black file was missing. He knew full well that even though others like him had access to the safe, nothing was to be removed from the room without authorization. He immediately phoned his boss, Johan Teichmann, and told him.

Teichmann was unnerved that, after the theft of the white file, the black file had now also gone missing. He replaced the receiver and after coming to grips with what he had heard, put on his jacket and left for John Kallis's office, two flights of stairs below. He felt Kallis was the only one he could trust in such matters, and he needed a man with determination and ability; it was the only chance of averting imminent disaster. The group leaders would be inconsolable when they heard the black file had gone missing.

John Kallis was on the phone when Teichmann entered his office and he instantly replaced the receiver. After sinking his corpulent frame into the spare chair, Teichmann said: 'I urgently need your help. The black file has disappeared.'

Kallis appeared to be stunned at the news. 'When was it taken?' he asked.

'It must have been last night,' said Teichmann. 'No one would have risked it this morning with people coming to work.' He breathed unevenly and went on. 'I want you to drop everything and give this your undivided attention. The only exemption is the work you are doing in tracing

172

the white file and that now has to run alongside this. I suggest you start by interviewing all those who have access to the safe, particularly the ones who were working on the files. They would all have known that the black file was complete and if they wanted to lift it now was the time to do it. And, importantly, see if any of these people has not turned up for work today.'

'I'll get onto this straight away,' said Kallis, his face suitably expressionless. 'While you are here may I ask if you have anything I don't know concerning the other file?'

'No,' said Teichmann. 'I will contact Jan Krige and tell him about the missing black file. He doesn't work for us but with his contacts he might hear something. You must meet Krige one day. He is a very capable man and an asset to any operation. Sadly, I heard this morning that his wife, Kirsty, has left him and is staying at the Plaza Hotel on the outskirts of Pretoria.'

Teichmann lifted himself out of the chair. 'My hopes are resting on you,' he said. He raised his hand slightly and walked from the office, leaving Kallis in thought.

Chapter 51

Pretoria

After he had given the file to Kallis, Rupert Bosch drove for nearly ten kilometres along the road away from Pretoria until he came to a small private hotel where he had previously booked a room for the night. He signed the register and when he reached his room he sat on his bed and reflected on the events of the past twenty-four hours.

The one thing that had occupied his mind was now becoming clear. He had no intention of walking away from what he had done, as Kallis had insisted. If Kallis was really doing his job, he would have gone straight to Teichmann, given him the tape and revealed what he knew. Kallis had absolutely no reason to get him to remove the black file and tell him to disappear. The more he thought about it, the more he became convinced that Kallis wanted the file for personal gain and had used him for that purpose.

Bosch pursued the line of thinking that was beginning to coalesce in his mind. He was coming to recognize that he was spending unnecessary time dwelling on what had occurred and not thinking about his future options. He knew that after a preliminary investigation, the group would quickly conclude that he was the perpetrator of the act. But they did not know where he was and if he was clever they never would. Kallis had unintentionally done him a big favour.

He started to work things out logically. It was to his advantage that he was the only one who knew that Kallis had File B. The last thing Kallis would expect was that he would appear out of nowhere and force him to give it to him. That might mean killing Kallis, but, if that was the only way of keeping the man quiet, he had to do it. With the black file in his possession, his next step would be to find and retrieve File A, and that meant going after Jan Krige. If Krige did not have it, he would have to look elsewhere, as others in the group had been doing. With both files in his hands, he was in a position of considerable power and he guessed that Kallis would now want the white file for that reason. He was annoyed with himself for not stealing the black file for himself in the first place.

While he was lying on the bed, Bosch's thoughts went to the two guerillas, Nofomela and Ngwenya. He certainly was not going to tell them that Kallis had forced him to remove the black file from the group safe and give it to him. They would then go after Kallis. They, too, would by now be aware of the power the files held if both were possessed by one person. He decided to contact the guerrillas and touch base with them. He phoned the number Nofomela had given him. Ngwenya answered.

'How are you?' said Bosch. 'I've been thinking of you guys, wondering if you have made any progress.'

'Not yet,' said Ngwenya, 'but we're ready to go after Krige. We wanted to rent a flat first so we have our own base but now we've decided to do that when we return. Is there anything you know that we don't?'

'No,' said Bosch, hesitating slightly. 'I'll phone you if there is. I'm meeting someone so I must go.'

'We'll contact you because we might not return here after visiting Krige,' said Ngwenya.

'Good luck,' said Bosch. He terminated the call.

When he heard the phone go dead, Ngwenya turned to Nofomela.

'I'm sure you know who that was.' said Ngwenya. 'It was Rupert Bosch.'

'Did he say anything interesting?' asked Nofomela.

'Nothing we haven't heard before from him,' said Ngwenya. He looked quizzically at Nofomela. 'I got the impression that he was keeping something to himself and that his mind was elsewhere. For example, he made

175

absolutely no comment when I said we are ready to go for Krige.'

Nofomela thought for a moment and then said: 'We'll phone him tomorrow at work and ask him to confirm Krige's address.'

Chapter 52

Pretoria

Late the following morning after Ngwenya had spoken on the phone to Rupert Bosch, John Nofomela stretched and shook Ngwenya to wake him up. The two men had gone to a pub after speaking to Bosch and had drunk beer and whisky chasers, a volatile mix. They needed something to relieve the boredom they were beginning to feel and knew they had to get after Krige. Life in Pretoria was a far cry from the life they had led in KwaZulu-Natal, where danger was a continual presence. Their delay in going after Krige was that they wanted their own accommodation and they had been hoping for more from Bosch. But now the waiting was over.

Nofomela picked up the phone and rang Rupert Bosch at work. The call was answered by a man whose voice was laced with authority.

'Can I help you?' the man asked. 'This is Rupert Bosch's number.'

'I would like to speak to him if I may,' said Nofomela.

'Who is speaking?'

'A close personal friend,' said Nofomela. 'I said I would phone him this morning.'

'My name is Jacob Marais. I'm head of office security and I am afraid Bosch has not come to work. We have tried his home telephone number repeatedly but there is no reply.'

'I am surprised,' said Nofomela, saying what he felt. 'We spoke to him last night and he sounded fine.'

'We would like to contact him urgently,' said Marais. 'An extremely important and valuable file was taken from a safe last night and we hope Bosch can shed some light on this. He is the only person we still have to contact who had unrestricted access to the safe. If you manage to find out where he is please let me know.'

'I will,' said Nofomela. 'Thank you for your time.' He replaced the receiver in its cradle and looked at Ngwenya.

'Something very strange is going on,' said Nofomela. 'I think you might have been right in the comments you made about Bosch last night. I just spoke to the head of office security for the group and he said Bosch has not turned up for work. He also said they have tried repeatedly to get him at home, to no avail.' Nofomela moved away from the phone and sat down. 'The most interesting thing he said was that an extremely important and valuable file was removed from its safe last night and that Bosch is the only person they have not yet contacted who had access. To me this is too much of a coincidence.'

'What do think is going on?' said Ngwenya. 'It looks as if Bosch is involved in the disappearance of the file. I wish he had elaborated and I can understand why. I suspect it was the black file.'

'I agree,' said Nofomela, unhesitatingly. 'But we cannot contact him and for the moment we have to forget about it and get this business over with Krige.'

'If Bosch took the file and did not tell us, he is definitely up to something,' said Ngwenya.

Nofomela stood up and put on his jacket. He picked up a small canvass bag that contained chocolate bars and drinks, and took a Ruger P85 semi-automatic pistol, chambered for a 9mmx19 Luger/Parabellum cartridge, from the top draw of the dresser. He inserted a 15-shot magazine into the butt and slipped the weapon into a cut-away holster concealed beneath his coat. Ngwenya did the same and together they left the room. They had hired a 3.5 litre BMW which they parked in the basement of the building. When they were in the car, Nofomela extracted an area road map from his pocket and rested it on his lap. He started the engine, drove out of the garage and picked

178

up the road that led to White River and the Kruger
Reserve.

Chapter 53

Plaza Hotel, Pretoria

After she walked out on her husband, Kirsty Krige drove fast along the dirt track to the main gate and then joined the main road to Pretoria. She reached the city in one hour and then skirted the centre to the far side. She had known after talking to her friend what she was going to do when she returned to the farm and she had booked a room for the night in a small, stylish city hotel, the Plaza.

As Kirsty had told her husband, she was far from sure whether or not they would come together again and that she needed time to think and be alone. She was an alluring woman, thirty-three, sexually appealing and with dark brown hair, usually pulled back revealing faintly pale skin and captivating beauty. She was very intelligent and had completed her formal education studying pure and applied mathematics at Natal University in Durban. After getting a first in her degree she stayed on in Durban for five years working for a firm of actuaries. She then returned to Pretoria where she had been brought up, met and married Jan Krige. He was already running the farm, left to him by his father, and she learned to love the way of life, keeping to herself fond memories of the rich social life she had enjoyed to the full in Durban.

On the second evening of he stay in the hotel, she received a phone call from a man who introduced himself as John Kallis. She was surprised because only two or three people knew she was there.

'Do I know you?' she asked, knowing she didn't.

'You don't,' said Kallis, smoothly. 'But I have heard of you and someone said you had left the farm and were staying at the Plaza Hotel.'

'I certainly didn't know my whereabouts were public knowledge,' she said, indignantly. 'What do you want?'

'I am sure your whereabouts are not public knowledge,' said Kallis, reassuringly. 'But I have heard of you, all complimentary I assure you. I would like to meet you somewhere in private. I think you will find what I have to say very interesting.'

'Can't you tell me over the phone?' she asked.

'A direct meeting would be preferable,' said Kallis, mysteriously. 'I could come round to the hotel.'

Kirsty was curious and knew she could only be satisfied by meeting Kallis She thought for a moment and then said: 'Come to the hotel lobby at ten tomorrow morning. I have dark hair and will be wearing dark blue denims and a white shirt.'

'Great,' said Kallis. 'I will be there.' His voice was without emotion and he replaced the phone. He was pleased. He was entering the second stage of his plan that he believed would satisfy his desire to possess the white file.

Chapter 54

Plaza Hotel, Pretoria

The next morning, Kirsty Krige caught the hotel lift to the ground floor and sat down in the lobby. At ten precisely she saw a tall man enter the hotel and, after a quick glance around, walked over to her.

'Mrs Krige?' he said suavely. 'John Kallis.'

'Yes, I'm Kirsty Krige,' she said. 'Shall we sit down?' They shook hands briefly.

'There is a place over there,' said Kallis. 'He indicated the extensive lounge that came up to the lobby and led the way to a small table and two chairs over on the side.

When they were seated he looked at her. 'I can imagine that you want to know why I contacted you. He shifted the position of his chair slightly and, before she could say anything, continued. 'I said I know a few things that will be of interest to you. They primarily concern your husband.'

She had guessed that was coming. She remained silent and listened.

'Some of this you probably know,' said Kallis, 'but there are parts in this drawn out saga that you do not. Three to four weeks ago your husband was asked by a political organization called the group of no name or group, to retrieve a file that had been stolen from their offices. The man who stole the file sent it to a leading trial lawyer in Durban, Andrew Cartwright. Your husband accepted the job and he was told he would be accompanied by two other men.' Kallis stopped and looked round the room.

Before he could continue, Kirsty Krige spoke. 'Who do you work for? Where did you get this information?'

'I don't mind telling you,' said Kallis. 'I used to work for the Directorate: Special Operations, the Scorpions, in Durban. I recently left them and now I work for the group on special assignments. Not everyone likes them, I know. My boss, the man who directs group operations, is Johan Teichmann.'

Her face was impassive when she said: 'You are right. Many people do not like them. They are racists, the type this country can do without.'

'I admit there are some racists in their ranks but the leadership or core of the group is made up of some very intelligent men who have the highest sense of honour,' said Kallis. 'They are certainly not racist. They only want to protect their own people.'

'Go on,' she said.

'Your husband duly went to Durban with the other two,' said Kallis. 'He could not stand them and the animosity was mutual. The two men bottled out after one attempt to get the file failed and your husband decided to go it alone. Cartwright was unfortunately killed and it appears your husband couldn't find the file. He left empty handed and went back to Pretoria.' Kallis leant forward in his seat and stared intently at Kirsty. 'I believe you have heard this before. Am I right?'

'I have heard it before,' said Kirsty. 'I suspected my husband killed Andrew Cartwright. Do you know he did?'

'He told the men in the group who organized the operation that he had killed Cartwright,' said Kallis. 'To the group the death of Cartwright was not important. It simply happened.'

'That is what I meant earlier,' said Kirsty. 'Death to them is of no consequence as long it achieves a specific goal and their own people are not killed.'

Kallis was quiet. He knew she was right. He broke his silence and said: 'The operation in Durban was a complete failure because the file was not retrieved. I will ask you a question, which I want you to answer. Did your husband retrieve the file? When Gerrit Viljoen of the group arrived at your farm after your husband had been shot there was a stranger present. He had spared your husband's life and escaped after being shot by one of Viljoen's men. I believe this man was working for the Scorpions. I also think your husband gave him his assurance that he had the file and would hand it over to the Scorpions. If what I've just told you is true, your husband knew where the file was and did not say. If the file was not on the farm it was with someone your husband could trust, like his lawyer David Staples.' Kallis changed position in his seat. 'A copy of the file was sent to the DSO. I came across it by chance and sent it to the group. I was found out and that is why I'm now in Pretoria.'

'I knew my husband had gone to Durban to retrieve this missing file but, like the group leaders behind the operation, I don't believe he ever found it,' said Kirsty. 'He would have told me if he had found it and been able to retrieve it. You are guessing and have no evidence.' She did not waver as she lied.

'Tell me something,' said Kallis. 'Do you trust your husband?'

She paled. 'Yes, I do trust him. Why do you ask?'

'Did your husband go away recently for a few days?' asked Kallis.

'Yes, he was away,' she said, knowing there was no point in lying.

'Do you know where he went?' said Kallis, persisting.

'He told me he was going to Pretoria to discuss a business deal,' she said.

'That quite frankly was a blatant lie,' said Kallis. 'Your husband and another man, John Dalton, were asked to go to KwaZulu-Natal to get rid of four blacks who were hated by the group leadership. Your husband complied and went after the blacks. One was a Zulu and a member of the provincial parliament, Moses Shozi, and the others were ex-guerillas. The Zulu and one of the guerillas were killed

184

and the other two escaped. They are now in Pretoria. I saw them the other night talking to a man, Rupert Bosch, from the group. I had his line tapped and heard him speaking to them about what I have told you. He was definitely an informer and I suspect he was working for a section in the African Nationalist Congress.'

'How do you know all this?' said Kirsty, visibly shocked.

'It's my job,' said Kallis.

'I am sure a man in your position has other things to tell me,' said Kirsty, mockingly, now determined to get everything she could out of Kallis.

'I will tell you something that might be related to all this,' said Kallis. 'The group has another file that is identical to the one that went missing. This other file, File B, refers to blacks. The first file, File A, refers to whites and was explicitly designed for their protection. I do not need to tell you what the other file is for.' Kallis grinned, beginning to enjoy himself. 'The black file was stolen two days ago from the group offices and they don't have any idea who took it and where it is now. Interestingly enough, the man, Rupert Bosch, who I saw talking to the two guerrillas, disappeared the day after the file was taken.' Kallis looked at his watch. He then told her how the original of each file could be ascertained.

When he had finished he said: 'I do not believe you know where the white file is held. If your husband can lie so brazenly to you and conceal his actions, I'm not surprised he didn't tell you if he had managed to get it. I was hoping you knew something and could have been of assistance to me in finding a document that rightfully belongs to the group. Now I must leave you. It has been a pleasure talking to you.'

Kallis rose from his seat and walked towards the doors. He was soon gone.

For a while Kirsty sat at the table, her head held in her hands. She knew a copy of the file was in the safe on the

185

farm and that her husband's lawyer had the original. To her this whole business was complex and, even though she felt she should become involved, she did not know how. She was certainly not going to contact her husband.

Chapter 55

Jan Krige's farm

The two guerrillas Nofomela and Ngwenya made easy work of their drive north towards Jan Krige's farm. If they saw more than two cars at the same time it was a lot. In forty-five minutes they reached White River and Nofomela pulled the car over and parked in the town centre.

'Let's stretch our legs,' he said.

Ngenya hauled himself out of the vehicle. 'That looks like a café over there. We can go there for something to revitalize us.'

They seated themselves in the near-empty café and gave their orders to the waiter.

'I take it we will stick to what we discussed when we meet Krige,' said Ngwenya. 'We don't want him to see us come in. Surprise is everything.'

'Agreed,' said Nofomela. 'According to Bosch, we should see the turnoff to the farm from this road. After parking some distance away, we will have to walk to get to the house. I'm sure we will find adequate cover for our approach.'

'It's hard to believe that here we are, five hundred miles from KwaZulu and about to confront the bastard who tried to kill us three days ago,' said Ngwenya.

'Don't be too hasty to put an end to him,' said Nofomela sagely. 'The aim of this exercise is not to kill Krige, but to get the file.' He smiled ruthlessly. 'If Krige gets in the way, it will be his fault if he falls foul of us and gets killed.'

After they had consumed what had been placed in front of them, the two men left the café for the car. Nofomela gunned the engine and they drove off. Twenty minutes later, he saw the sign they wanted. It said Krige.

Nofomela laughed. 'Our guy certainly gets full marks for imagination.'

'Something has just come to me,' said Ngwenya, stopping the car, engine running, at the side of the road. 'Bosch said Krige has a wife. What do we do about her? We can't kill a woman.'

'That should not be a problem,' said Nofomela confidently. 'We will just have to play our cards as they come, whoever we get to first. Krige wouldn't do anything that endangers his wife and the same applies to her.'

Nofomela swung the car into the road, expelling a cloud of dust as they sped off down the dirt track to the main gate of the farm. When they saw it, Nofomela stopped and reversed off the track into some undergrowth.

'The less conspicuous we are the better,' he said, cutting the engine. 'Let's move before it gets dark.'

The two men half-ran towards the gate and, when they were near it, climbed through a barbed wire fence onto Krige's land. What they saw in front of them resembled a small valley. They could see part of the house poking out from behind a rocky outcrop that loomed before it. Farm buildings reared up next to the house and acres of prime tobacco extended from the little oasis before disappearing beyond carefully planned fire breaks.

After they had surveyed the scene, Nofomela said: 'I think we should follow that ridge. It goes beyond the house and the dense vegetation should provide excellent cover all the way there.'

Together they made for the ridge, climbed halfway up and moved in single file towards the house. As they neared their goal, they heard the engine of a vehicle disturb the tranquillity of the valley and they dropped to the ground. A Land Rover soon appeared, the noise from the engine a high-pitched scream, and they watched as the driver, hanging over the wheel, drove along the single stretch of track to the house.

'That guy's in a hurry,' said Nofomela, getting to his feet and brushing off flecks of earth and dead leaves. 'It must be Krige. You don't drive on just anyone's land like a madman. Give him a minute to get out of the Land Rover and then we'll go in.'

After a short wait, the guerillas left the ridge and, using the *kopje* as a screen, approached the house. When they reached the mound of rock, they at last had a full view of the house. To them it was an attractive building and they were quiet as they absorbed its solitude. There was no one in sight.

'Be patient,' said Nofomela, knowing what his friend was thinking. 'Unless he's gone off for a nap he will soon appear, either on the verandah or in that room adjacent to it.'

They sat still for what seemed an age, only their heads showing, and then their patience was rewarded. A tall man came on to the verandah, a glass of whisky in his hand, and sat down in a rocking chair that could easily have coped with someone twice his size. From the brief view of the man's face and the way he walked, Nofomela instantly recognized Jan Krige.

'Now's the opportunity we wanted,' said Nofomela. He went from the *kopje*, Ngwenya behind him and walked casually up to the verandah steps. Krige was reading from a magazine when Nofomela stepped onto the polished stone. He quickly turned and rose to his feet, slowly placing the magazine and unfinished whisky on a side table.

'Who the hell are you?' said Krige. 'Don't you know this is private property?'

'Surely you recognize us,' said Nofomela softly.

'Why should I recognize you?' said Krige. 'Are you saying we have met before?'

'A week ago you tried to kill us in Malakazi township, KwaZulu-Natal,' said Nofomela, bluntly. 'You put a bullet into our sick friend, Ngubane, and then tried to do the same to us. You and your friend failed and we escaped into the night. Do you think that is an accurate description of your antics Major Krige?'

'You are mistaken,' said Krige, calmly. 'I've never been near this place you call Malakazi.'

Nofomela went on. 'After we had escaped I remembered seeing you previously. You've had your photograph in the press and, when you were head of the Johannesburg murder and robbery squad, you once came so close to me in the cells of Pretoria central prison I could smell you.'

Krige knew there was now no point denying what the black had said and he knew he had to remain calm until he could either overpower them or escape. He noticed their guns were still in their holsters and he was aware that he had to act before they could bring them into play. He had to keep them talking.

'What do want?' said Krige, asking the obvious question. 'Spit it out.'

Nofomela indicated to Ngwenya to take over and the man moved forward.

'Before you went on this mission to kill us and Moses Shozi, at the behest of the group command, you did another job for them in Durban. You were sent with two other thugs of the group to retrieve from Andrew Cartwright, a distinguished lawyer, what is known as File A. During the operation the men with you fled and you went in alone. Cartwright was killed by you but you returned to Pretoria without the file. You told your group masters that you had been unable to find it and they believed you. But if you didn't get the file, someone else did and shortly after the operation a copy of the file, that was meant for the DSO in Durban, was intercepted and sent to the group. The word copy means just that and the all-important original is still missing.'

Ngwenya stood still, his eyes never leaving Krige. 'Now, I will get to the guts of why we are here. We do not believe anyone else took that file from Cartwright's house. First, if they had broken in and taken it before you got there, Cartwright would have had the police at the place. Second, you, with your experience, would not have killed Cartwright before getting him to reveal where the file was, and he certainly would have given you what you wanted rather than die.' Ngwenya smoothly put his hands in his pockets. 'We conclude, Major, that you did receive the file that night and managed to evade any possible pursuit. To us that means the file is either on this farm or with someone you trust implicitly, like your lawyer. You also decided not to return the file to the group and to send a copy instead to the Scorpions. We want that file Major. You can either give it to us freely or tell us where we can get it. If you don't cooperate we'll relieve you of it by force, something you won't like.'

Krige knew he could not hold them off by denying what they said was true and his only options were to fight his way out or reveal that David Staples had it. The two men were armed, tall and powerful and his chance of overcoming them was not good. He had to play along until the right opportunity arose.

'I do not have the file here on the farm,' said Krige. 'There was only one copy made and that was sent to the DSO. The original is in the hands of my lawyer.'

'What are his name and contact details?' said Nofomela.

'His name is David Staples. He works in the centre of Pretoria and has a house on the outskirts. I can get that information for you.' He pivoted slightly to go through the doors into the lounge but before he could take a step, Nofomela rapidly moved towards him.

'We'll come with you Major,' said Nofomela, lifting his hand to grab Krige by the arm. But before he could take hold, Krige back-peddled and spun into the lounge with the agility of a ballet dancer. He adroitly corrected his balance and, like an antelope ahead of the lion, skipped

191

and ran down the passage to the doors in the kitchen that led to the back yard and the open veld beyond.

'I'll follow him,' shouted Nofomela to Ngwenya who was already moving. 'Get round to the back.'

Ngwenya vaulted down the verandah steps and sprinted to the rear of the house. Nofomela, running as if his life was at stake, quickly reached the kitchen. He saw Krige through the wire screens. He was nearly across the yard and heading for the nearest line of trees and scrub. Nofomela bolted through the back door and gave chase, beginning to enjoy what to him had become an exciting game. Before he reached the trees, he slowed for Ngwenya, who had just appeared at the corner of the house, to catch up with him.

Together, the two guerrillas continued their pursuit. At first Krige appeared to have vanished and then he re-appeared, altering his direction and driving towards the north-western section of the farm. The vegetation and trees were becoming more congested and progress for Nofomela and Ngwenya was not as good as it had been earlier. At times they had to slow down to a walk, as they brushed aside the foliage in their path.

When the guerrillas had gone 500 metres, the bush became so dense they had to stop. They had lost sight of Krige and as far as they knew he could well have changed direction again.

'What should we do?' asked Ngwenya, bending over and resting his hands on his knees. 'He must know this land like the back of his hand. To lose sight of him in this thick bush means we can kiss him goodbye. We'll never find him now.'

Nofomela leant against a tree, his arms folded in front of him. 'We shouldn't have lost sight of him. But that's history and to nail him now will require use of our brains. I think we can only achieve our objective by drawing him into a trap.'

'What do you suggest?' said Ngwenya, sometimes slow to think, preferring to leave it to Nofomela.

'The way I see it is this,' said Nofomela. 'Krige will soon realize that we are not on his trail anymore and that we have lost him. After a while, he will think we have given up and got out of here. He won't want to sit it out here in the bush doing nothing. Impatience will set in and drive him crazy.'

Nofomela scratched the incipient growth of stubble on his face. 'My bet is that he will plan on getting out as quickly as possible and that means reaching his Land Rover. He will know that our vehicle is not on his land and that we will have to walk some distance to get to it. That will give him an advantage if he can make it to his Land Rover without us seeing him.'

'Why don't we just leave?' asked Ngwenya. 'We only have to go to his lawyer and the file is ours.'

Nofomela shook his head. 'By the time we get to the lawyer, Krige will have told him we are coming. If that happens we will never find the man. The only way of knowing he is telling the truth is to threaten him with his life. Even then we will not be sure, but it is our only chance. Besides, we must not lose sight of the fact that we still want to kill him. The only way we will be satisfied is to get hold of him.'

'Where do we go now?' said Ngwenya, beginning to see the logic in what Nofomela was saying.

'We head for the house. The Land Rover is parked in front of the verandah. I am certain Krige's wife is not on the farm otherwise we would have seen her earlier. When we're at the house, we go inside and split up. You go to the kitchen, which has a good view of the back and I will take up position in the lounge. From there I will be able to see if he goes in a circle and approaches the house from the other side of the rocks.'

'What about servants?' said Ngwenya.

Nofomela looked at him and said: 'Kill them if they interfere. I don't think any are here. Now let's go.'

The two guerrillas started to back-track in single file, keeping low, and after a while they saw the barns that were adjacent to the house. No one was in sight and they swiftly crossed the yard to the back door. They slipped through and stood quietly in the kitchen, listening for any sound.

'I'll give a faint tap if I spot him,' said Nofomela. 'You do the same. Good luck.' He gave a thumbs-up and disappeared down the passage to the lounge.

Chapter 56

Jan Krige's farm

After constantly checking his trail, Jan Krige became aware that he had lost the guerrillas. There was no sight of them. He watched his trail for a while and then moved off in a steady run at right angles to it. He was alert, physically very fit, his mind on the unexpected confrontation he had experienced with the two guerrillas. He knew he had the advantage of knowing the area very well and he could go where he wanted to undetected. He regretted not having his pistol with him and he thought about how he could get hold of one. He did not relish facing the two men unarmed. He was certain that if the guerrillas still wanted him they would go and watch the house and his Land Rover, if they were still on the farm. If that happened they would block his way out.

As he neared the side of the house and the barns, still concealed by foliage, it came to him that there had always been a snub-nosed .38 Smith and Wesson revolver in a small office, standing alone and hidden from the house by the buildings. It was kept for protection only, but this time, if it was still there, he would use it to kill.

Krige waited in the bush for a while longer and then went quickly to the outbuildings. He was soon at the small office and he slipped inside. He rapidly jerked open the only drawer in the single desk and delved with his hand through an untidy assemblage of notes and receipts. With a feeling of quiet satisfaction his hand found the gun and he extracted it, simultaneously rotating the cylinder to see if it was loaded. It was full and he stuck it behind his belt to keep his hands free. After leaving the office, he went with consummate stealth to an adjacent barn that, through a side window, provided an excellent view of the entire side wall of the house from the kitchen to the verandah.

Krige waited, his eyes probing for the slightest movement, the silence and stillness a void He did not see anyone, but he had no intention of assuming they were not there. He was now certain they weren't still out in the bush looking for him and that they had not left the farm. They could be cleverly concealed in the house and have the patience to wait until he appeared which to them would be a foregone conclusion.

Krige gave it ten minutes and decided to take his chance and go for the rear door leading into the kitchen. He left the barn through the single set of doors, hidden from the house, and moved round to the corner. After a final look at what lay ahead, he ran across the yard towards the kitchen. When he reached it, he grabbed the handle and flung the door open, sweeping into the kitchen. There, rising like a ghost, was Ngwenya, the pistol pointed at his heart, a supercilious grin on his traditionally scarred face.

'You are too impatient,' said the black, sardonically. 'We knew you would come.'

As Ngwenya drew breath, Krige glanced past him, diverting his attention, the oldest evasive technique in the book. Ngwenya, thinking Krige had seen Nofomela, turned, saw only the vacant passage and made to swing his gun back onto Krige. But he was too late and, leaping forward, Krige hit him with brute force in the stomach, his fist sinking into the unused muscle. The guerilla tried to regain his footing, the gun partly hanging, and Krige came in again, beating him viciously to the floor. He pulled his gun from his waist and callously fired two rapid shots into the black's head, killing him instantly.

'You haven't lost your touch Major. Drop the gun.'

Krige stepped from Ngwenya, his back to the voice, knowing immediately who had spoken, hoping he had not been outplayed. He released the gun, turned, and standing in the doorway leading to the passage, pointing a pistol at his heart, was the tall, proud figure of Nofomela.

Nofomela took a couple of steps into the room. 'You took your time coming here,' he said. 'For a moment we thought we had lost you and would never see you again. That would have been most disappointing.' He was deathly calm, grinning fleetingly, his face alight with satisfaction. 'We have unfinished business.'

'What do you want?' said Krige. 'I told you my lawyer has the original and I gave you his name. Surely a man of your education can use a phone book.'

'Tell me where I can contact him,' snapped Nofomela. 'I want to get out of this place. You go first.' He waved the barrel of his pistol towards the passage.

As Nofomela swung the weapon back into play Krige moved rapidly taking two measured steps and driving his knee into the guerrilla's groin. Cradling the body as it fell forward, he swept Nofomela's feet from under him, sending him crashing to the floor, an unwanted mass of flesh and bone. Wrenching the pistol from the guerilla's hand, he fired two shots into the man's chest, killing him where he lay in a grotesque heap.

Krige stared for a moment at the dead bodies, finding it ironic that here on his own farm he had finally killed the two men who had escaped him in KwaZulu-Natal, 800 kilometres away. He collected the guerillas' pistols, placed them on the table and dragged the bodies in turn out into the yard, where he placed them against the rear wall of the house.

He went inside, poured a Scotch and walked out onto the verandah. Everything was peaceful, in stark contrast to the violence that had just occurred. He was drained, mentally and physically, and craved sleep, but that had to wait while he selfishly savoured the prowess he had so adeptly exhibited in slaughtering two men he had come to hate. It was now clear why the group wanted them dead and all the other murderers who were in the black file he

197

had been told existed. He had little remorse. He had become a ruthless killer, ready to destroy life without compunction and devour the satisfaction that came with the work. Kirsty was a forgotten part of his life and had served his desire for sexual gratification. He had discovered his alter ego and it suited him.

Krige slept for an hour after killing the blacks, enough to replenish his depleted mental and physical strength. He had a bath, changed his clothes and went to the phone in the lounge. He dialled Johan Teichmann's number.

'Teichmann,' said the group leader.

'It's Jan Krige. I would like to see you on the farm. You will find what I've got to tell you very satisfying.'

'Can't you tell me over the phone?' said Teichmann, a little curious. Krige had never phoned him unless it concerned business.

'I'd rather not,' said Krige. 'I'd like to move quickly.'

'I'll be there in an hour,' said Teichmann and replaced the receiver.

Krige sat down in his rocking chair. He was proud of himself for completing the job in KwaZulu-Natal, even though the two men in the yard had willingly and incongruously come to him, the killer. He never imagined in his most bizarre dreams that he would indulge in the satisfaction that now coursed his body, a potent drug. He did not regret now his lies and acts of duplicity. They had been necessary to find his hidden self, a part of him he never knew existed.

In a little over one hour after his phone call to Teichmann, the man arrived and drove his car up to the house. He hauled himself out of the vehicle and came round to the verandah steps where Krige stood, arms folded.

'I'm glad you could make it,' said Krige, guiding Teichmann onto the verandah and indicating one of several seats.

'It sounded urgent,' said Teichmann, releasing his bulk onto soft cushions. 'I came straight away.'

'You are aware that two of the guerrillas we went to kill in KwaZulu-Natal escaped, when Dalton and I thought we had them,' said Krige. 'Unknown to me they fled Malakazi township and came to Pretoria. Two hours ago they turned up here on the farm.' Krige clasped his hands behind his neck and leant back in his chair, as relaxed as a cat after devouring a nocturnal meal.

Teichmann sat upright, staring at Krige. 'Where are they now?' he asked, half-expecting the men to appear.

'They're dead,' said Krige. 'I put them in the back yard for a couple of your men to come and remove. I would like them to do it today and I suggest you make the calls now. My phone's through there in the other room. This will look good in the press and when you say it was self-defence, you won't be lying.'

Teichmann got up and went to phone in the lounge. In five minutes he finished the call and returned to the verandah. 'They'll soon be here,' he said. 'Now tell me the story.'

'I was sitting out here when they appeared,' said Krige. 'I recognized them immediately but did not admit it. That did not help me because they recognized me and knew I was one of the whites who tried to kill them in Malakazi township. They knew I had killed their friend Elijah Ngubane and had been rightly told I had got rid of Moses Shozi, not one of their bosom pals. They proceeded to tell me about my past deeds, almost as much as I know myself. They knew I had killed Cartwright and that I had gone to Durban to retrieve the white file.' He wrapped his hands around his belt. 'I told them I had not been able to find it and that I had come back to Pretoria empty handed. They did not believe me and said they would force me to tell them the truth and reveal where I was keeping the file. I played for time and said my lawyer David Staples had the original. They asked for his contact details and that was

199

when I got away from them. When I returned to the house they were lying in wait. We fought and I killed them. It's as simple as that.'

Teichmann looked at Krige in admiration. 'I always knew you were one of the best operatives I have known. It must come from your training in the police and your ingrained ability. So the job is now complete.' He rubbed his hand over his prodigious stomach. 'You probably don't know that a copy of the file was sent to the DSO. It was intercepted by one of our plants, John Kallis, and sent to me. Kallis was found out and fired. He has excellent credentials and is very street wise. I took him on as a special operative reporting only to me.' He leaned forward. 'I am glad you called because something very embarrassing has occurred. The black file, File B, that you know exists and which is identical to the white file, File A, in concept was removed from its safe. It has not been found.'

Krige suspected what was coming but this time had no fear of being asked by Teichmann to get involved.

'I once said I would not ask you again to do anything for me,' said Teichmann. 'I also said that I don't always have control of some of the leaders in the group. There are things that are extremely important which they leave me to solve, and I keep them informed when I think it appropriate.' Teichmann scratched his cheek. 'They do know the white file went missing and has not yet been found. I assured them I have the best man on the case. They also know the black file is missing. The fact that two documents of vital importance have been stolen concerned them a lot more than if it had only been the one. It makes them very uneasy.' Teichmann came out of his chair and took a step towards Krige, his hands in his pockets. 'I again assured them that both files would be retrieved. I do not want to disappoint them and neither do I want to disappoint myself. But I have one problem that I believe could be seriously detrimental to success. I don't know if I

200

can trust the man to whom I have now given the sole responsibility of finding File B as well as File A.'

'Who is he?' asked Krige.

'His name is John Kallis, the ex-DSO man I mentioned earlier.'

'I don't know him,' said Krige. He brushed a tiny leaf from his shirt. 'Let me understand this. You have given the job of solving these two cases to one man who you now feel you can't trust. When did you decide you couldn't trust him?'

'Shortly after I had assigned him the job of also locating the black file and dealing with the guilty parties,' said Teichmann, embarrassed.

'Has anything occurred to substantiate this belief?' asked Krige. He laughed ruthlessly. 'I would never have given another job of such importance to one man.'

Teichmann tacitly accepted the criticism. 'You have worked with people and sensed that something is not right. I started to feel that about Kallis. For a while I didn't think any more of it until the second file was stolen. I remember telling Kallis to start the interrogation process of all those who had been working on the file and who had access to the safe. There was no reason for him to have access but he had the list of all those who did. Since then he has never spoken to me about our inability to find one man, Rupert Bosch. To me Bosch has to be the prime suspect and yet it is strange that Kallis has not once made reference about him to me. It is as if the man never existed.'

'That is strange,' said Krige. 'If I were in Kallis's position, I would certainly keep my boss informed concerning progress in finding the prime suspect. It implies that Kallis found Bosch and got hold of the black file for himself. If that were the case it would have meant nullifying Bosch. I assume everyone else on the list is clean.'

201

'Yes,' said Teichmann. 'I have the greatest confidence in our methods.'

'I bet you do,' said Krige. 'Let me ask you a question. Why are you telling all this to me?'

'I would like you to help me and become directly involved in sorting out this mess,' said Teichmann bluntly.

'I knew that was coming when you first told me the black file had gone missing,' said Krige. 'I take it the job would also entail finding the white file.'

'Yes,' said Teichmann. 'If you accept you will be working alone.'

'What about Kallis?' asked Krige. 'We can't just run around in the dark and pretend the other doesn't exist. That could be dangerous.'

'I think you can handle that quite adequately,' said Teichmann. 'Kallis knows of you but he would never suspect you are involved. I will also keep you informed about anything he uncovers, if of course he tells me.'

'You certainly don't trust him,' said Krige. 'What do you think he will get out of all this by playing a double game?'

'Personal gain,' said Teichmann. 'Many men would sell their mothers for it.'

'Or their wives,' said Krige in a whisper. 'I accept the job. I want to know everything you've got on these cases, including the contact details and profiles of Rupert Bosch and John Kallis. I want 100 000 pounds sterling to be transferred to an account in Switzerland for each of the originals of these files that I retrieve. You don't have to pay me for dealing with the people involved, whether or not I get the files. And, I am not obliged to reveal their identities if I find them.'

'Agreed,' said Teichmann. 'You have my word. You can start when you like.' He got out of the chair and peered down the track that led to the front gate. 'Those guys should be here by now.'

As Teichmann uttered the words they saw lights appear near the gate and a large Ford van was driven at speed up to the house. It stopped in front of the verandah and two men got out. They clearly knew Teichmann and waited for instructions.

'Come with me,' said Krige walking past Teichmann and going down the steps. 'The bodies are round the back.'

In a little over five minutes the two blacks were stretched out in the rear of the vehicle and it left the farm.

'Thank you,' said Teichmann, turning to Krige. 'I will be in contact.'

The group man had soon gone, leaving Krige alone, not sure what he had got himself into. But he was getting used to it and he liked it.

Chapter 57

Pretoria

After meeting John Kallis in the lounge of the Plaza Hotel, Kirsty Krige spent hours going over what he had said. It was clear that Kallis was after both files and that his reason was not to gain favour with his boss and the group. It was to satisfy his vanity and above all acquire personal wealth. She had no doubt that the files were of great value and that they had the power to bring white and black leaders of whatever persuasion to their knees. She kept saying to herself that she had to become involved in the whole sordid business and reveal what she knew to someone of influence. But no one would believe her unless she had the originals of the two files in her possession and she could not in her wildest dreams see how she could get them. She was up against men who lived in the world of darkness, the most dangerous breed of all. Against them she was impotent, even if she knew who they were and how they operated. It still galled her that her husband had been so stupid to stray and do their work. By now he was certainly converted and she had no desire ever to see him again. She was reviled by him and she now wanted a divorce.

On the morning after the two guerrillas, Nofomela and Ngwenya, had gone to Jan Krige's farm, Kirsty went down to breakfast. She was not one to lie in bed after she woke up, a habit she had acquired on the farm, and now having left the place she still liked an early start to think about where she was going in life.

When she reached the lobby and started to walk across to the dining room on the other side of the lounge, she picked up a copy of the newspaper she preferred to the others. Half-way through the lounge she chose to have a

204

cup of coffee before going into breakfast. She seated herself at one of the many empty tables and ordered a pot of coffee from a waiter. She rested the newspaper on her knee and casually started to skim the front page. Near the bottom she saw a headline that made her gasp in disbelief. It said: Guerillas killed on White River farm. When she had recovered she lifted the paper and read the article. She sat with her hand to her mouth as the words told their story. When she had finished she left the table and took the lift up to her room.

In her room, Kirsty sat on the bed and read the newspaper article again. She couldn't believe it and for her it was like reading the script of a surreal play. She felt debilitated and very much alone. The game never stopped, driven by a strange force controlling people like pieces on a board. She let the paper fall onto the floor and sat bent over, elbows on her knees, feeling as if she was going to vomit.

For minutes Kirsty Krige remained in that position, thoughts flying randomly round in her head. But slowly her spirit induced a sense of calm and the determination to pull herself together and think clearly. She started to feel bitterly angry that people like those in the group were set on destroying others rather than working for the common good and prosecuting blacks and whites through the courts when the evidence was there. But they would not use the evidence that had been meticulously compiled by intelligent men. It had only been a game. They preferred exacting their own sense of justice.

As she sat on the bed, her emotions becoming more cohesive, a man appeared in her mind, a man she would never forget. For a moment she was still and then she sprang from the bed and went to the phone. She called directory enquiries and after a short wait she was given the phone number and address of the man in her thoughts. His name was James Steiner.

Chapter 58

Durban

Since returning from Japan, James Steiner got back to his way of life, dedicating himself to his insatiable passion, karate. He trained early in the morning when the city was quiet and still. His movements were simple, fluid and precise and many who had seen him practice knew he had gone beyond technique. For seemingly endless hours he sat in *seiza*, meditating and breathing deeply to calm his mind and strengthen his centre. This was the source of his power and for him pure *zen*.

Steiner met up with Sophie Carswell frequently and they enjoyed dining together, dancing at the city's nightclubs and sometimes at weekends going for walks in the local countryside. She had fallen deeply in love with him and to her he was unlike anyone she had ever met, tall, handsome in a ruthless way, intelligent and with a strong sense of care for others. How he could easily change into someone so dangerous and powerful, as she had witnessed, was a mystery to her but all that interested her was that she loved him. She had come to accept that at times he kept his feelings to himself as if he was part of another world, and that he never told her he loved her. But deep inside she felt he did, and she couldn't help thinking he held back because someone had badly hurt him earlier in his life.

Sophie's parents were now living in England where her father had been born and one day she told Steiner that she was taking time off work and going to visit them for six weeks. He was pleased for her and when she left he told her how much he looked forward to seeing her when she returned and how empty his life would be without her.

After Sophie had gone Steiner spent even longer in the *dojo*, updating student records and giving private classes. One evening at a little after nine he returned to his flat and when he was about to insert the key a woman stepped from the shadows. She was beautiful, wearing a red dress, navy blazer and carrying a small bag.

'James Steiner,' she said softly. 'Do you remember me?' She took a step closer.

'Kirsty Krige,' said Steiner, amazed at seeing her so far from home and standing outside his flat. 'What are you doing here?'

'I need to see you,' she said. 'I believe you are the only person who can help me.'

He opened the door and stood aside for her to pass. 'Please come in. I'm afraid it's a bit untidy.'

'It's great,' she said, as she seated herself. She went silent and looked at him, not knowing exactly where to start and explain her presence.

Steiner had last seen her and her husband on their farm three weeks ago when he had thought the affair concerning the missing file had been resolved. She was the most attractive woman he had ever seen, with dark brown eyes that matched the colour of her silken hair and a figure that would ignite the flame of any man who had the good fortune to meet her. He ignored his feelings. He could never have her. He walked a few steps closer. The expression on her face portrayed a state of abject turmoil.

'You're in trouble,' he said. 'Tell me about it.'

She sat back, still looking at him. 'I am not in trouble but I want the business in which you were involved to end. For whatever reason, it is driving me insane with confusion and anger. I am referring to the work my husband did in Durban for the group and the things that have occurred since.' She paused, drank some water he had placed next to her and then continued. 'You will remember that my husband said he had retrieved the file. He was telling the truth because he showed me a copy of it

207

the next day, a copy that was made by his lawyer, David Staples. You will also recall that he said he would instruct Staples to send a copy to the DSO. I believe a copy was sent but it was intercepted by someone in the DSO and sent to the group. The man you were working for in the DSO, Peter Smith, phoned my husband and told him the copy had not arrived. My husband knew nothing about it and Smith then phoned Staples. He asked for the original and Staples refused. Smith then asked for a copy but Staples told him to find the one that had been sent.'

'I know everything you have just told me,' said Steiner. 'But I am not doing any work for the DSO and as far as I am concerned the matter is closed.' He thought for a moment. 'I admit I am a little curious when you speak of things that have gone on since we last met. What do you mean?'

'Three days ago a man phoned me in the hotel and said he wanted to see me,' she said. 'Like you I was a little curious.' She smiled, contrasting white teeth against red lips. 'I agreed to meet him the next morning in the hotel. When he arrived we sat at one of the tables in the lounge.' She drank some more water and adjusted her dress. 'I will be brief. He related what I have told you and what you already know. He then said he believed my husband had in fact retrieved the file from Cartwright's place and that he was lying when he told the group he hadn't. I of course knew this but when he asked me I denied it. He then said a file called the black file, File B, had been removed from its safe in the group building two days before. He said it was identical in structure to what he termed the white file, File A, except that it was for elimination. I am sure you know what that means. He also told me something I had wondered about when my husband retrieved the white file. He said the original of each file can only be determined by checking to see if there is a small Oriental seal stamped on the back cover between the attached synthetic backing and the cover itself.'

'That is very interesting,' said Steiner. 'Presumably only a few men know that. And, I do know what elimination means.'

'Before I continue, my husband and I are separated and I am suing for divorce. I have already contacted my lawyer.'

'You surprise me,' said Steiner, wondering how that was connected to the meeting in the hotel with the man. He waited for her to go on.

'This man then asked me if I trusted my husband. I said yes when in fact I don't. I wondered what he was getting at. He asked me if my husband had recently spent a few days away from the farm. I said he had gone to Pretoria for three days on business. He then told me what I feared. He said that was a lie and my husband had gone to KwaZulu-Natal with a man, John Dalton, at the behest of the group to eliminate four blacks, a Zulu member of the provincial government and three ANC ex-guerillas. Three of the men were killed and the other two escaped. I was literally torn apart because it reinforced my belief that he was doing another job for the group. Before I was told this I had challenged my husband about his business trip and I accused him of not telling me the truth. I said the group had a hold over him and that I was going to leave him. That was when I went to Pretoria.'

'And now you are going to divorce him,' said Steiner, understanding her sentiments.

'Yes,' she said. 'Even though I had no proof of the operation in KwaZulu-Natal I believed he was involved and that is enough for me. Quite frankly I can't stand the sight of him anymore.'

'Do you believe he has changed irreversibly?' said Steiner.

'Yes,' she said without hesitation. 'When someone continues to commit such a crime and deny it I believe they have found their alter ego and it has taken over. That has happened to my husband.'

'You've certainly put some thought into this,' said Steiner, impressed. 'I have seen this happen before and I believe you. What else did the man say?'

'He said the two guerillas who escaped were in Pretoria and that they were in contact with a man, Rupert Bosch, who works for the group. He also said he had arranged for Bosch's line to be tapped. When he later heard the recording of a conversation between Bosch and the guerrillas he said it was obvious they had already been told that my husband, who the guerillas had recognized in Natal, had done the job for the group. He also said the guerrillas knew about Cartwright and the missing white file, and that my husband had said on his return that he had not been able to find the file. He also believes there is an outsider involved in all this. You know who that is.'

'What comes next?' said Steiner. 'You tell quite a story.'

She continued. 'The guerillas expressed a real interest in getting hold of the white file and they were planning to go to the farm to speak to my husband. It was obvious they also wanted to kill him. The guerrillas are keen to get hold of the black file as well because it lists them and provides the evidence that would convict them.' She smiled, glad she had got all that off her chest. 'That was all the man said. He was clearly only interested in finding the file and when he thought I could not help him he thanked me for my time and left.'

'He obviously worked for the group,' said Steiner. 'He was too well informed not to be. What was his name?'

'He gave it as John Kallis,' she said.

'This really is a small world,' said Steiner, finding it hard to believe what he had just heard.

'Do you know him,' she asked.

'I met him once when he was drunk,' said Steiner. 'That was before he joined the DSO. He was the man who intercepted the copy of the file meant for Peter Smith and sent it to the group.'

210

'It certainly is a small world,' said Kirsty. She smiled, feeling more secure in his presence than she felt with anyone else. Then she said: 'You've got to help me.'

'What else is there?' said Steiner phlegmatically.

'This morning it was reported in the press that two ex-guerillas had been killed by Jan Krige when they attacked him on his farm outside White River. That was when I decided to see you.'

'Why did you want to see me?' said Steiner. 'I told you I don't work for the DSO. I still see Peter Smith now and then but the Cartwright affair was a one-off job for me. I am not used to that kind of work and I don't like it.'

'That means you're not interested in the truth,' she said. 'You're quietly content with your own little life.' She had played her last card and she went silent, staring at him, her lovely eyes distracting.

He looked away. 'How did you get here?'

'I flew down this afternoon,' she said. 'I got your address through directory enquiries.'

'When are you returning?' he asked.

'That sounds as if you don't want to get involved in this business,' she said. 'If that is the case I'll find someone else.'

'I didn't say that,' he said, admiring her determination and spirit. He poured water into her empty glass and stood in front of her, his arms folded across his chest. 'You'll never find anyone else.'

'You're so arrogant,' she said sardonically.

'I'm not,' he said, wondering why he had said that. It was not his style. He turned away. 'I will help you.'

She came off the sofa and went to him. As much as she wanted to put her arms round him she resisted.

'Where are you staying?' he asked.

'I'll find somewhere. That is unless you are willing to let me sleep here.'

He smiled, giving nothing away. 'I see you came prepared,' he said, looking at her bag. 'I suggest you return to Pretoria tomorrow.'

'What about you?' she asked.

'I'll see you up there in two days. There are some things I have to do before I go.'

'Great,' she said, rubbing her hands together. 'Where's my bedroom?'

'You're lucky,' he said. 'I managed to buy a place with two bedrooms. You're in the master suite.'

Kirsty Krige and Steiner were both up early the next morning. After breakfast, she confirmed a reservation on the mid-morning flight to Pretoria. She left the flat at eight-thirty after she and Steiner had arranged to meet at the Plaza Hotel in two days at noon.

When she had gone Steiner contacted two of his senior students and told them he was going away for a short time. When asked, they agreed to take the classes while he was gone. Later in the day he phoned Peter Smith at the DSO.

'I am going away for a few days,' said Steiner without elaborating. 'I thought I would I give you a ring and see if you are having any luck getting the original of the file.'

'No,' said Smith. 'I would give anything to get hold of it but, as I guessed in the beginning, I would never have got the authority I needed to get Staples to release it. I don't even know for sure that he's got it. If he was asked for it by anyone else in authority he would deny ever having seen it and I would have sweet nothing to substantiate my belief. For all I know, Krige could still be sitting on it.'

'It's the type of case people in your position hope never comes their way,' said Steiner. 'Perhaps you should have used a little force.'

'That's too dangerous,' replied Smith. 'I never told anyone about your nocturnal habits in the Cartwright case. You never existed. If we had got the original they would

212

have leapt on it with glee and they would never have bothered to ask where it came from or how I got it. But when I fail and they know about it, everything I have done is turned inside out and I'm hung out to dry.'

'It's an unjust world,' said Steiner. 'But I believe you will get what you so badly want and more.'

Before Smith could say anymore Steiner said goodbye and replaced the receiver.

Late the following afternoon, he packed a small canvas bag with a change of clothing and personal items. He had decided to drive to Pretoria in his recent acquisition, a five-year-old Mercedes Benz, and at seven he was on the main freeway heading inland.

After three hours at the wheel, Steiner stopped at a motel for the night. At nine the next morning he left the motel and reached Pretoria without stopping. He made his way to the Plaza Hotel. It was close to twelve and he went in and asked at the desk for Kirsty Krige. The receptionist buzzed her and in minutes she appeared in the lobby where he was waiting. She was casually dressed in jeans and a black T-shirt.

'It's great to see you,' she said as she walked up to him. 'I'm so glad you came. You're actually on time.'

He liked her mocking sense of humour. 'It's good to see you had a safe return. I got here sooner than I thought.'

'Perhaps that is because you drive too fast,' she said. 'Would you like something to drink in the bar before we have some lunch?'

'Sounds great,' said Steiner.

They seated themselves on stools at the bar that was surprisingly quiet for the time of day, and ordered drinks, a dry martini for her and tap water for him. She took a sip from her drink and looked at him with surprise.

'Don't you drink?' she asked.

'I used to drink,' said Steiner. 'I gave it up when I started to like it too much.'

213

'That's the first time I have heard someone speak with such conviction,' she said. 'I am impressed. I know a lot of woman who would love to hear that from their husbands.' She was quiet for a moment and then changed the subject.

'What have you been thinking about since I last saw you?' she said.

'You mean about this business?' said Steiner.

'You know what I mean,' she said. 'You are too intelligent to come all the way up here and not give the business, as you call it, any more thought.'

'I guessed that would get you going,' he said, smiling. 'Of course I've been thinking about it. It is clear to me that before I start I need to know the names and contact details of those involved and gain some understanding of what they hope to achieve, what they have achieved and who they are working for. I can't just run around in the dark.'

'What do you mean by I?' she said. 'We are in this together or don't you know.'

'I can't work effectively and look after a woman at the same time,' he said, deliberately drawing her out. He had realized during the conversation in Durban that she was the type who would want to be actively involved.

'I am up to here in this mess,' she said defiantly, holding her finger against her throat. 'If you don't want me with you I'll work alone.'

He thought for a while. She was intelligent, strong and could be a real asset. He did not think she would give in at the first sign of danger which he was sure would come in whatever form. He could not think of anyone else he would rather have with him on the job that he knew lay ahead. He shifted to the edge of his stool and turned to her.

'We will work together,' he said. 'I just wanted to see if you have spirit as well as good looks.'

She laughed. 'I honestly don't know why I'm doing this with you.'

'I do,' he said. 'Let's get some lunch and then we'll get started. I don't want to drag this thing out anymore than I can help. I'm sure that applies to you.'

After a lunch of filet steak, new potatoes and salad she and Steiner went up to her room. They seated themselves, Kirsty on the bed and Steiner on a chair near the window. Steiner began.

'As we firm up on what we know it is a good idea to make some bullet points,' he said.

'I'll do that,' she said going to the desk and getting a pen and paper. 'Not that you can't write.'

He carried on. 'The points are no more than a way of getting the information we have on these people into our minds. It is merely preparation for the job ahead. It should only take us a couple of hours. After the list is complete we will study it until we know the contents off by heart. We can then throw the list away because we have to move on and keep pace with the men we are interested in. It sounds to me as if things are really beginning to get going. At this stage we have to try and put ourselves in the position of our antagonists, know how they think, and be aware that there are things they are doing which we know nothing about. We'll just have to pick those up as we go. Does that make sense?'

'Don't tell me you were a shrink in your previous life,' she said. 'If you were you must have been pretty good at it.'

'Thanks,' he said. 'I hope that was a compliment.' He continued.

'It is important to remember you are not writing a novel. You are only making points. We will begin with John Kallis, the group operative. He wants to get hold of both files. He knows as much as we do about your husband's handiwork in Durban and later with John Dalton in KwaZulu-Natal. He believes the white file is held either by your husband or by his lawyer. Therefore he knows where to get it. We think he is in some way linked to Rupert Bosch, the man suspected of stealing the black file. It is possible Bosch stole the file for Kallis, who knew about his dealings with the blacks and threatened him. We think Kallis now has the black file. He wants both files for personal gain. This applies to nearly all the key players.'

Steiner sat back in his chair. 'How was that?' he said.

'It will serve its purpose,' she said, pleased. 'Who's next?'

I suggest we go onto Krige, your husband. As with Kallis, I will tell you what I think is fact and what is conjecture. Feel free to add or change anything.'

They completed the first draft of the list in a little over two hours and it covered John Kallis, Jan Krige, David Staples, Rupert Bosch, Johan Teichmann and the dead guerillas, John Nofomela and Paul Ngwenya. After they had reworked parts of it they had the final copy. They then spent another forty-five minutes reading and re-reading the contents. When Steiner felt they had gone as far as they could he looked at Kirsty. He really admired the way she worked.

'You did a great job,' he said. 'I feel I can get inside the head of any one of these men and know what he is going to do next.'

'I know you can perform miracles but that's stretching things a bit,' she said, laughing. 'It has certainly been a valuable exercise.'

Steiner got to his feet. 'Let's have a break,' he said. 'Would you like a cup of coffee downstairs?'

'Yes,' she said. Working with Steiner was an experience she was enjoying even though they had only just started. He was so aware and prepared to listen.

In the lounge they placed their order for a pot of coffee and a plate of sandwiches. After it arrived Steiner said to Kirsty.

'When do you think you will leave the hotel? I assume you do not intend to return to the farm.'

'I'll leave when this work is over and rent a flat somewhere, probably away from the city,' she said. 'When I returned from Durban I filed for divorce. That should go ahead pretty quickly without my having to appear in court. I'll have to discuss with my husband what happens to the farm but in any event I do not intend to live there again. Where are you going to stay while you're up here?'

'I'll book a room here,' he said. 'Ideally I would like the space and privacy of my own place but I won't be here long enough. This thing will soon be over if we know what we're doing.'

She looked at him, pensively. 'How would you like to share a flat with me?' she said, smiling. 'We can get one now and I will stay on after you've gone. You won't get many other offers like that.'

He thought for a moment then said: 'I'll take you up on that. We can try some agents now and see what's available. How does that sound?'

She got up. 'You know the answer to that.' she said. 'We'll make the calls from my room.'

They went up to her room and started going through the list of estate agents in the yellow pages. There were five well known agents near the hotel and they decided to give them a try. They went to each agent and were shown two-bedroom flats and houses available. Nearly all the two-bedroom places were flats in the city area and as far as they were concerned they left a lot to be desired. They were about to give up for the day and when they were shown details of a small period house five miles out of Pretoria and on the road to White River and the Kruger Reserve.

'That's the one,' said Kirsty. She spoke to the agent who said the house was vacant and on a one-year let. He agreed to show them before it got dark. Twenty minutes later they arrived at the house in the agent's car and he wasted no time in showing them around. It was in good condition and fully furnished.

'What do you think of it,' said Kirsty when they were alone and the agent had gone round the back. 'I like it.'

'It has been well maintained, has a good view of the mountains and is far enough from the main road for you not to be bothered by noise,' said Steiner. 'It is also very quiet and has privacy. But I'm no expert, having spent a lot of my life in flats, some good and some bad. It really is your call since I won't spend much time in it before completion of the work up here and I head for Durban.'

'You sound very confident,' she said. 'I will be lonely when you go but I can always move on. I'll get the agent to fill out the papers in my name. He told me that if I like it we can move in first thing tomorrow morning. He will also have the telephone connected. Let's find him and return to the hotel.'

When Kirsty and Steiner reached the hotel it was early evening and they decided to have a drink in the bar before going into the restaurant for dinner.

After they had been served she said to Steiner: 'Have you decided what we are going to do tomorrow? I get the feeling you think it is time to get to know those men out there. Am I right?'

'Yes,' said Steiner. 'Unfortunately we have to face them if we are going to come out on top in this case and get hold of those files. Sometimes I wish I had never heard of them.'

'Is that all you want?' she said.

'Yes,' said Steiner. 'Retrieving the originals is the only way of totally deflating these men. They will quite literally be destroyed, with nothing to offer anyone. If I had to create my own file, those people would be in it and at the top of the list.'

She laughed. 'I'm glad you're on my side. I wouldn't like to have to face you.'

'Don't have too much confidence in me,' said Steiner. 'I still experience fear. I did when I had to go against Richter and Koch in the Cartwright case.' He looked into

218

his glass. 'There is a saying that I used to try and instil in my unconscious mind. It was: The intellect toys with the concept; only the intuition understands.' He smiled.

'I don't care if you feel fear,' she said, her eyes alight. 'All I know is that I've seen you in action. You move as if you're in a void and no one else exists, total isolation. That is alright with me.'

'We should be concentrating on the job.' said Steiner, smiling.

'I'm waiting,' she said, mischievously.

'There are four men out there who either have one of the files, File A or File B, or have nothing,' said Steiner. 'I think it reasonable to assume that no one has managed to get hold of both files. If they have, we will soon know about it.'

Steiner ordered another drink for Kirsty and poured water for himself. 'The four men are Krige, Kallis, Bosch and Staples. Now, we can't deal with them all simultaneously. We have to take them one at a time, remembering their association if any with the others, and which file or files they need to complete their haul. Tell me who you would tackle first and why?'

She thought for a while, running her finger round the rim of her glass. 'I would first work on Rupert Bosch,' she said. 'He probably stole the black file and Kallis might have got it from him. He knows of Krige and Staples and we think he wants both files. But the black file comes first. I would contact him and give my name, and by using bait ask him for a meeting, preferably at his house when he thinks it's safe. We both go together but I am the one he will expect to meet. You will stay in the shadows. I will tell him that Kallis phoned me and said he had stolen the black file. We think he will admit taking it and say Kallis took it from him. If he doesn't it might be necessary for you to appear and take over. I will ask him if he wants the white file. I will tell him that Krige has it. I will also say I know how to get it.' She sipped her drink and then carried

219

on. 'Bosch's importance to us concerns the black file. If he asks me why I'm doing this I will say revenge and the file should go to the proper authorities. Basically we are playing him along and selecting our moves accordingly. There are no hard and fast rules in this game. What do you think?'

'I would also have picked Bosch and your approach is the way to play him,' said Steiner. 'You have the best chance as a woman of getting a reaction out of him. Tell me how you will contact him in the first place? You were told by Kallis that he has disappeared.'

'I think the only way of contacting him is to leave a short message on his answering machine. It will say I have something very interesting to tell him concerning the files and that I can help him. I will ask him to phone me so we can meet. I'll leave my name and the numbers of the house and my cell phone.'

'Excellent,' said Steiner. 'It's short and sweet. You will make that call tomorrow. I am getting a little excited by all this.'

'Bullshit,' she said. 'To you it is a dangerous game. I believe it really lights your fire. It's mother's milk to you.'

He made no reply. 'Let's get something to eat,' he said. 'We need an early night. Who knows what might happen tomorrow?'

After dinner they went up to their bedrooms. In the passage Steiner said: 'Give me a ring in the morning. Sleep well.'

'You to,' she said. 'Good night.' When she was alone she again thought how great it was having Steiner with her.

The following morning they went round to see the agent. He told them the phone had been connected and the papers were ready for her to sign. Minutes later they picked up their cars and headed for the house.

'We were lucky to get this place,' said Steiner after they had arrived and were seated in the compact reception room.'

'I agree,' she said. 'Let's not waste time and get down to business. I feel that at last we are entering the dark world of the unknown.'

'Don't talk like that,' said Steiner, grinning. 'You send a shiver down my spine.' He walked over to the phone and picked up the receiver. 'It's all yours. Give Bosch a ring.'

Kirsty took the phone and dialled Bosch's number. The phone was still in service and she waited. Seconds after she knew there was no one there the answering machine came to life. She waited for the click and then left the message she had agreed with Steiner.

'We now have to wait,' she said to Steiner, perched on a stool.

'Yes,' said Steiner, getting up and walking across the room to the window. 'Who is next?'

'You tell me,' she said. 'It's your turn.'

'I think you should go for Johan Teichmann,' said Steiner. 'He's the head of field operations in the group and boss. I'm sure he knows Bosch and he is the one who sent Krige to Natal.'

'Isn't it too soon to go for him,' she said. 'Surely he will alert Krige and Kallis and tell them I made contact with him.'

'No,' said Steiner. 'It's not too early. He is the only one who is close to Krige and Kallis. He will know virtually everything we need to know about them and we have to get it from him. For example, we don't know if he is satisfied with the way Kallis operates and we have no idea if Krige is now working for him. You said Krige has tasted blood and wants more. Who better to go to than Teichmann?

'Teichmann will also have an idea of the progress made so far in retrieving the files and who he has assigned the task of getting them. Kallis is one but are there are others

221

such as Krige. You can also tell him Kallis phoned you and that he believes Krige has possession of the original white file. You can say Kallis is right and the file is in the hands of Krige's lawyer. He will worship the ground you walk on when he hears that. Finally, you can ask him if he trusts those who are looking for the files to return them to the group if they manage to get hold of them.'

Steiner glanced out of the window. He went on. 'As with Bosch, it is vital you gain Teichmann's complete trust and that he believes you are doing this for him and the group. If you get his trust and he confides in you, he won't tell anyone he has spoken to you. What you exactly tell Teichmann is largely up to you, but it should be along these lines and really interest him. As with Bosch you are playing a game and the direction you take when dealing with him depends on how he reacts to you.'

'Perhaps we should be working on Teichmann first,' said Kirsty.

'No,' said Steiner. 'I have the impression that Bosch is merely a foot soldier and I would like to get him out of the way. The other guys, Krige, Kallis, Staples and Teichmann, are the main operators and dangerous.'

'It's all just a game of chess,' said Kirsty.

'Exactly,' said Steiner. 'And, it is a game we are going to win.'

'When do I contact Teichmann?' asked Kirsty. Steiner planned things as if he was on a war footing and she could see the value of this. They would be groping in the dark without being tactical and strategic in their thinking.

'Let's sit tight and see if Bosch answers your call,' said Steiner. 'He knows he is being hunted and that he's got to lie low but I think he would take a chance and be prepared to meet you at his house at say midnight when he wouldn't expect the people after him to be there. If he fights shy of that then you can suggest this place.'

'He might want somewhere public.'

'No,' said Steiner. 'That's too risky unless it is 800 kilometres away like Durban.'

She laughed at the thought of going all the way to Durban just to meet Bosch. 'And I suppose you would just sit up here while I went and did all the work,' she said.

'Yes,' said Steiner, grinning humourlessly.

'We're forgetting one thing,' she said. 'Before Bosch rings me, if he does, he or someone designated by him will have to go to his place to read the messages on his machine.' She sat down despondently in one of the chairs. 'This could take ages.'

'I thought of that,' said Steiner. 'I think Bosch will have arranged for someone to go and check his messages at least once a day, someone who masquerades as a cleaner but doesn't know him or where he can be contacted. Bosch would then contact this person for any messages.'

'And what if the men in the group are also checking his messages?' asked Kirsty. 'They will come after me.'

'If it's Kallis I doubt he would bother,' said Steiner. 'If it's someone else you could easily bluff your way out. All you have to say is you had spoken to Kallis and that your work has nothing to do with them.' After a moment he then said: 'It might take a while for Bosch to receive your message but we will have to be patient. If we don't hear anything in two or three days you can leave another one in case the group got there first. When and if you do that you should also contact Teichmann to keep the ball rolling.'

'Well, I hope it all works,' she said. 'I think I'll go and have a soak in the bath.'

'You will have to answer whichever phone rings,' said Steiner. He looked at her with a smile on his face. 'I hate to admit it but I couldn't do without you.'

Chapter 59

Pretoria

John Kallis was sure Kirsty Krige was lying when she said she had no knowledge of the whereabouts of the white file and that she did not believe her husband had got his hands on it. As he thought about it he realized his only way forward was to go first to Krige's lawyer, Staples, and see what he could get out of him. If he got nothing out of the man his next move would be to keep him quiet while he went for Krige.

Kallis also thought about Rupert Bosch. He was the only one in the group who went round to Bosch's house every two or three days so he could at least tell Teichmann he was still determined to get him and it was not plain sailing. But every time he went to the house Kallis felt uneasy. He was beginning to believe Bosch would not disappear and never be heard of again. He would, like any normal person, have felt the value of the black file before he had reluctantly been compelled to hand it over to him in the car park. The file must have cast its spell over him and he would want it back. As these thoughts festered inside him, Kallis decided on impulse to go to Bosch's house before paying a visit to Staples. He knew he could only give his full attention to the white file if he got rid of the potential threat imposed by Bosch's existence, and that meant finding him.

It was four days after meeting Kirsty Krige in the hotel when Kallis went again to Bosch's house. He had his own set of keys and let himself in, certain that Bosch was not there. He went through the rooms looking for disturbance or anything unusual. He knew a cleaner came in every couple of days but as far as he was concerned everything was as it had been on his previous visits. As he passed through the lounge on his way to the glass doors he noticed the message light on the telephone was flashing. He went over to the phone and pressed a button. He was told there was only one message and he waited to hear it. When the message came he immediately recognized Kirsty Krige's voice. This was confirmed and he listened to the rest of the message. At the end the light on the phone turned off automatically and Kallis made a note of the contents of the call and Kirsty's phone numbers. There was no address given but he was sure he could get it with relative ease.

Kallis quickly left the house, locking the doors, and drove to his flat. He had some thinking to do and needed to be on his own. When he was in the flat he sat on the sofa and replayed the call. It confirmed he was right when he guessed Kirsty was lying about the white file and he was now certain Krige had retrieved it from Cartwright's house. Also, her assertion that Bosch had stolen the black file was obviously correct but it implied he had given it to someone else and was not now in possession of it. Kallis suspected Kirsty new a lot more than what she had said on the phone and that is why she wanted the meeting. It was abundantly clear to him that Kirsty was involved concerning the missing files and she was working to a plan she had devised. He wondered if she was together in this with another person. One thing was certain. She had to be neutralized and kept out of the way until he had achieved his objectives.

Kallis switched his thoughts to Rupert Bosch. He felt Bosch had somehow regained his depleted confidence and now wanted both files for himself. If he was right it would mean Bosch had become dangerous. He would also have to be neutralized but in his case that meant being killed.

Kallis thought hard about his decision concerning Kirsty Krige and Bosch and he concluded that to put it into effect efficaciously he would need the help of another man so that the two of them could act independently if necessary. The man would have to do as he was told and ask no questions. He would only tell him as much as he needed to know. If he already knew two files had gone missing it would have been by chance since only a few at the top had been informed. Kallis thought about the men he knew and could trust. One man came to mind. It was John Dalton, the guy who had done the job with Krige in KwaZulu-Natal. Kallis hardly knew him but Teichmann thought enough of him to send him after the blacks. Although Dalton had a fairly nondescript job with the group, Kallis seemed to recall he used to be an operative in a South African special forces regiment. Kallis went to the phone and called Dalton at the group offices. He answered.

'John Dalton?' said Kallis.

'Yes,' said Dalton. 'Who are you?'

'John Kallis. I work for the group under Johan Teichmann. I remember meeting you a couple of times at group social gatherings.'

'I remember you,' said Dalton, a little surprised. 'How can I help you?'

'I don't want to speak on the phone,' said Kallis. 'Can we meet somewhere a bit private?'

'There's a smart bar three blocks from the office going south,' said Dalton. 'It is in Waldemar Avenue and called the Black Panther. It's ideal.'

'Excellent,' said Kallis. 'I will give you my flat and cell phone numbers in case you need them.' He gave Dalton the numbers. 'How does eight this evening suit you?'

'I'll see you there,' said Kallis, terminating the connection and feeling he was getting somewhere. When he had first heard the call from Kirsty Krige his confidence had taken a beating.

Kallis arrived at the bar a little after Dalton. He saw him seated on the far side against a wall adorned with old hunting photographs and went over to join him. Dalton had already been served and he ordered another beer for Kallis.

'I haven't seen you at work for a while,' said Dalton. 'What exactly do you do?'

'I'm a field operator,' said Kallis. 'As I told you on the phone my boss is Teichmann.'

'That sounds interesting,' said Dalton, sure that Kallis wanted him to do something for him.

Kallis leaned over his beer. 'The reason I wanted to see you is that I need you to do some work for me. It concerns a high profile job I am involved in for the group. No one knows what I have been doing on the case except Teichmann. But at the moment he is not aware that I want you to help me part time for about a week on a specific aspect of the case. I want it to stay like that.'

'What you tell me will be between the two of us,' said Dalton, becoming interested.

'There are a few people in this case who could irreversibly destroy group aspirations,' said Kallis. 'Of these, two pose an imminent threat and they must be removed now from the equation. They are a man and a woman. The man is someone you have probably met, Rupert Bosch. It is highly likely that he stole an extremely important file from the group offices, the black file as it is called, and we have since found out he was an ANC informer.'

'I know of him,' said Dalton appearing not to have heard of the file and not interested in what it contained. This pleased Kallis. 'He was a strange sort of character and kept mostly to himself. We have only exchanged a few words together. Who's the woman?'

'Before we go onto her there is something else that I should tell you,' said Kallis. 'It might come in useful when you speak to Bosch. A similar file, the white file, was removed from its safe before the black file and I am also responsible for finding it. In that sense the two files are connected. I explained how Bosch is connected to the black file but I believe he is also linked to this white file, exactly how I'm not yet sure.'

227

Kallis sank another mouthful of beer. 'Now let's get onto the girl. Her name is Kirsty Krige, wife of Jan Krige. I believe you and he were together on the KwaZulu operation.'

'Yes,' said Dalton. 'I was surprised he was chosen because of his political views. He certainly believes in full integration between black and white. Where is he now? What is his wife's connection to these files?'

'Krige's on his farm and I understand the two of them are separated. She is presently living in Pretoria. Let me explain her connection in this case. She knows about the black file and has made reference to it. That is enough for me but she is also interested in the white file. I believe Krige, or his lawyer, Staples, has the white file in his possession and for that reason she must in some way be connected to it. She has to be removed even if she is interested in only one of the files. That also applies to Bosch. It should be clear to you that the job I am involved in concerning retrieval of both files is first a process of elimination, which is where you can help me, and a second phase when I can give my full attention to the ones who really count, or the key players.'

'I understand,' said Dalton. 'I have never met Kirsty Krige. I'm sure she hasn't heard of me. Krige would have kept that quiet. How do you plan to remove them?' Dalton wondered who, if not both, was going to die.

'Bosch will have to be killed,' said Kallis. 'When it was discovered the file was missing he had already disappeared and has not been found. One way of finding him that we have not tried is to leave a message on the answering machine at his house. I am convinced that he checks it regularly or, more likely, he gets someone else to do it for him, someone like a cleaner. Another way is to contact the local offices of the ANC and ask how and where he can be contacted. But that is a long shot for obvious reasons.'

'I think we should try both methods,' said Dalton. 'If he answered the machine would he recognise your voice? I assume you would leave your numbers.'

'He would recognize my voice,' said Kallis. 'That is where you come in, if you want to do the work.'

'I'll get involved,' said Dalton. 'We should get going now if you give me the message. If he thinks I'm being open he will relax and contact me.'

Kallis was beginning to take to Dalton. He pulled a piece of paper from his pocket. On it he wrote: Do not trust anyone who calls you about the files; please phone me urgently. He passed the note to Dalton and said: 'I use the word files because I want to draw him in. Add your name and the numbers of your house and cell phone. You have mine.'

Dalton had a quick look at the piece of paper. 'There's a pay phone over there,' he said. 'Let's do it now.'

The two men went to the phone and in minutes Dalton had left the message. They returned to their seats.

'What do I do if I receive the call from Bosch,' asked Dalton, silently rebuking himself for not asking the question earlier. He didn't want Kallis to think he was a fool.

'You soften him up with a few appetizers and then say the two of you must meet,' said Kallis, surprised Dalton had not asked before. 'Bosch would want a public place and you must tell him you know of one just outside the city. There are several restaurants cum bars that I'm sure you know. Decide on one so that you are prepared.' Kallis cleared his throat then carried on. 'If Bosch wants to make his own choice emphasize that it must be quiet and private for your own protection. I am sure he will come up with the goods. Let me know and I'll be waiting for him.' Kallis smiled. 'You won't even have to appear.'

'It will be done as you suggest but I'll be there,' said Dalton. 'What about the woman?'

'I would like you to collect her, by force if necessary,' said Kallis. 'I don't have her address but you should be able to get it from the Plaza Hotel where she was staying. When you pick her up take her to an isolated place. Do you know of any?'

'Yes,' said Dalton. 'I own a small holding just outside the city and no one ever goes there. It would be ideal. I bought it primarily for the land.'

'I would like to give Bosch several hours before you go for the girl,' said Kallis. 'I might go to his house and see if the message has been read.' Kallis finished his beer. 'Let's go and just wait. I'll take the day off tomorrow and be at the flat all day. It might be an idea if you also took some time off. It would also give you a chance to visit the Plaza Hotel and see if you can get Kirsty Krige's address. If that fails we will have to try directory enquiries but unfortunately they are not always obliging. I recently asked a friend of mine in the telephone exchange to tap a line for me, but I'm reluctant to contact him again when I still owe him one for the work he did then.'

The two men left the bar and went their separate ways, Kallis satisfied with the progress he was making.

Chapter 60

Pretoria

When David Staples, Krige's lawyer, read about the killing of the blacks on Krige's farm his sixth sense told him they were after revenge or something else, like the white file.

After Staples had made copies of the file, he had locked the original in a well-concealed safe at his house. Now, with news of the killings, he phoned Krige on the farm. Krige answered.

'Jan, David Staples. I have just read about the killings on your farm. Do you know what they wanted? I think I can guess but you tell me.'

'They think that I had something to do with a recent job in KwaZulu-Natal, which I rightly denied,' said Krige, calmly. 'I was nowhere near there. They had also heard about my involvement in the Cartwright case and the existence of the white file. They said I had it, which again I denied. I sensed they were not in the mood to accept my defence and that at some stage they were going to kill me. I took my chance and after chasing me through the bush, they returned to the house. I had to reach the Land Rover and when I came to the house they jumped me. It was a bad mistake.'

'I'll be quite frank,' said Staples. 'All this makes me uneasy and I would rather you kept the original of the file. You have a safe that would take a lot of experience and a cutting torch to crack. Alternatively, you could hide it somewhere away from the house.'

Krige thought for a moment. He had thought about collecting the original before Staples phoned. 'That's fine by me,' he said. 'I can understand how you feel. I'll collect it in a few days if that's alright with you.'

'Good,' said Staples. 'Phone me before you come and I'll have it ready.'

After the call Staples felt an enormous weight had been lifted from him. He was not known for his guts.

Chapter 61

Pretoria

In the early morning after meeting Dalton in the Black Panther bar, John Kallis was sitting in his lounge drinking a cup of strong coffee without really enjoying it. He was already becoming impatient and his desire to hold the white file in his hands was stronger than ever. At ten when he felt he needed something to relieve the waiting, he went downstairs to his car and began the three-kilometre drive to Bosch's house. He had to see if someone had read the message on the phone that had been left by Dalton the previous evening.

When he was a short distance from the house, he drew up at the curb, switched off the engine and waited. He remained in the car for five minutes, looking for the presence of anyone in the vicinity of the house. He saw nothing and after leaving the car went along the grass verge next to the road. Just before reaching the gates he vaulted the fence and approached the house, using carefully planted trees for cover. He left the trees and went across to the front verandah and up to the glass doors. Inside the house he went to the phone; the light was off. Excited, Kallis sank into a chair. It was exactly what he wanted to see. His message had been received. After a few moments in the chair, Kallis crossed to the doors and let himself out of the house. He was returning to his flat to wait for an update from Dalton.

Chapter 62

Pretoria

Two days after speaking to David Staples, Jan Krige decided to go into Pretoria and get the file. He phoned Staples and agreed to meet him at his office in three hours, time for him to go to his house and collect the file.

At the appointed time Krige reached the offices in Pretoria and was shown through to the lawyer who was sitting pompously in a buffalo-hide chair that was close to suffocating him.

'Jan,' said Staples, rising from the leather. 'I was glad to hear you on the phone. I'm sure you understand my position.'

'I do,' said Krige, extending his hand and wanting to leave as soon as he could. 'I'm sure it is of deep concern holding something of such value that is desired by people who we would not exactly call our friends. Where is it?'

'Right here,' said Staples, bending over and removing a large plastic carrier bag from the lowest draw in his desk. He handed the bag to Krige who took one look inside before placing it firmly under his arm.

'You've helped me a lot with this,' said Krige without meaning it. 'But it is time I took responsibility for it. Do not be surprised if people pay you a visit. The good thing is you are clean.'

Staples paled. 'If they come here they must think I have either got it or know where it can be found. What do I tell them?'

'The guys in the DSO are the only ones who know for certain that you have the original,' said Krige. 'I told them you have it and I'm sure they believe me. I know for a fact that the group do not have a clue regarding the whereabouts of the file. They are playing in the dark. If they come here you can say you have never heard of the file and certainly haven't got it. They will have absolutely nothing to go on and will leave you alone. Trust me on this.'

'I feel reassured by that,' said Staples. 'If I can be of any further help on this or any other matter, please contact me.'

'Thanks,' said Krige. 'I will.' He went to the door and was soon gone.

Chapter 63

Pretoria

Dalton arrived at the Plaza Hotel and went directly to the main desk. There was a woman on duty and she looked up as he approached.

'Good morning sir,' she said. 'How may I help you?'

Dalton smiled, disarmingly. 'I'm sure you can,' he said. 'My name is John Dalton and I am up here from Durban. I believe a very close friend of mine has been staying here. I have tried several times to contact her but to know avail. Her name is Kirsty Krige.'

'I do know her,' said the woman. 'I made the reservation for her when she first came here and I have spoken to her several times. She is so charming.' She opened her register and after a short while said: 'I am not surprised you couldn't contact her. She booked out early yesterday morning. A man I had seen her with, James Steiner, also cancelled his reservation.'

'Did she leave a forwarding address?' asked Dalton. 'I was hoping to surprise her. Please don't tell me this trip has been in vain.'

'Just a minute,' said the woman. 'I'll see if she left an address in the log.' She went through a door behind her and after a while she returned, a wide smile on her face. 'You're in luck,' she said. 'I have the address.' She read it out to Dalton.

'Fantastic,' said Dalton. 'Thank you very much. You have been most helpful.' He left the hotel.

When Dalton reached his house he squatted on a stool in the kitchen and rang Kallis. He answered.

'I got the woman's address from the Plaza Hotel,' said Dalton. 'I haven't heard anything from Bosch.'

'It is good news about the woman's address,' said Kallis. 'I think we might be getting somewhere with Bosch.'

'Why do you say that?' asked Dalton.

'I went to his house this morning and the light on the machine was out,' said Kallis. 'That means it is highly likely he has received your message through his cleaner. I know of no one else who goes near the place and that includes Bosch.'

'Very good,' said Dalton. 'By the way, the receptionist told me Kirsty Krige was seen with a man, James Steiner, and that they had booked out on the same day. Do you know anyone of that name?'

'No,' said Kallis. 'I once had the unpleasant surprise of meeting someone in Durban with that name but I am sure it is not him. It would be too much of a coincidence. But before you burst into her house it would be smart not only to make sure she is there but also that she is alone.'

'What do we do next?' asked Dalton.

'Patience is a virtue,' said Kallis, sagely. 'Remain at home for the rest of the day and then go and get her. Just before you do that there is no harm in leaving another message on Bosch's machine. Make sure you tell me before you try for the woman. I hope you've cleared up the small holding so that it's ready for her.'

'It's suitable for a princess,' said Dalton. 'I'll ring you.' He replaced the receiver and went into the lounge. All the excitement made him thirst for something strong.

Chapter 64

Jan Krige's farm

When Jan Krige returned to the farm with the white file he had retrieved from his lawyer, he went to a large safe down a side passage in the house and locked the file inside. The safe had originally been police property but when a periodic update of hardware, vehicles and equipment was conducted Krige had managed without difficulty to acquire it. It had been manufactured to the most demanding specification and he was surprised when it was earmarked for replacement. The only answer was that everything regardless of condition came under the axe.

With the file virtually out of bounds to anyone without the safe's combination, Krige went and sat in his chair on the verandah, his feet on the rail. His mind soon returned once again to the conversation he had had with Teichmann. Krige knew he and John Kallis were in unique positions in that they were each in possession of one of the coveted files. After listening to Teichmann's account concerning the files, Krige was sure Kallis had received the black file from Bosch. Bosch then disappeared because he was still wanted by the group and like any sane person he was not going to hang around and risk being caught and killed. Krige was convinced Kallis in his investigation of the missing white file had concluded that only he could have removed the file from Cartwright's house. Kallis would therefore have deduced he or his lawyer had sent the copy of the file, which Kallis had intercepted, to the Scorpions. It would then have been crystal clear to Kallis that the unknown man in all of this would have got him to admit removing the file from Cartwright's place and that the condition imposed on him was that he send a copy to the DSO. The corollary was that the unknown man was in effect working for the Scorpions. It wouldn't have taken a genius to realize that when the file was intercepted, the DSO would have gone directly to him and his lawyer, David Staples, and asked for the original. Staples would have refused because he knew the value of the file and the DSO could not prove he had the original even though he had told them he did. It was their word against his.

Krige realized Staples was a weak link and would figure in Kallis's plans. He would readily abdicate if and when Kallis got hold of him and, regardless of what Staples said to the contrary, he would, under duress, reveal that he had the file. Krige knew that Staples had to be silenced at all costs to prevent Kallis from ever having it confirmed that he had the file and informing Teichmann. If Teichmann believed Kallis, and he would, Kallis would come after him with a vengeance. Kallis would be cleared of all suspicion and become a god in Teichmann's eyes. He would have a completely free hand and authorization to kill him and retrieve the white file. If Kallis then achieved what he so fervently wanted he would disappear with both files. Krige was acutely aware that he had to silence Staples to prevent Kallis gaining favour with Teichmann. As soon as Staples had been eliminated he would hunt Kallis down with the hate that was eating into him like an incurable disease.

For a while Krige formulated his course of action. When he was satisfied he went into the lounge and phoned Staples on his private office number.

Chapter 65

Pretoria

John Dalton was on his second whisky when the quiet in the room was split by the strident ringing of the house phone. He leapt from his seat, converged on the instrument and lifted the receiver, glad he hadn't had anymore to drink.

'John Dalton,' he answered, sure who was on the line. 'May I help you?'

'My name is Bosch, Rupert Bosch. I received your telephone message.'

Dalton changed his grip on the phone. 'Thank you for getting back to me. As I said in the message I would like to meet you. There is something I'm sure you will find interesting.'

'How do you know me?' said Bosch. 'I don't remember having met you before.'

'I work for the group,' said Dalton. 'I know who you are even though we've never met.'

'Tell me briefly why you phoned me,' said Bosch. 'You mentioned files. I'm sure you are aware the group are searching for me and it's not that they are worried about my health.'

'I have heard about the missing files, File A and File B, and that the group want to contact you to see if you know anything about the latter,' said Dalton calmly. 'I want to retrieve the white file. I am sure I know the person who has it.'

'Why are you telling me?' said Bosch. 'You could easily go to the group and be revered as an icon. Alternatively you could get the white file for yourself, vanish into thin air and make a lot of money.'

'I need someone to help me,' said Dalton. 'One is not enough. If this person and I manage to get hold of the file we would split the spoils equally. The problem is I don't know anyone I can trust and who has some understanding of what all this is about. That means that the person would need to know the names and contact details of past and present group field operatives and which of these men are responsible for retrieval of the files. You come into that category.'

Bosch was silent for a moment and then he spoke. 'I already have a shrewd idea who has the white file,' he said. 'And now I will tell you something else that only one other person knows. I did remove the black file because I was forced to do it.'

'So someone else was involved,' said Dalton, probing. He was beginning to realize Kallis had kept a lot to himself, but exactly what he didn't know.

'Yes,' said Bosch.

'You must want it back,' said Dalton, already guessing the reply. He and Bosch were of the same breed.

'I do,' said Bosch, his determination obvious. 'For that reason I am prepared to get involved with you. Between us we know the men who have the files and we can help one another.'

'I'm glad to hear that,' said Dalton. 'We will have to meet to discuss how and when we make a start and finally get our hands wet.'

'I suggest we meet at eight this evening,' said Bosch. 'The place I have in mind is the bar at a hotel called the The Wanderers' Haven. It's on the coast road and is quiet and very private. I am sure you will appreciate why I have selected a public place. I hardly know you.' Bosch laughed down the line, causing Dalton to shift the receiver slightly away from his ear.

'I've been there before,' said Dalton. 'It's very nice. I'll be there at eight.' He replaced the receiver and took a seat in the nearest chair. Things were going exactly as planned. He returned to the phone and rang Kallis.

'I've got some news,' said Dalton, as if he was about to report a routine daily event. 'Bosch has just contacted me. We've agreed to meet at The Wanderers' Haven on the coast road at eight this evening.'

'I know it,' said Kallis. 'It is a quiet place with a large car park at the rear. It's ideal for our purposes.'

'Bosch chose it,' said Dalton. 'We spoke for about ten minutes and he appears driven by a desire to get the black file. I told him I want the white file and we could help one another to get both files. He wants to be involved.'

'I see you did a good job enticing him to enter the lair,' said Kallis. 'He won't lie down and it's precisely the reason why he has become so dangerous. Now, I'll be in the car park well ahead of time. He owns a large, silver Mercedes. When he arrives I'll move as soon as he opens the door. No one will have the faintest idea what is going on.'

'What will you do with the body?' said Dalton.

'I'll leave it in the car and get out of there,' said Kallis. 'As I said, you don't even have to turn up.'

'I'm sure you can handle it,' said Dalton, 'and it is time to pull in the woman. What do you think?'

'That's good thinking,' said Kallis. 'It will be perfect if you can get her today and the sooner you reach her house the better. You might have a long wait for the right opportunity. The guy from the hotel might even be there and if he is it could complicate things. But you'll be the man in control. Keep in touch and good luck.'

'Thanks,' said Dalton. He terminated the call.

Chapter 66

Jan Krige's farm

On the day that John Dalton heard from Rupert Bosch, Jan Krige phoned his lawyer in Pretoria on the private number. Staples answered.

'David, Jan Krige. Something very important has come up and I would like to see you.'

'It's nice to hear from you,' said Staples. 'Why don't you come to my office? I'm available for the rest of the day.'

'I don't want anyone to know I have spoken to you and that you are meeting me later,' said Krige. 'This is very urgent and must be treated in the strictest confidence. Could I meet you at your home?' David Staples was divorced and Krige knew there was little chance of anyone else being at the house during the day.

Staples wondered what could be so urgent. 'I can meet you there in forty-five minutes,' he said. 'Does that suit you?'

'Thank you,' said Krige. 'I'll be there then.'

Immediately after the call, Krige changed into a dark jacket and matching trousers that were more in keeping with the city style. He unlocked his gun cabinet and removed the Beretta 93R 9mmx19 Luger/Parabellum semi-automatic pistol that he favoured and the silencer. He locked the cabinet and went through the lounge to his Land Rover at the front of the house.

He built up a good speed on the fairly deserted main road and reached the outskirts of Pretoria in a little under forty minutes. Staples lived on the north side in a palatial house, the norm for successful lawyers. When Krige came to the road he wanted he drove slowly along it until he saw the house and then parked against the curb 200 metres further on. Staples' car was not in its usual position and Krige knew he hadn't arrived. He let himself into the grounds through a side gate and went to the front of the building to wait.

Staples arrived at the house a few minutes after Krige and he smiled when he saw the farmer's Land Rover parked in the road beyond the gate. Krige clearly liked the spot because he always parked there. He opened the gates and crawled up to the house. When he alighted Krige stepped forward from behind a pillar and casually walked up to him. They shook hands and Staples led the way into the beautifully furnished front room of the building. When they were seated Staples faced Krige.

'Well, what is so urgent that you leave your farm and come all the way here?' he said. 'Whatever it is I'm glad to see you because I need to discuss a few things concerning your divorce. When these matters have been agreed by you and signed the divorce can be settled without delay.'

'I thought I had made everything clear,' said Krige. 'But let's get that stuff out of the way. Kirsty wants this divorce finalized as quickly as I do.'

For nearly an hour the two men went over the outstanding issues, with Staples typing and printing everything of relevance using his personal computer. When they had completed the job and signed the papers Staples passed them to Krige and went to the chair he favoured.

'Now, with that cleared up we can get to the reason for this meeting,' he said. 'I must say I am intrigued.'

Krige was silent for a while and when Staples was about to ask if there was anything wrong he came to his feet. He walked across to the lawyer and stood directly in front of him.

'I said on the phone that this was urgent,' he said. 'But there are some very serious men out there who will not rest until they have the file. I intend to disappoint them and eliminate any potential risk that stands in my way. Unfortunately you are such a risk because you know too much. I am sorry.'

In a blur of speed Krige drew the pistol from his belt and fired twice, the soft-nosed bullets hitting Staples in the centre of his forehead in a tight grouping, killing him. As the lawyer's head fell forward Krige, without a glance at the body, went swiftly to the doors and let himself out. He ran across the slate slabs of the verandah and onto the lawn. Without a change in momentum he wheeled to the right and went down a winding gravel path to the side gate. After a quick look up and down the road he bolted for the Land Rover. Once in the seat he accelerated onto the tar, disgorging earth from the thick tyres in a fine spray, and headed for the farm. He grinned wolfishly and quietly said: 'That leaves two of us.'

Chapter 67

Pretoria

It was mid-afternoon when John Dalton had the brief conversation with Kallis and on completion he got ready to go and get Kirsty Krige. He put sandwiches and a flask of coffee in a sports bag and after pulling on his boots and jacket went to his car parked in the drive. He ignited the engine, reversed into the street and was soon on his way to the house on the Kruger road where he believed Kirsty was staying.

The journey took him thirty minutes and he soon saw the house situated at the base of a small hill, half-a-kilometre from the road. He stopped on the grass verge and using a pair of binoculars he kept in the car scanned the area around the small building. There was no sign of life but he knew his only real option regardless of what he saw was to approach the house on foot, using the available vegetation for cover. He started the engine and drove the car past the gate to a lay-by from which he could gain access to the property. He left the vehicle and started on a circular route through the grass that he calculated would bring him close to where he wanted to be before he made his final move. It bugged him he had not seen anyone and the woman was either not doing anything or she was not there. He was also aware that if she was there he would have to assume she was alone.

When he was as close to the house as he dared go, he halted. He was facing the side elevation. For the first time he had a rear view of the house and he soon saw a small car parked up against the back wall. He was sure it belonged to the woman. He was motionless for a while and then, driven by impulse, went silently to the back door. He turned the handle and when the door opened he slipped inside, finding himself in a kitchen with a passage leading to the rest of the house. He went along the passage, past the bathroom and two empty rooms. As he came to the last door he slowed and cautiously peered round the frame. Seated and facing away from him was a woman he knew must be Kirsty Krige. She was reading a book.

As Dalton started walking towards her she turned round. When she saw him she quickly came to her feet and took a step backwards.

'Who are you?' she said, forcing herself to keep calm. 'Don't you know this is a private house?'

'I was able to figure that out,' said Dalton, stopping a couple of metres from her. 'My name is John Dalton and I'm here to take you away with me. I hope for your sake you don't resist.'

'You're out of your mind,' she said. 'A friend of mine will soon be here. He won't be happy when he sees you and I tell him you're here to abduct me.'

'Well, we'll just have to get out before he appears,' said Dalton. 'Is his name Steiner by any chance?'

'No,' she lied, wondering how he had heard the name and wishing above all else that Steiner would walk through the door.

Dalton moved closer to her. 'Let's go,' he said. 'You're testing my patience and I don't like it.'

As he completed the last word she darted to the left and ran towards the door. When she thought she was going to get past him he reached out with the speed of a hungry cat and threw himself at her in a dive that had his full weight behind it. His powerful arms encircled her waist in one quick movement and, unable to help herself, she fell heavily to the floor, her red skirt rising immodestly to her thighs. She struggled to free herself but he was too strong. He stood up and lifted her to her feet. With his one hand holding her arm and the other gripping the back of her neck, he half-dragged her across to the passage before forcing her to walk upright to the back door and through to the yard outside.

Dalton didn't waste any time getting Kirsty into the undergrowth and she didn't say anything, realizing it was pointless. They moved at a steady pace until he slowed and changed direction for the main road and the lay-by. The house was now partly obscured and he started to feel satisfied at the way things had gone. He relaxed his hold and kept her going at his pace with only one arm round her waist. When he saw his car he increased his speed until they reached it. After pushing her into the co-driver's seat he got in, started the engine and with the tyres squealing mutely drove off towards Pretoria.

Kirsty remained silent and when they were on the outskirts of the city Dalton picked up a ring road that led to the area where he had his small holding. After another ten minutes he left the road and finally came to his destination. He parked out of sight at the back of the unattended house and when he had cut the engine he looked at her.

'This is where you'll be staying until the job is complete,' he said, grinning, the proverbial Cheshire cat. 'The sooner you get used to it the better it will be for everyone.'

'Where am I?' she said, staring ahead. 'You haven't told me why you are doing this. I've never seen you before.'

'You're very attractive,' he said, feasting his eyes on her large breasts and then down to between her legs. 'I can't wait to get you alone.'

'The thought of you feeling me is revolting,' she said, her strong spirit fuelling his desire. 'Where the hell do bastards like you come from?'

He laughed. 'You'll soon be begging me for more,' he said. 'Now let's get into the house. I'm sure you will find it comfortable.'

He waited for her to leave the car and then they went into the house. Dalton had cleaned it the previous evening and bought items of food that he had stored in the kitchen. He led Kirsty into the front room, frugally furnished with a rug, table, three chairs and the essential liquor cabinet that had seen better days.

'Would you like a drink,' he asked in his most civilized voice. He had read that women liked refined, well-spoken men and he was confident he came up to scratch.

'No,' she said disdainfully. 'I want to get out of here and never see you again. I hope you burn in hell.'

He walked to the liquor cabinet, poured himself a neat Scotch and then sank a third of the spirit in one crude gulp. 'That was just what I needed,' he said. 'Are you sure you won't have a drink? It will help you relax.'

She didn't reply and stared through the window, again wishing Steiner would walk through the door.

Dalton put his glass down and went slowly to where she was standing. 'Perhaps this will relax you,' he said. 'It's part of the service.'

In a flash he took hold of her and swung her round to face him. He grabbed her with both hands and pulled her to him, tearing her cotton shirt open down to her stomach and then throwing her to the carpet in one neatly executed movement. Consumed by lust he unclipped her bra and slid it up, revealing her firm, beautifully proportioned breasts. They were as he liked them, exceptional.

Kirsty lay still, knowing that she was powerless against him, forcing herself to accept what would surely come. She moved a little on the carpet, wanting a position that would relieve the incipient pain in her shoulder, the result of the fall. When she became still he opened his mouth like a dying fish and started sucking her nipples, moving alternately between her breasts, leaving a glutinous trail that glistened in the fading light. He was in his element and he soon wanted the prize between her legs.

As Dalton reached for her skirt his cell phone came to life, emitting a shrill whistle and vibrating in his pocket. He swore and released her. He got to his feet, pulled the phone free and stuck it to his ear.

'Who is it?' he said, angry that he had been disturbed. 'What do you want? I'm busy.'

'Did you get the girl?' said Kallis, without introducing himself.

Dalton turned his back on Kirsty. 'Yes,' he said. 'It went as smooth as silk. We got here fifteen minutes ago.'

'Good,' said Kallis. 'It's just after six-thirty and in another half-hour I'll make my way to the bar and wait for Bosch.'

'How long should I stay here?' said Dalton.

'Why don't you let her have a bath and cook her some food?' said Kallis. 'After that, and when she is locked up in the bedroom, you might as well go home. I'll touch base with you later.'

'I'll do that,' said Dalton. 'Good luck.'

'I won't need it,' said Kallis arrogantly. He cut the line.

Dalton put his phone in his pocket and looked at Kirsty, still lying on the floor. The call had disturbed his concentration but he was determined to get from her what he wanted. He couldn't see Kallis completing his work in under a couple of days and that gave him plenty of time.

'Why don't you go and have a bath?' he said. 'I'll cook you something to eat.'

'I'll have a bath,' she said. 'But I don't want any food. After that just show me my room and leave me alone. I'm not sleeping out here.'

'I don't feel like cooking anyway,' he said. 'Follow me and I'll show you around.'

In addition to the lounge, the building comprised two bedrooms, a kitchen and a bathroom. When she had seen where she was going to sleep she admitted that at least it was clean, with new sheets, two pillows and a duvet on the

250

only bed. After showing her the bathroom and giving her a towel, Dalton returned to the lounge and his whisky.

When she was completely alone she took the towel and went into the bathroom. There was no lock on the door but that was of no concern. What she was going to do would only take a matter of seconds. She put her ear to the door and when she heard nothing she extracted the phone from her pocket. Like her keys and some money it had not been removed. She quickly dialled the phone in her house but there was no immediate reply and she waited for the answering machine to kick in. When it did she whispered: 'Dalton has me. I need you.'

After her bath Kirsty went to her room and Dalton soon appeared.

'I'm going now,' he said. 'But before I do I want to see what you've got on you. I should have looked earlier.'

She was sitting on the bed and he went over to her, making her stand up. He frisked her, airport style, front and back, and then went for her pockets. There were two, one in her shirt and the other in her skirt. The first was clearly empty and he slipped his hand into the second. With a look of triumph he dragged out her keys, money and cell phone.

'I'm glad I got that,' he said, holding up the small, compact Nokia. 'You would have had every man and his dog after me if I hadn't found it. I'll take it with me. I'll be here early tomorrow morning. The door will be heavily locked and I'm sure you have noticed the bars on the window.'

Dalton left the room, double locking the Banham and sliding two bolts into their closed positions. A while later she heard him go out the rear door and leave the premises in his car. She lay on the bed, fervently hoping Steiner would soon get her message. She was convinced that someone else was also involved in her abduction and she began to fear what they would eventually do to her.

251

Chapter 68

Near Pretoria

At seven-fifteen that evening John Kallis put on his jacket and removed a silenced Ruger P85 9mmx19 Luger/Parabellum semi-automatic pistol from the draw in his desk. The weapon was fully loaded with a fifteen-cartridge magazine and he stuffed it, with the silencer fixed in position, behind his belt above the hip. After making sure the gun was covered by his jacket he left the flat and went down the two flights of stairs to the basement car-park. In his car he started the V8 engine and crawled up the exit ramp to the street outside. He turned left and in ten minutes filtered into the main road that, in a little under five kilometres, passed near the bar where he expected Bosch to arrive at eight.

After twenty minutes at the wheel Kallis finally saw the bar and restaurant some 500 metres from the main road. He took the nearest turn-off and then drove steadily until he reached the building. He swung through the gate of the car-park and after looking around parked as far as he could go from the entrance, carefully ensuring the area behind him was relatively free from other cars. He turned off the engine, reclined his seat slightly and waited for Bosch to appear.

Several minutes after eight, when Kallis was beginning to wonder if Bosch was going to show, a large, silver 350S Mercedes Benz entered the car-park. Kallis watched the car do a circle and then park near the exit. He knew it was Rupert Bosch and as soon as the lights and engine were switched off he left his car. He walked down a line of vehicles to within a few metres of his target and halted, watching like a hawk.

When the door of the Mercedes opened, Kallis made his move. In four giant paces he was alongside Bosch, positioning himself to prevent the door from being closed. Bosch looked up at him, not believing he was again seeing Kallis's leering face.

'What do you want?' he said harshly, placing his hands on the wheel. 'Our business is over.'

'No it isn't,' said Kallis. 'You have become greedy and you want the files for yourself.'

'What about you?' said Bosch, regaining a measure of the confidence he had felt before the appearance of Kallis, a man he detested. 'You're no angel.'

'I know,' said Kallis, 'but that's what makes life interesting.' He briefly looked around, drawing the pistol smoothly from behind his belt. 'I'm afraid you're a nuisance I can do without.'

Before Bosch grasped the deadly meaning of the words, Kallis fired twice, hitting him between his eyes and killing him. His hands continued to hold the wheel as his head fell forwards onto them, his glazed, lifeless eyes still looking at Kallis.

Kallis reclined the seat as far as it would go and, freeing Bosch's hands, heaved the torso backwards into a resting position. He pulled it over a bit towards him, partly hiding the head behind the roof pillar, and closed the door. Anyone passing the Mercedes would with the usual glance think Bosch was sleeping off too many drinks before driving. Satisfied, Kallis walked to his car, got in and drove through the exit onto the road. He turned left and started on the route he had used earlier when coming to the bar.

As he neared the city perimeter, Kallis was tempted to call in at Dalton's smallholding to see if he was there, but he thought against it and carried on to his flat. He had decided he would not let Kisty know he was involved in her abduction unless necessity prevailed.

When Kallis reached the building where he had his flat, he parked his car and used the fire escape to go up to it. In the lounge he seated himself, poured a double Scotch and dialled the number of Dalton's cell phone.

Dalton answered and was pleased this time to hear Kallis's voice.

'Did you get him?' he asked. 'I was wondering how you were getting on.'

'He won't be looking for group files again,' said Kallis. 'He might still be resting in his car. How's the girl?'

'She's alright,' said Dalton. 'Obviously she doesn't like being forcibly abducted but I've told her she will be released as soon as we get what we want.'

'Don't build up her hopes too high,' said Kallis. 'If I decide she poses too much of a risk to be released, I might have to think again.'

'You wouldn't kill her?' said Dalton, in disbelief. 'What kind of risk would she present when she's free? You would have what the group wants and be beyond reproach. No one would be able to prove she was abducted.'

'I told you I would think about it when the time comes,' said Kallis. 'Let's forget about it for the moment. Did you mention my name?'

'No,' said Dalton.

'Good,' said Kallis. 'Leave it like that. Keep her in the dark.'

'What are you going to do now?' asked Dalton.

'I'm going into the next phase,' said Kallis, cryptically. 'Your work on this job will soon be over. Just make sure the girl has what she needs. I'll ring you tomorrow.'

Before Dalton could say any more Kallis cut the call.

After Kallis put down his phone he knew that if there was any chance of Kirsty Krige positively naming him as the man behind her abduction and revealing anything that went against him before he had decided what to do with the files, he would have to silence her for good. He also

254

thought about John Dalton and he was beginning to realize he was also a potential threat. If Dalton wanted the files for himself he could effectively nullify Kallis by threatening to reveal he had been forced by Kallis to abduct the girl, an action not sanctioned by Teichmann, and that Kallis had killed Bosch, also not approved by Teichmann.

But before giving these issues more thought, Kallis had decided that the next phase, as he'd described it to Dalton, was to pay a visit to Krige's lawyer David Staples. If, after that visit, he didn't get the white file he would go for Krige.

Chapter 69

Near Pretoria

An hour before Kirsty Krige was abducted by Dalton, James Steiner left the house they were sharing and drove into Pretoria. He needed to buy some clothes and go to the bank. From what he had seen he liked Pretoria as a city and he was in no hurry to get back to the house. Kirsty was there if Bosch phoned, which was becoming less likely by the minute, and he felt she needed some time alone to help build her confidence. She was clearly dispirited by the slow pace of things and sometimes she told him that they were getting nowhere. He sympathised with her, knowing her broken relationship with Krige only compounded things. He tried to reassure her by saying that preparing a plan of action and patience were the foundations in all successful operations, particularly the one in which they were involved, with its multiple protagonists.

At seven in the early evening Steiner returned to the house. As he drove down the driveway to the small building he was a little surprised to see there were no lights on when it was already starting to get dark. He parked in his usual place at the rear next to Kirsty's car and entered the house through the kitchen door, making enough sound for Kirsty to know he was there. But she didn't show and after taking a quick look in the bathroom and bedrooms he went to the lounge. She wasn't there either and for the first time he started to become worried. After a closer look around the house he could find no sign of any unusual disturbance. He was now uneasy because her car had not been moved, the house was unlocked, when they always locked it before going out, and the surrounding countryside was not inspiring enough for her to have gone for a walk. These factors implied she had left under force.

He returned to the lounge and sat down, suddenly remembering her cell phone. He was about to call the number when he noticed the house phone message light flashing. He sprang towards it, pressed the button and at once heard Kisty's message. It was the only one and he felt a chill go down his spine. He replaced the receiver. She was in real danger. He thought of the name Dalton and soon realized that Kirsty had mentioned his name previously. It came from her conversation with John Kallis when he had said Jan Krige had gone with John Dalton to eliminate the blacks in KwaZulu at the behest of Teichmann in the group.

After going through the main people linked to the missing files, Steiner concluded Dalton was not working alone and he had abducted Kirsty for Krige, Kallis or Teichmann. He immediately ruled out Krige and doubted Teichmann would get directly involved in abducting her. That left Kallis but Dalton had to be dealt with first because it was highly likely he was guarding Kirsty, until Kallis decided what to do with her. Now that he had received the message, Steiner decided against phoning Kirsty on her cell phone because if she was with Dalton he would immediately remove it, if he had not already done so. Neither did he want Dalton to answer the phone. But to tackle Dalton, he had to know how to find him, and that meant paying Teichmann a visit.

Steiner phoned the group. A night porter picked up the phone and when he asked for Teichmann he was told he had left. He asked for Teichmann's home number and it was not available. There was no alternative other than wait until the morning.

Early the next morning Steiner again phoned the group and asked for Teichmann. He was connected and after a few rings Teichmann answered.

'Teichmann. Who is calling?'

'You don't know me,' said Steiner, 'but I would like to see you urgently. I have something to say concerning the files that I'm sure would be of great interest to you.'

As predicted, Teichmann was very interested. 'Who do you work for?'

'I am working independently,' said Steiner. 'That will be clearer when we meet.'

'What do you have in mind?' asked Teichmann. 'I can meet you in thirty minutes. You could come to my house. There's no one there.'

'That suits me,' said Steiner. 'What's the address?'

Teichmann gave him the address, glad Steiner didn't mince words. 'I'll see you there.' He replaced the receiver and minutes later left his office.

Steiner left for Pretoria and Teichmann's house soon after the call. As well as the address, Teichmann had given him general directions once he reached the city and had told him the house was very near the university on the west side. With his existing knowledge of Pretoria, he had a good idea where that would be.

Ten minutes after coming to the outskirts of Pretoria, Steiner came to the road he wanted. He drove slowly up it, noting the numbers, and when he was in front of the house he cut the engine and went through the gate up to the front door. The building was one of the most impressive he had seen and after pressing the bell Teichmann appeared, still dressed in his suit. They greeted one another and Teichmann led him through the entrance hall into a study. He closed the door and when he was seated he looked intently at Steiner.

'Now what is your name?' he asked. 'I can't talk to someone whose name I don't know.'

'James Steiner. I am sure you haven't heard of me.'

'You are right, I haven't,' said Teichmann. 'With that out of the way tell me how you know about the files and your connection with the group? You told me you are working independently. Does that mean you are still working for others or does it mean you are totally alone in what you are doing? I'm sure you appreciate the distinction.'

'I was directly involved in the Cartwright case and doing the work for a senior operative in the Scorpions,' said Steiner. 'I was not employed by them in the strict sense of the word. I know you have people working for you in the same way.'

'We do,' said Teichmann, impassively. 'They do a job and then disappear with no strings attached.' Teichmann leant forward and stared at Steiner. 'Are you telling me you are the unknown man in all this?'

'You could put it like that,' said Steiner, phlegmatically. 'I don't always reveal my presence.'

'Until you kill someone,' said Teichmann.

Steiner ignored the comment. 'I have no connection with the group,' he said pointedly.

Teichmann sank back into his seat, momentarily thinking about his part in the operations and the justification for his actions, issues he had gone over many times before. 'You said you are working independently. How does that involve the files and what is your interest in them?'

'When my work on the Cartwright case was coming to an end at Jan Krige's farm, I briefly met his wife, Kirsty Krige,' said Steiner. 'After I returned to Durban she contacted me and said a black file, File B, had also been stolen from the group offices, allegedly by a man named Rupert Bosch, and that both files, the white file, File A, and the black file, had not been found.' Steiner deliberately did not say a copy of the white file had been sent to by Krige to the DSO because Teichmann didn't know Krige had retrieved it from Cartwright's house. He had to be careful in how he got what he wanted from Teichmann.

'Who was keeping her informed?' asked Teichmann. 'It wouldn't have been her husband.'

'John Kallis,' said Steiner. 'He went to her hotel.' Things were getting going. 'I'm sure you know him.'

'I do,' said Teichmann. 'He is directly involved in finding the stolen files. Now will you tell me your personal interest in the files?'

'I'm coming to that,' said Steiner, keeping his eyes on Teichmann. 'Do you trust Kallis?'

'What the hell is this?' said Teichmann. 'You get me all the way out here without telling me what you want and then ask me if I trust one of my agents.'

'Trust me,' said Steiner patiently. 'You will soon understand the reason for the question.'

'I'm not sure,' said Teichmann, candidly.

'Kirsty Krige has been abducted and I believe Kallis is behind it,' said Steiner. 'To be more precise, he instructed John Dalton to do the dirty work. You will remember he is the person you sent to KwaZulu-Natal with Krige to kill four blacks.'

Teichmann paled under his tan. Steiner had the uncanny ability to squeeze where it caused pain. 'How do you know?' he asked, regaining a measure of composure.

'I found her missing from her house an hour ago. She left a message saying Dalton had her and asking me to help. For that reason I am here. The files are of no real importance to me.'

Teichmann was not sure he believed what Steiner said about the files. They were important to anyone who knew about them. 'What do want from me?' he said. He felt he had to show he was concerned for the woman before finding out anything more Steiner could tell him. There had to be more.

'Does Dalton work for the group?' said Steiner. 'If he does, is he there now?'

'He works for us,' said Teichmann. 'I didn't see him before I left this morning. I know he took yesterday off.'

'I'm not surprised,' said Steiner. 'He must find abducting women quite demanding. I would like you to give me the address and phone numbers of his home and any other place where he might be staying. That also goes for Kallis. Do you have the details here?'

'I'll get them,' said Teichmann, getting up. He walked over to a desk, consulted a thin folder and wrote briefly on a sheet of paper. He returned to his seat and handed it over to Steiner. 'You'll find the information on that including this number and that of my cell phone.'

'Thank you,' said Steiner, running his eyes down the sheet before folding it and putting it into an inside pocket in his blazer. He looked at Teichmann. 'So Dalton has only one address and he is single. Do you know the colour and make of car he drives and can you give me a brief description of him?'

'He drives a three-year-old light blue Ford sedan and he is about five-eleven, well built, not particularly good looking, and with dark hair worn in a crew cut.'

'Just my type,' said Steiner. 'Finally, I don't want you to tell anyone about this visit. That includes my name and what we spoke about. I will deal with Dalton and Kallis.'

'Before you go I have something to tell you,' said Teichmann. 'Yesterday afternoon Jan Krige's lawyer, David Staples, was shot dead at his home. The killer hasn't been caught but a dark green Land Rover that needed a wash was seen parked near the house at about the time Staples died. It wasn't there for long and it is unusual to see any vehicle that is not a limousine in that neighbourhood.'

'Krige,' said Steiner.

'I came to the same conclusion,' said Teichmann. 'Also, it appeared Staples had been working on Krige's divorce papers. It's not much but I doubt it was a coincidence and to me that means Krige must have been there.'

Steiner had been hoping to get something about group progress in locating the files and what he had just heard

261

was totally unexpected. 'Have you got anything else?' he said, half-joking.

'Yes,' said Teichmann. 'When you hear it you won't forget this meeting.'

'Go on,' said Steiner, listening intently.

'This morning, half-an-hour before you phoned I had a call from someone telling me that Rupert Bosch was found dead in his car. It was not a case of drink driving. He was slumped over the wheel in the car park of a bar on the coast road, five kilometres from the city. He had been shot twice in the head.'

Steiner stared at nothing in particular. Then he faced Teichmann. 'Do you know who killed him?'

'I have an idea,' said Teichmann. 'But I wouldn't be surprised if you told me.'

'I think it was John Kallis,' said Steiner.

'Why him?' asked Teichmann.

'I am reasonably sure Rupert Bosch stole the file to give to Kallis because he had some sort of hold on him,' said Steiner.

'What was that?'

'I seem to be doing all the talking,' said Steiner. 'I am not really interested and I must find Kirsty Krige before Dalton does something to her.'

'You are interested,' said Teichmann. 'Obviously you are pretty sure she won't be harmed otherwise you would have bolted out of here when I gave you Dalton's address.' He rubbed his cheek and studied Steiner closely. 'You still haven't answered my earlier question which I will repeat. Why are you interested in the files?'

'I have a reason for that,' said Steiner. 'And, it is not financial.'

'Evasive as ever,' said Teichmann smiling. 'Now I'll tell you where I'm coming from. I am convinced Krige, who I also asked to go after the files, and Kallis want the files for financial gratification. They have no intention of ever returning them to the group.'

'They are nearly there,' said Steiner. 'Kallis has the black file and Krige lied when he said he had failed to retrieve the white file from Cartwright's house. The blame you and your friends in the group pinned on the outsider was clearly wrong because if I had it I wouldn't be standing here now. Krige has the white file in his possession. He gave it to Staples when he returned from Durban but Staples didn't have it when he died. Krige wouldn't have killed him unless he had access to where Staples kept it, unlikely, or that he already had it.'

'And I believed him all this time,' said Teichmann. 'Let me continue from where I left off. I will reward you handsomely if you retrieve the files for me, even if you have to kill Krige and Kallis. Each is definitely playing a double game. What is your answer?'

Steiner had prepared himself for this. 'I will get them,' he said. 'You will be the first to know when I do.'

'Thank you,' said Teichmann, not quite sure exactly what Steiner meant but refraining from asking him. He had no one else he could trust.

'Goodbye,' said Steiner. 'That was very interesting.' He turned and without a backward glance walked out of the house to his car. The meeting had taken longer than expected. When he reached his car he started it, did a three-point turn and, after checking his map, headed for Dalton's house.

Chapter 70

Near Pretoria

Fifteen minutes before Steiner met Teichmann at his home, John Dalton left his house in his car and picked up the ring road that led towards his smallholding. He was soon at the turnoff he wanted and in another five minutes pulled up in front of the house where Kirsty Krige had spent the night. He went through the front door, down the passage and stopped in front of her bedroom door. He knocked, waited for a reply, and when it didn't come he unlocked it, slid the bolts to the open position and entered the room. She was sitting on her unmade bed and staring through the window. He approached her and she faced him.

'I'm sure you would like to use the bathroom,' he said, trying to be as gentle as he could manage. 'Did you sleep well?' He grinned, his teeth crying out for dental treatment. He would have been the first to acknowledge he hadn't been near a dentist in ten years.

She gathered her towel and without looking at him went through the door to the bathroom further along the passage towards the kitchen. She had never felt so depressed and she looked forward to a hot bath that would at least help to lift her spirit. The man she trusted more than any other had let her down and not answered her cry for help.

She went to the toilet and then after running the bath stayed in the steaming water with no desire to leave and go back to her room. After what seemed an age she got out, dressed and with one hand holding the partly torn shirt together at the front returned to where she had spent the last sixteen hours.

Dalton was there when she entered and he looked at her, his hands stuffed in the pockets of his jeans. She went to her bed and sat down, the same position she had been in when he arrived.

'Are you still on a hunger strike?' he said. 'The sooner you accept that you will be here for at least a few days the better you will feel. You are acting like a child.'

'I'll never get used to this place,' she said. 'I'm not surprised you have given up on it and live elsewhere. I suppose it's too much to ask who you are working for. You haven't got the brains to be doing something as complicated as abducting a woman on your own. The sight of you makes me sick.'

The jibes were finally more than he could bare and he took a long step forwards, grabbing her by the arm and striking her viciously across the mouth, drawing blood that seeped from her red lips. She cried out with pain, feverishly trying to break loose from the grip that held her like a vice. Her struggling only nurtured his desire and he knocked her other hand away from where it was shielding her proud breasts, revealing mounds that held him rigid under their spell. And then he suddenly went still, seemingly not knowing what to do, and after mere seconds thrust her back onto the bed.

'You're not worth it,' he said with a sneer. 'You remind me of a whore who can't find a client.' He walked to the door and turned. 'I'll be back later.'

Dalton left the room, locking and bolting the door behind him. Moments later she heard him leave the premises in his car. The relief engulfed her and she broke down, crying unashamedly in her desperation, silently begging Steiner to come and remove the pain.

After leaving the smallholding Dalton drove faster than usual to his home. He had got divorced several years ago and he found life as a single man vastly better than he had experienced when he made the mistake of getting married. He was in his mid-thirties, intelligent, streetwise and

265

athletic with the strength of a hungry beast. For sexual gratification he favoured women in their early twenties, but sometimes when it was necessary to have an older woman they were also fairly good. He sometimes regretted leaving the South African special forces but he knew when he made the decision that by staying he would never have the good life he now enjoyed and for which he had craved.

As Dalton sped along the road his thoughts went to John Kallis. When Kallis had asked him to do the job of luring Bosch to the slaughter and abducting the woman, he hadn't realized Kallis was playing a double game, with his prime aim personal financial gain. He had no intention of returning the black file to the group, the file Dalton now believed Kallis had forced Bosch to give to him, and he was convinced Kallis was also intent on getting the white file for himself. The thought of Kallis disappearing into the sunset with the spoils was enough to drive him to distraction. He realized after speaking to Bosch that, ironically, he should have dumped Kallis, told Bosch that Kallis had asked him to persuade him to go where he could be killed, and joined forces with him. But even though he had lost his chance then, with Bosch dead and Kallis no doubt crowing, he was not finished. All he had to do was go with the flow and seize the opportunity of destroying Kallis and anyone else in his path when the opportunity presented itself.

When Dalton reached his house he parked his car outside in the road and went in through a side door. He watched television for the next two hours and when he had finished his third whisky he left the house and headed again for the smallholding. He had decided to buy a pizza for Kirsty Krige and after he had stopped and bought one he resumed his journey.

Chapter 71

Near Pretoria

When Steiner came to the road where Dalton lived he found the house and then parked round the corner in a neighbouring street. From his position he had a clear view of the property. Dalton's Ford sedan was nowhere in sight. He thought about trying him on the phone but it carried the risk of alerting him and he decided to wait.

Steiner didn't have to wait for long before he saw the blue sedan drive up to the house. Dalton got out and went down the side of the building, presumably to another door. Steiner felt his stomach tighten when he thought of Kirsty and he decided to give Dalton at most two hours before he went in.

Nearly two hours later when Steiner was preparing to move, Dalton appeared, got into his car and drove off along the road. Steiner gave him a lead of a couple of hundred metres before he followed. After a kilometre Dalton stopped, bought a take-away and when he continued his journey, Steiner again took up position behind him.

As Steiner followed Dalton, the route twisted and turned progressively as if Dalton was taking a short cut, and he knew that to keep him in sight he would have to shorten the distance between them. He closed the gap accordingly and Dalton continued at his pace until he reduced his speed, went through a gate and drove up to a small house. For Steiner it was now or never. He accelerated and followed. He was almost on Dalton and about to stop and get out of his car, when Dalton did a U-turn. He careered past Steiner, went through the gate and disappeared down the road.

Steiner ran to the front door, entered the house and when he saw no one went to the short passage. Only one door caught his attention and he ran to it.

'Kirsty,' he shouted when he reached it. 'Are you there?'

'Steiner, I'm here. Open the door.'

'Keep back, I'm coming through,' said Steiner, not seeing a key for the Banham. He slid back the top and bottom bolts, took a long step back with his right foot and then without changing the position of his feet swung his hips, using the first two knuckles of his fist to strike the door above the lock with devastating force. The lock burst, the door swinging smoothly inwards, revealing Kirsty, standing well back, her hands held to her mouth.

'You came.' She rushed to him and they embraced, she smothering him with kisses, the tears streaming down her cheeks. Her shirt fell open but she didn't care, holding him tightly, her head finally resting on his chest.

'Why didn't you come sooner,' she said, smiling for the first time. 'I thought you had given up and returned to Durban.'

He was glad she still had her sense of humour. 'I wouldn't have left you.'

'What did you use to open the door,' she said. She looked at his hand. It was smooth, the skin unscarred after the beating to which it had been subjected through the years. 'It's all in the mind, isn't it,' she whispered. She stared at him with her beautiful eyes. It was so good seeing him.

'Dalton must have gone,' she said. 'You wouldn't be standing here if he hadn't.' She thought of the items Dalton had removed from her pocket and after telling Steiner, led him into the lounge. After a quick search she found them in the liquor cabinet. 'Sorry for the interruption,' she said. 'I'm so glad he didn't take them with him. Where is Dalton?'

'I followed him from his house close to the front door. He then showed initiative, went past me and shot off up the road.'

'How did you get his address?' she asked.

'Teichmann. I'll tell you more when we leave this place. Let's go'

They went to his car, leaving the front door open and were soon on their way to the house. When they arrived he made some tea and gave her a cup in the lounge.

'How did Dalton treat you?' he asked.

'He twice tried to screw me,' she said. 'The first time he was disturbed by his cell phone and if I had had the strength I would have burst out laughing. The next time he unbelievably lost interest. That was when he went home and later returned.'

'He was certainly working for someone else,' said Steiner. 'Your abduction fitted into a wider plan.'

'Who's he working for?' she asked. 'I bet you are going to say Kallis.'

'Yes. You're becoming as clever at deduction as I am.'

'Actually, I think you have quietly been learning from me,' she said, smiling. 'Do you think Dalton will try and get me again?'

'No,' said Steiner confidently. 'He had his chance and blew it.'

'What do we do now?' she said, not sure Dalton wouldn't come again. 'We must be nearing the end of this business.'

'I will go after Kallis,' said Steiner. 'But first I must tell you what Teichmann told me.'

'Go on,' she said, wondering what Teichmann knew that they didn't.

'Yesterday, David Staples was shot dead in his home. The killer was not apprehended but a couple of things point to your husband, Krige.'

'What things?'

'A dirty Land Rover was seen near Staples' house at the time of death. Vehicles like that are seldom, if ever, seen in the neighbourhood. Also, it appears Staples had been working on your divorce papers and that indicates Krige was there. Was it coincidence? No.'

'What does Teichmann think?' she asked.

'He agrees with me particularly after I told him Krige had retrieved the file from Cartwright.'

'He must have loved hearing that. What's going to happen next? Can there possibly be anymore?'

'Yes,' said Steiner. 'Last night Rupert Bosch was found dead in his car in the car park of a restaurant. He had also been shot. Teichmann and I agree that this time the killer was Kallis. That makes sense for the simple reason that we believed Kallis forced Bosch to steal the black file to give to him. After Kallis received it Bosch became ambitious and Kallis killed him. Now comes the interesting part. Teichmann had asked Krige to help him get the files, as well as Kallis. But after the killings and after hearing from me that Krige surely had the white file before he killed Staples, he now believes each is playing a double game. Unsurprisingly, he wants to keep them on ice and bring in someone else. He asked me.'

She broke out laughing. 'Did you say yes?'

'I told him I would get them and he would be the first to know.'

'That means nothing,' she said. 'I have to admit I am learning from you. Are we finished with Teichmann?'

'Yes, unless something unforeseen comes up and I have to contact him. Quite frankly I just want to retrieve the files and get out of here.'

She looked at him, an unusual expression on her face. 'I must have a bath and wash my hair. I had one at Dalton's house but I want another. I hope you don't mind if I sleep for a couple of hours. The bed at Dalton's kept me awake for most of the night. After that we'll go for Kallis.'

'I knew you would come up with that,' said Steiner. 'But we leave in two hours. I've a paperback I want to read again.'

'What's it called?' she asked. 'Is it about sex?'

'No. Its title is The 47 Ronin. Before I get to the end of this business I might do what they did.'

'What's that,' she asked.

'They committed *seppuku.* That's the honourable term for killing yourself.'

She smiled, slowly shaking her head. 'You, James Steiner, are the last person who would ever do that, so don't talk bullshit. I've never known a man with your mental strength, the spirit to overcome anything that stands in your way. And, I'm sure you won't leave me now.' She smiled again and then left the room.

Chapter 72

Pretoria

After evading Steiner, John Dalton drove to a bar he knew in the centre of Pretoria. It was quiet and he had never seen anyone from the group in there. He found an isolated table and before ordering a beer phoned Kallis, wondering what he would say when he heard the girl had probably been freed. Anyone with the right tools could break down the door. The call was answered.

'Kallis. Who is that?'

'John, it is Dalton. I'm glad I got you. I'm phoning from a bar in the city. Something has gone wrong.'

'What?' asked Kallis.

'Someone followed me to the smallholding and I got out of there. I couldn't risk him catching me.'

'So he freed the woman,' said Kallis, unexcited. 'This alters my plans slightly.

'How?' said Dalton, again feeling he was just a pawn.

'I have a nasty suspicion the person who followed you was the guy James Steiner, seen with the girl at the hotel. I'll bet anything they have gone or will go to her house. You and I will go there and eliminate them.'

'Why not go directly for Krige as you had planned?' said Dalton. Sometimes, when it suited him, Kallis had difficulty giving a straight answer.

'If they reveal everything they know before I get the white file, I might have to come clean prematurely. That also goes for you.'

'Are you saying you have the black file?' said Dalton.

'No,' said Kallis.

'What do I get out of all this?' asked Dalton, venting what had become uppermost in his mind.

272

'If you help me sort out the woman and retrieve the white file, I'll inform Teichmann,' said Kallis. 'I will also tell him you've helped me considerably in my efforts to secure the black file. Does that satisfy you?'

'Yes,' said Dalton, lying. He was now convinced he could not trust Kallis and that his aim was to get the files for himself.

'Good,' said Kallis. 'Give me the name and address of the bar where you are now. I'll meet you there in a couple of hours. Go for a walk around the town.'

Dalton passed on the information. 'I'll see you later,' he said. He cut the call and walked to the bar. He needed a stiff drink.

Chapter 73

Pretoria

After the call from Dalton, Kallis started packing two suitcases with things he had in the flat. There was hardly anything of value and nearly all the stuff he chose to take with him, were clothes and an extra pair of shoes. The last item he packed before closing the cases was the group black file, secure in its thick envelope. Finally, he stuck his fully loaded pistol behind his belt on the right side, making sure it was concealed by his jacket, and dropped the spare magazine, also full, into one of his deep pockets.

Kallis had decided before Dalton phoned that as soon as he got hold of the white file he would leave the flat with the door locked and drive to Durban. He had told Dalton that if he assisted him in dealing with the woman and retrieving the white file he would inform Teichmann. But Kallis had no intention doing anything of the sort because he alone was going to retrieve the white file before disappearing and he had at some stage to lose Dalton. Going after Kirsty Krige with Dalton could well give him the opportunity to escape from Dalton after he had helped him with the dirty work. Everything depended on how well he executed the plan he had already started formulating.

It was growing dark when Kallis vacated his flat for the last time. He knew he wouldn't miss it because it was not up to the standard he was used to. When he had locked his cases in the boot of the car he drove up the ramp and headed for the bar where he was to meet Dalton. It took him just over five minutes to reach the place and after he had parked his car outside the entrance he entered. Dalton was seated against the far wall and after buying a beer he joined him.

'It's good to see you,' said Dalton, ingratiatingly. 'I'm sure you're looking forward to tonight.'

'Why?' said Kallis. 'The woman and the guy are hardly worth the bother. I only want to pay them a visit to reduce the risk of further interference on their part.' He belched, wanting to emphasize his control. 'After we've finished our beers we'll get going. I hope you've got your gun. If not we'll go and fetch it.'

'It's in the holster on my belt,' said Dalton. 'Don't worry, I'm well prepared. How do we get to the woman's house?'

'We can go in my car,' said Kallis. 'I will drop you off at your house after we've dealt with the girl. I've decided we should make a move on Krige tomorrow rather than tonight. We want to be fresh for him. Getting the white file is what this is all about.'

'You certainly know when to change your mind,' said Dalton, standing up. 'But we'll do your way.'

Chapter 74

Near Pretoria

After Kirsty had finished her bath, she dressed in a blue skirt, white shirt and went into her bedroom to rest. She was still tired mentally and physically and when she lay down she soon dropped off to sleep.

Steiner had seated himself on the sofa and was reading his book when he thought he heard the sound of a car's engine. It was too quiet for it to be near the house and when the sound went he became interested. There was nothing around that anyone would stop for, except to visit the house. He waited a few moments and then turned out the only lamp in the room. He went over to the drawn curtains and after taking the edge and slightly shifting it to reveal the glass looked outside down the narrow drive. A little less than 200 metres from the house a car was parked. He tried to make out if there was anyone inside but it was already too dark and after a short while he released the curtain and let it fall into place. He walked into the centre of the room wondering who was out there. The front door was locked and when he was about to do the same in the kitchen, Dalton appeared in the passage doorway, a semi-automatic pistol held steadily in his hand and pointed directly at his heart.

Dalton grinned and said: 'You must be James Steiner. You are the one who followed me to the smallholding.' He half-turned and called down the passage. 'He's here. Have you got the woman?'

As if on cue, Kallis entered, leading Kirsty by the arm. He was also carrying a pistol and when he was a few steps into the room he stopped and pushed her forward. 'Stand still and shut up,' he said to her. 'You've already caused enough trouble by rejecting the hospitality provided by

John Dalton.' He faced Steiner. 'When Dalton told me that a James Steiner had been seen at the Plaza Hotel in the company of this woman I didn't think it was you. You were with Sophie Carswell when I turned up to take her out on a date.'

Kallis arrogantly walked in a small circle, his head bent forward. 'If I remember correctly you rudely told me to leave. That was poor behaviour in such a civilized area.'

'You wouldn't take no for an answer,' said Steiner. 'You deserved what you got.'

Kirsty was quiet sensing Steiner was drawing things out, waiting for his chance. But she was scared, of Kallis and Dalton. They were totally unpredictable.

Kallis was becoming impatient. The wrangling was not in his script, even though he enjoyed it. 'By the way I played back the message your woman left on Rupert Bosch's answering machine. Congratulations, you appear to know where the files are being kept. I am particularly interested in the white file, File A.'

'That doesn't come as a surprise,' said Steiner. 'Tell me. Was it hard to get Bosch to hand over the black file, the one you forced him to steal from the group? Why, when you had it, did you kill him last night? It sounds to me as if you're losing your nerve. Perhaps this type of work is too complex for you.'

The words pushed Kallis over the edge, his mouth going dry, and he had become his most dangerous. 'It's time you learnt some manners,' he said. 'With lightning speed he moved the weapon slightly and fired two shots in rapid succession, the soft-nosed lead running together as one, hitting Steiner with full impact to the left of his heart and bringing him to his knees, his face a symbol of pain.

Kirsty cried out and started to go to him, the fear that Steiner would die too much to bear. But before she could take a step, Dalton faced her, his pistol held with menacing intent. 'Stay where you are,' he said his eyes hard, merciless. 'Try to help him and you'll get the same.'

Kallis lowered the gun and stared at the stricken figure before him, the blood expanding concentrically, the petals of a morning rose, staining the white shirt. For a moment his mind was elsewhere and then he took a step forward, keeping the others clearly in sight, a smile parting his lips.

'Things are at last fitting neatly into place,' he said quietly, regaining his calm. 'I now recall that I also heard Steiner's name mentioned by my ex-boss at the DSO in connection with the Cartwright case and the missing white file. I knew very little about the case at the time but I heard Steiner had been assigned the job of finding the file and tracking down those in the group who were intent on retrieving it. The group found that someone was slowly killing the men who were involved in the Cartwright operation, sparing only Krige. They never found out the killer's identity and to this day he is always referred to as the unknown man.' Kallis cackled inanely. 'That is until now. The killer is now before you, one James Steiner. Everything points to him and he is with us now because he failed to get the white file from Krige when he had the chance.' He looked at Steiner, on his knees, his body bent over, a man in prayer. Kirsty was standing still, as near to him as she dared go, a figure of all-consuming despair.

Dalton looked at Kallis, thinking over what he had said. 'I believe from what you say that everything points to Steiner as the unknown man but how do you know Krige has the white file?'

'When I left the DSO and joined the group, Johan Teichmann gave me the job of locating File A,' said Kallis. 'Krige had said on his return that he'd killed Cartwright alone and claimed he had not been able to retrieve the file. But the group soon found out someone had got hold of the file because a copy was later sent to the DSO, intercepted by me and sent to the group. I realized Krige had lied because it was highly unlikely someone else had collected the file from the house. The person who sent it to the DSO could only have been Krige or his lawyer

278

and Krige had been spared by Steiner because he had given his word that he would send a copy of the file he had reclaimed from Cartwright's to the DSO. Krige certainly has the white file now because yesterday he killed his lawyer, David Staples, and he wouldn't have done that unless he already had the file in his possession or knew precisely where he could get it.'

Kallis looked at Dalton. 'Are you satisfied? If you are I'm going to the car to phone Teichmann. It is time he knew exactly what was going on.' He grinned, confident. 'I can't wait to see his face when he hears that Krige lied and has the white file. Keep that gun on Steiner and I'll soon be back.' Without waiting for a reply from Dalton he left the room.

As soon as Kallis disappeared Dalton walked closer to Steiner who was still in the same position, his face hidden. The blood had congealed and his breathing was deep and even. Kirsty was still looking at him, hoping above all else that he would recover. She wanted so much to hold him, but if she did she had no idea what Dalton would do. He would probably go mad and have another go at her. The way he had acted at the smallholding was still engraved on her mind. She didn't like seeing that he was beginning to show he was losing patience.

Dalton was less than a metre from Steiner when he stopped, the gun still directed at him. 'Get up big boy,' he said. 'It's time to stop pretending.' As he spoke they heard the sound of an engine coming to life and for a moment he turned from Steiner and looked to where they had parked the car, even though he couldn't see anything because of the curtains.

'The bastard's leaving,' he said. 'I had a feeling he would do something like this.' For a moment he was distracted and Steiner seized his chance, coming to life, rising like a man returning from the dead. Feverishly, Dalton twisted at the waist, trying to level the gun but he was too slow and Steiner struck him, a rapid combination

279

of blows that brought him down. In a continuous movement he knelt at his side and dispassionately hit him once on the side of his head with the edge of his hand, killing him.

For a while he remained in the position of his last strike, his hands hanging at his sides, and then he got to his feet. He faced Kirsty, still standing in the same place, staring at him.

'You killed him,' she whispered. 'He deserved to die. I was terrified every time I laid eyes on him.' She walked over to Steiner and put her arms around him, holding him tightly. 'Thank God they didn't kill you. I would have missed you so much.'

He didn't say anything, only too glad to hold her in his arms. He looked down at Dalton, a spent heap, disposable flesh and bone. He felt no regret and knew only one of them could have lived. Dalton was of that type and as Kirsty had said he deserved it.

'You need someone to look at this,' said Kirsty, breaking the silence and exposing the wound. 'Fortunately it has stopped bleeding and I don't think you have lost much blood. I'll remove your shirt and wrap it with some of the bandage I have in the car. You were very lucky.'

'We'll have to move quickly,' said Steiner. 'Kallis has definitely gone to the farm to pay Krige a visit and get hold of the file. Once he has it I doubt we'll ever see him again. The dream Dalton must have had of getting it has turned to ash.'

'What do we do with him?' she asked. 'If we contact the police we would have to explain everything and kiss goodbye to Kallis and Krige.'

'You saw the group collect the body of Koch after I'd killed him when he tried to rape you. They offer an efficient service when one of their own goes off the rails and pays the ultimate price. They can do the same with Dalton. I'll phone Teichmann later and tell him what I'm sure he expected.' He thought for a moment and then said: 'I think you should stay here. It's too dangerous.'

'I'm certainly not,' she said. 'You nearly got yourself killed and you give me that crap.'

'Get the bandage and a shirt and after you've got me looking like a mummy we'll stick him out the back and go. By the time we leave, Kallis will have had a forty-minute lead and be near the farm.'

Fifteen minutes later after the bandage had been applied in layers around his chest and he had on a fresh shirt, Kirsty walked over to the body. The pistol was still in Dalton's hand and held loosely.

'Do you have a gun?' she asked. 'I remember you carried a Glock 17 semi-automatic.'

'I don't have one,' he said. 'The Glock was on loan from the Scorpions. Besides, I'm not in the habit of walking around with a pistol at my side like many of you people.'

'So you're not a South African. I thought you had some strange ways about you.' She smiled. 'Where're you from?'

'I'm English, born in West London. I still own a mews house in Knightsbridge that was left to me by my father. He was a South African and my mother English.'

'Very interesting,' she said. 'I'll talk to you about that later. What should I do with Dalton's gun?'

'Stick it in that drawer over there,' he said. 'I'm sure he wouldn't mind if you removed it from him, although he might need it where he's gone.' He walked over to a chair to pick up his blazer. As soon as his back was turned she took the gun from Dalton's hand and went to the drawer. She opened it, stuck the pistol inside her belt under her coat and closed it. She then returned to the body. Dalton hadn't used the gun and she was sure it was fully loaded. No one was going to shoot Steiner again.

After Steiner had put on his blazer they dragged the body outside. It was pitch dark when they drove down the drive and headed for the farm.

Chapter 75

Jan Krige's farm, near the Kruger Reserve

Kallis was in a good mood after he had left Dalton at the house with the others and set off to see Krige. He knew Dalton and the woman would have heard him departing but they were now a depleted force. Dalton didn't have the brains to decide on a course of action, Steiner couldn't move and the woman was nothing to be reckoned with. The only thing Dalton would be capable of doing was to taunt the others and he would soon get tired of that. If he took one of the cars he wouldn't go to the farm for fear of being wiped out by either Krige or himself and he would run the risk of the woman singing like a bird and him being hunted down like a dog, unless he killed her. When and if Dalton managed to get his act together he would have disappeared.

After thirty minutes Kallis finally reached the main gate leading onto the farm. He parked the car, climbed over the fence and in the dark could just see the house in the near distance, only the one wing jutting out from behind a *kopje*. He went over to the side of the track that led to the house and when he was reasonably well concealed by the wild vegetation he started his approach. The going was fairly easy and after a few minutes he was in line with the *kopje* and had a clear view of the house. There were no lights on in the building and the only light came from the outside where a lamp had been attached to the roof overhang. Krige was either not there or he was asleep. To Kallis, Krige's absence was more likely because the front yard was ideal for parking a car or utility vehicle and nothing was there. He was prepared to wait rather than go looking for him in the house and sat down behind a rock where he had a good view of the track and the house. In the dark he was close to being invisible.

Kallis waited for nearly forty minutes before the lights of a moving vehicle appeared at the start of the track near the gate. The driver was going fast but being the only one around he was obviously confident there was no danger and he was in his element. As the vehicle neared the *kopje* he saw it was a Land Rover and it momentarily went out of sight before appearing again in front of the building. It swung in a circle and then stopped. Kallis had not seen Krige before but he had a general description of him and when the driver got out he was definitely Krige.

Kallis was transfixed by the sight of the man who had recently occupied his thoughts with a feeling of ambivalence, on the one hand admiring him for his determination and on the other despising him because he had the white file.

In two giant strides Krige went up the front steps onto the verandah and then into the house, switching on some side lamps and transforming the front reception room into an oasis of light. He poured a drink and sat down, taking a magazine from a rack. For Kallis it was a perfect setting, his target quietly seated, no one else in sight. It was time to move and Kallis, at last feeling the white file in his hands, left the *kopje*. He walked casually towards the verandah, climbed the steps and stopped just before the wide doors. Krige was three metres away and still reading when Kallis spoke.

'Jan Krige,' he said. 'At last we meet. John Kallis.'

The look of surprise on Krige's face when he twisted in his seat and saw Kallis could not have been easily imitated. For a moment he stared and then he got to feet, his eyes never leaving Kallis.

'I've heard of you,' he said, throwing the magazine onto the chair. 'Now get off this farm.'

Chapter 76

Jan Krige's farm

Steiner drove at well over the speeding limit until he and Kirsty finally neared the gate of the farm. 'What do you think I should do?' he said. 'Kallis has still got his lead and we want to reduce it by as much as we can. Mere minutes can alter the balance in this game.'

'Go through the gate and drive along the track that leads to the house,' she said. 'When you near the *kopje* you will see a relatively unused track that veers away to the right and comes out at the side of the building. No one would go down that side of the house at this time and we can leave the car there.'

'Perfect,' said Steiner. He drove through the gate and followed the track. When he was close to the second track to which Kirsty had referred she pointed to it. It wound round in a semi-circle through thick undergrowth and in less than a minute they reached the side of the house. He cut the engine and before getting out placed his hand on her arm.

'This is where we part company,' he said softly. 'You know this place as well as anyone and I would like you to enter the house from the rear. You saw the lights are on in the front room and that indicates Krige is there. But we don't know, and it could be to our advantage if he isn't because you know the combination to the safe. That is where I think he is keeping the file.'

'What about Kallis?' she said. 'If he was coming here he must have arrived by now. If he is here, his car is probably hidden near the gate. But, he might have come and gone.'

'We don't know,' said Steiner, 'and that is why we will have to very careful. I'll go round to the front. Take care of yourself.'

She watched him go and then started for the rear of the house.

When Steiner came to the front corner of the house he saw Krige's Land Rover and walked slowly towards the front doors. The windows of the lounge were high enough above ground level for him not to be able to see inside and he had covered three-quarters of the distance to the doors when he heard Krige speaking. As Steiner listened, Krige stopped, and then came the unmistakeable voice of Kallis. Steiner couldn't believe his luck.

'I want you and more specifically the white file,' said Kallis. 'Don't drag this out. I've already waited too long for it.'

'Your audacity amazes me,' said Krige, calmly. He had faced many situations like this before and he had always come out on top. 'You have obviously missed your vocation.'

Kallis levelled his pistol at Krige's chest. He had already noticed the holstered gun on Krige's belt. 'I'll show you who's missed his vocation,' he said, part of him enjoying the foreplay and the other losing patience. 'I'll count to three and if you don't give me the file I'll slowly go to work on you with this gun until you do. I've not seen anyone who can stand pain like that. I'll get the file in the end. There is no one to stop me.'

'It's not here,' said Krige. 'My lawyer has it.'

'You're lying,' said Kallis. 'Yesterday you killed him. Your Land Rover was seen near his house at the time of his death. It's in the papers. Don't tell me you went there without already having it in your possession. You killed him for some other reason.'

Krige thought of the Beretta at his side. Somehow he had to stall for time until he could get it into play. 'You are the last person who should talk about killing,' he said. 'I have heard from a reliable source that you got Rupert Bosch to steal the black file for you from the group offices. Last night someone shot him dead in his car. I believe it was you and you killed him because he posed a threat. With the black file in your hands, and I think it is outside in your car, there is only one thing that is missing from your collection. It is File A and you are convinced I've got it.'

'So what if the black file is in my car,' said Kallis, grinning confidently. 'You won't get it and I'm getting tired of your shit.'

With amazing speed for a heavily-built man, Kallis dropped to one knee and fired. The bullet hit Krige in the shoulder, causing a stab of pain, and as his free hand went involuntarily to the wound, Kallis fired again, the bullet penetrating high up on the right thigh. The leg bent and Krige stared at him. 'What's next,' he said, staying on his feet with difficulty. 'You'll never get that file.'

Steiner had heard and seen enough. Using the rail, he swung himself onto the verandah and sprang through the doors. Startled by the sudden intrusion, Kallis took his attention off Krige and spun round. When he saw who it was, he took a step to the side, raised the gun and fired. But Steiner was already moving and as the bullet flew past his cheek he turned, and with consummate ease delivered a high, venomous kick that struck Kallis on the side of his head, killing him before his body reached the floor.

For a while Steiner looked at the body and then he faced Krige. 'So, I've done your dirty work for you,' he said, unemotionally. 'You must be pleased.'

Krige had already drawn his gun, which was hanging at his side. 'You did it for yourself,' he said. 'What made you come back?'

'I think you know the answer to that,' said Steiner. 'What will you do with it now that you again have it in your hands? Teichmann will hunt you down as if you were a rabid dog.'

287

'I work for him,' said Krige, smiling. 'When he sees Kallis and hears the story he will be standing in the queue to congratulate me. By that time I will already have retrieved the black file from Kallis's car.'

'Teichmann couldn't care about stories,' said Steiner. 'Why do you think he asked me to help him? He didn't trust you and Kallis and all he wanted was the return of the files. You two failed to deliver and whatever you tell him he will still ask for them. If he doesn't get them you'll become history. And, you won't have the files with you.'

'Where will be they be?' asked Krige.

'I'll have them,' said Steiner, smiling. 'Surely you must know we're all in this for what we can get.'

Krige grinned. 'The white file is in my safe, for which you don't have the combination, and I'll soon have the other. I'll tell Teichmann I know you spoke to him and that you were playing a double game on behalf of your masters, the DSO. He'll believe me when I also say I do not know who has the files, and I'll ask to be released from the job of finding them. The group trust me completely.'

'The first thing he'll do is contact me,' said Steiner, getting ready to move. He knew what was coming and he wanted it, the sooner the better.

'You won't be available,' said Krige, stepping backwards to increase the distance between them. He had seen how fast Steiner could act.

'Where will I be?' asked Steiner.

'Dead,' said Krige, slowly raising the pistol, certain that Steiner couldn't reach him before he shot him.

But before he could detonate the charge, Kirsty's voice came from behind him. 'No he won't. I'm here to make sure. Get rid of the gun.'

Krige knew it was Kirsty. 'Come and get it,' he said, turning rapidly, desperately trying to level the gun. But she was ready and without hesitation fired two shots, hitting him in the centre of the forehead, killing him and then watching him fall. She stood still, looking at the man she

288

had killed, feeling no remorse. He had deserved it, as had the others who were now going stiff. She looked at Steiner, the man who was so gentle, so dangerous and who was always there when she cried for help. He had killed but it was self-defence. They had left him no choice, men like Kallis, Dalton and those who had gone before, Koch, Richter and there bosom friends. They were all of the same type and there would always be men like them.

Steiner stood looking at Krige, and then he walked to her. He took her in his arms.

'For a moment, when all that was about to end, I thought you weren't coming,' he said. 'I don't like it when you leave it so late.'

'I wanted to see if you could come out alive,' she said.

Thank you,' he said, smiling. 'The next time you dream up something like that let me know so I can come prepared. You're a very good shot. Where did you get the gun?'

'I wondered when you would ask,' she said. 'It belonged to Dalton.'

'I thought you put it in the drawer,' said Steiner.

'I was worried they would kill you,' she said. 'I was there to protect you.'

'I've never heard that before. Do I look incompetent?'

'No,' she said. 'But I've now seen you shot by two people. One was when you were in this room three weeks ago and the other was when Dalton got you. You will just have to accept that you attract bullets.' She broke out laughing. 'I'm sorry. All this is my weird sense of humour. Forgive me.'

'With difficulty,' said Steiner, his face creasing with mirth. 'You had me going.'

When she had stopped laughing she said: 'What do we do with the bodies?'

'One of them is your husband.'

'He is no different from the other two. He had his chance and blew it.

289

'I'll phone Teichmann,' he said. 'I'll also tell him to collect Dalton. I don't want to return with him still there. But first I want to retrieve the files. We'll start with the black file and use my car. Kallis would have parked beyond the gate. I'll get his keys.'

After Steiner had found Kallis's keys in one of his pockets, they went to the Mercedes and drove down the track to the gate. Once through Steiner went slowly along the road that came in from the left. They soon found the car and after stopping next to it Steiner went to the boot and opened it. They started their search, looking in the cases, and were rewarded when, in the second case they tried, they found a package.

'Have a look,' said Steiner, handing the package to Kirsty.

She opened the envelope, extracted the bound file with State Security 1960 to Present, File B embossed on it and went to the inside of the back cover.

'This is what really counts,' she said. She stuck her finger nail just under the corner of the synthetic backing and carefully peeled it away. Staring at them was the deep, round indentation of the Oriental seal.

'God, it is actually the original File B,' she said. 'Like the other one, it kills those who get involved with it. Just the sight of it makes me go cold.'

'Don't lose sight of it,' said Steiner. 'Let's get back to the house. All we need now is File A. Are you sure you remember the combination?'

'Yes,' she said. 'I only hope he hasn't changed it.'

'We'll see.'

They soon reached the farmhouse and went through the lounge to the study. The safe was in the corner of the room and Kirsty immediately went to it. She dialled the combination and then tried the door. It yielded and right in front of their eyes was a package, similar to the one that housed the black file. After she had removed the file from inside the envelope she turned to the back cover and peeled away part of the synthetic backing. The seal was there and she returned the file to its envelope.

She put the file under her arm but before she shut the safe she noticed a similar package on the bottom shelf. She took it out, removed the file that was in it and looked for the seal inside the back cover. She glanced at Steiner. 'The seal is not there. I feel like a detective.' She replaced it, shut the safe and turned to Steiner. 'Do you want to phone Teichmann?' she said. 'There's a phone on the desk. I would like to hear what you say.'

They went to the phone and Steiner pulled up two chairs. 'Please sit down,' he said.

After they were both seated she said: 'I am really interested in what you say about the files, particularly when you used those nebulous words when you spoke to him.'

He dialled Teichmann's home number and he answered.

'Teichmann.'

'Johan. It's James Steiner. Do you remember me?'

'My memory's not that bad,' said Teichmann. 'How can I help you?'

'I and Kirsty Krige have retrieved the originals of the two files,' he said. 'But before I go any further I'd like you to arrange for something to be done.'

'You actually got them,' said Teichmann quietly. 'What do you want done?'

'I would like you to send some of your people to the house where Kirsty and I have been staying and collect John Dalton's corpse. They will find it against the wall at the back.'

'What's the address?' said Teichmann as if he was arranging to meet someone for tea.

Steiner gave it to him.

'Is that all?' asked Teichmann.

'No,' said Steiner. 'After collecting Dalton I'd like them to go to the Krige farm. At the front of the house they'll find the bodies of Jan Krige and John Kallis. They must also be removed. I would like all this to be done now. Kirsty and I will soon be returning to her house and we don't want to see Dalton lying in the back yard.'

'What do you want them to do with the three bodies?' asked Teichmann.

'Tell them to follow your standard operating procedures,' said Steiner. 'That is, make the bodies disappear. It is probably smart to make a brief statement in the press concerning their disappearance but all I am really interested in is that there is never any reference made to Kirsty Krige or me in connection with this case.'

'I understand,' said Teichmann. 'I'll get onto it straight after this call. Now tell me about the files. You said you have retrieved them.'

'Yes we have,' said Steiner. 'But we are not going to return them to you. If you want to be an acceptable political organization with something to offer this country you should exclude this kind of stuff and your insidious methods from your portfolio. There is no harm in compiling racially unbiased, well-documented evidence against people, black and white, who you believe have committed serious crimes against humanity but the group should not be the judge, jury and executioner. The evidence should be submitted to the National Prosecuting Authority. We are giving these files to Peter Smith of the DSO.'

Steiner terminated the call. He faced Kirsty. 'I'm glad that's over.'

'You were brilliant,' she said. 'I felt proud of you.'

'Thank you. I'll remember that. I suggest we do a bit of cleaning up before we leave. I don't want to meet those guys, at your place or here.'

'Nor do I,' she said. 'Let's get started.'

Chapter 77

Pretoria

Steiner and Kirsty Krige left the farm an hour after Steiner had made the phone call to Teichmann. They had dragged Krige and Kallis into the front yard, next to the verandah steps, and had locked the house after extinguishing the lights. There was no sign of foul play, they had the files and, as Steiner had told Teichmann, he was going to give them to Peter Smith of the Scorpions.

When they reached the house, they sat in the lounge, Kirsty with a gin and tonic and Steiner with a glass of water.

'Do you think you will ever drink anything stronger than water?' she asked.

'No. If you drink you have to control the amount you take. I decided it was it was easier to give up. I prefer using my mental strength elsewhere.'

'You're so disciplined,' she said. 'But tell me a bit more about yourself. Why have you never married? Don't you like women?'

'Some of them are great. They just don't give me a chance to get to know them.'

'When are you going back to Durban?' She stared at him.

'I was thinking of sometime tomorrow afternoon. There's nothing in Pretoria to make me stay longer.'

'Isn't there?' she asked. 'What's wrong with me? I thought that by now you would have known I'm in love with you.' She smiled. 'I hope you're not embarrassed.'

He smiled and said: 'When I first saw you on the farm I remember saying to myself that you were the loveliest girl I had ever seen.'

'You were as cold as ice but I knew I wanted you even then. Do you still think I'm the loveliest girl?'

'Yes,' he said, smiling. He got up, walked over to her and touched her on the cheek. 'Would you like to come to Durban with me? You can stay in my flat. I've got two bedrooms.'

'That sounds perfect,' she said, giggling like a precocious school girl and rubbing her cheek softly against his hand. 'When do we go?'

'I'll wait for you.'

'I haven't heard that for a long time,' she said, holding his hand. 'I'll be ready tomorrow. Don't try and leave me behind.' She came to her feet and held him in her arms. She kissed him softly on the cheek and slowly moved her lips down to his. 'I love you so much,' she whispered. 'You are everything to me.' She took him by the hand and said: 'I've made my bed.'

Late the next day Kirsty and James Steiner travelled to Durban. They arrived in the morning and after breakfast were sitting in the lounge when Steiner looked up from the newspaper he had been skipping through.

'We should go and see Peter Smith and get rid of those files,' he said to Kirsty. 'The sooner I give them to him the better I'll feel.'

'What will he do with them?' she asked.

'When I told Teichmann we were going to hand them over to the Scorpions he knew exactly what that will mean and I'm sure he is now a very scared man and going through an intense process of damage limitation. The DSO will inform the National Prosecuting Authority or NPA of what they find in the files and prepare cases for prosecution. When the DSO acts, I doubt the group will have the time to prepare for what the DSO has in mind, even if they had been tipped off by Teichmann. They would be caught napping with no time to hide and the heads would start rolling. All the records collected by the

294

group and referred to in the files would be sequestered. The white and black files would become documents for prosecution rather than protection and persecution.'

Steiner walked over to the phone. 'I'll give Smith a ring. If I tell him it's urgent he will drop everything and see us.'

'Do I have to go?' she asked.

'Yes,' said Steiner. 'If it was not for you the DSO and NPA would still be creeping around in the dark. From what I've heard they don't even know File B was stolen even though they might vaguely be aware of its existence.'

When Smith heard Steiner on the phone he was surprised.

'Where the hell have you been?' he said. 'I thought you were only going out of town for a day, not a week. I have heard from a very reliable source that the black file you once said existed has been removed from the group offices. Apparently it is even of greater value to the group than the white file.'

'A friend and I would like to see you urgently,' said Steiner. 'Can we come round now?'

'Certainly,' said Smith. 'I'll see you in a few minutes.'

'Let's go,' said Steiner to Kirsty after he had replaced the receiver. 'He's waiting for us.'

Ten minutes later Steiner and Kirsty were at the DSO offices and were taken up to Smith.

'Good to see you,' said Smith 'Who's your pretty friend?'

'Her name is Kirsty. It's nice meeting you.' She smiled.

'Please sit down,' said Smith. 'Now tell me what's so important.'

'A few minutes ago you told me the original of a valuable black file was stolen from the group,' said Steiner. 'I also know you haven't found the original white file.'

'How do you know that?'

Steiner placed the two packages he was carrying on Smith's desk. 'In these packages you will find the originals of both files.'

'Where did you get them?' asked Smith.

'We'll tell you the story later,' said Steiner. 'We've just returned from Pretoria and need a break. I thought I was going on holiday but I got diverted. You will find them more than interesting.'

The following day, Kirsty took steps to change her surname to her maiden name of Callard. She also contacted her two sons at Bishops and told them of their father's death. She didn't say she had killed him, and arranged to fly to the Cape to see them.

Steiner phoned Sophie Carswell and told her about his relationship with Kirsty. They agreed to meet.

After a few months in Durban, Steiner and Kirsty started spending most of their time in London where he had a mews house in Knightsbridge.

Examination of the files resulted in the prosecution, conviction and incarceration of a number of leading figures who had committed serious crimes during and after the apartheid era. For them, there was no place to hide.